DEAD WITCH ON A BRIDGE

Sonoma Witches #1

GRETCHEN GALWAY

Eton Field

DEAD WITCH ON A BRIDGE

Eton Field, Publisher
www.gretchengalway.com

Cover design by Gretchen Galway
Stock art images: Depositphotos

All characters in this book are fictitious. Any resemblance to actual persons, living or dead, is purely coincidental.

eBook ISBN-13: 978-1-939872-19-7
Paperback ISBN-13: 978-1-939872-41-8
v.20230206

Chapter One

As soon as I saw the body in the middle of the bridge, I knew I was too late.

Shivering, I rubbed my arms and looked around me. Surrounded by redwoods, my tiny village of Silverpool was usually quiet, remote, even boring.

Not tonight.

Edging closer, I aimed the flashlight of my phone on Tristan's crumpled form and sent out a probing spell to confirm he was dead.

Yes, very. It looked like a car had hit him. My stomach recoiled, but years of training kicked in. I could keep it together for a few minutes. I had to.

Tristan's home was a short distance from the river, and he'd always enjoyed late-night walks. But this couldn't have been an accident. The fairies wouldn't be making so much noise if magic hadn't been involved.

I had to hurry—whoever had killed him might still be nearby. I could feel a hint of magic, but that might've been Tristan's remaining powers, lingering before they were snuffed out forever.

Hand shaking, I moved the light to his face. In life, he'd looked like a handsome man in his early forties with curly blond hair. But death had erased that illusion, making it obvious he'd been much older. Even smart people like Tristan had their vanities. And a lucky few, like Tristan, had the power to indulge them.

When I'd dated him last year, he'd accused me of being overly emotional. Too softhearted. Would he say that now, given that I was staring at his dead body without shedding a tear?

Maybe. I would be crying soon enough when the shock wore off.

Poor Tristan. Run over and left for dead. And he was going to be left twice—I couldn't stay either. Silverpool was in a small, remote corner of Sonoma County, but this was the only road into town. Somebody would be driving by any minute.

I wanted to call the police, but how could I explain why I'd run out of my house in the middle of the night in my pajamas? I had no information I could give them. None they could use, anyway. And it was too late to help Tristan.

The frenzied fae voices that had woken me from sleep and led me to the river were louder than ever. The fairy under the bridge wasn't the only one sending up an alarm, but his voice was the loudest, the one that had made me run out of my house as if it had been on fire.

Maybe he would talk to me. As much as I wanted to hide, I needed to know if the bridge fairy had seen anything —for Tristan's sake and my own. I hurried to the far side and crept through the grass and bushes to the path that snaked down to the riverbank. The Vago River was low after months without rain, and the dirt path was dry and rocky.

Even though he was calling for help, the creature was hostile. I could sense his bad mood from ten feet away.

Brownish-green sparks sizzled above his hiding spot under the concrete approach span.

I put my hand on my beaded necklace and called out to him, "Are you all right?"

He stopped screaming. Without his high-pitched whine, the night suddenly seemed peaceful.

I ducked under the bridge and lowered my voice. "Were you here when the Protector was attacked?" The fae in this area would only know Tristan by his official title. Tristan had been the local agent for the Protectorate, the international body of witches that protected fae and humans alike from supernatural dangers.

The fairy didn't respond to my question. He probably assumed I wouldn't be able to hear him. Most people couldn't. Not even other witches.

"Are you hurt?" I asked.

Lit by its own fairy light, a narrow face the color of a Granny Smith apple appeared. He looked unharmed. When he saw me, he scowled but relaxed, as if recognizing I was no threat to him.

"I'm a friend of the Protector's," I said. "Did you call for me?"

He shook his head. "You are child."

"I'm twenty-six," I said.

"Child." The fairy pinched his face together until his chin nearly touched the tip of his pointy nose.

"Did he say who did this? Did you see the car? Anything?"

"His spirit," the fairy said. "Didn't want to go."

A chill went through me. "Was there magic?"

"Everywhere is magic," the fairy said.

"Did you see a witch?" Talking to most fairies was useless, but I had to try. "Maybe a demon?"

"Help!" He opened his mouth, revealing pointy yellow teeth, and began to wail again.

Although the sound wasn't real, I slapped my hands over my ears. "Please stop. Nobody can hear you but me."

"Help. Coming." He looked up.

Overhead was the sound of a large vehicle approaching. "That's probably a nonmag."

"Nonmag?"

"Just people. Not witches. The first of many," I said.

"Help."

"They'll see the body and call others. More humans will come. You might be safer with them around."

Shooting bright green sparks, he retreated into the shadows just as the vehicle rumbled onto the bridge above.

I was stuck. It would look suspicious to be seen hiding near the scene of a hit-and-run. In my haste, I'd put on running shoes but no pants. I wore a long T-shirt and shorts, but no underwear. And I'd run down the hill from my house on foot instead of taking my car because I couldn't protect myself with magic while I was driving.

With a hand on the beads around my neck, I cast a darkness spell about me. It wouldn't be powerful enough under close scrutiny, but hopefully nobody would be looking down in the river. They'd be distracted by the body.

Had Tristan been distracted when the car hit him? Had that been how one of the most powerful witches in Sonoma County had been struck down and left for dead?

When a second car arrived and I heard people running and shouting for somebody to call 911, I crept into the river, glad the water level was low at late summer, and began my wet hike home.

Chapter Two

"Willy, are you around?" I whispered, twisting the water out of my shirt. Although my house was less than a mile from the bridge, I'd had to cross the river and hike downstream to the gravel beach behind Cypress Hardware to get back up to the road.

A small voice—small but deep—spoke from the base of the biggest redwood tree in my backyard. "Where else would I be?"

I'd begun to shiver in the cold, and my teeth chattered. "I-I m-might be having company."

Willy lit a candle and held it up in the air. Since he was only about as tall as a two-liter bottle of Diet Coke, his candle failed to illuminate anything other than the redwood sorrel around his feet. "Human?"

"All kinds." I squatted down to address him eye to eye, or at least eye to elbow. He'd become my friend over the couple of years I'd lived here, and I wanted to warn him to be extra careful with Tristan gone. "Willy, the Protector is dead."

"I heard the mourning songs," he said. "Did you kill him?"

"Of course I didn't kill him!" I sat on the ground and plucked a stem of the sorrel, twirling it between my fingers until the three leaves of the shamrock turned to four. "Why would— How could you think—"

"I know females," Willy said. "Females never forgive."

"Forgive him for what? Being annoying?"

Willy nodded, gazing at me solemnly over the tiny flame. "When he was your husband, you spoke often of killing him."

"He was never my husband. We were only—" I rolled my eyes. Gnomes were very old-fashioned. "Courting. It wasn't serious. I never really got involved." Tristan had dated every available woman in a ten-mile radius. And most of the unavailable ones too.

"He was your husband," Willy insisted. "And you his wife. Just as I had a wife who is now dead."

I stopped twirling the stem. "What you had with your wife was very different, Willy." Before he could light the pipe he was taking from his red velvet coat—and then launch into a two-day poem about his departed beloved, a creature I suspected had died in the Old Country centuries before—I handed him the shamrock. "Keep your eyes open over the next few days, will you? With Tristan gone, anybody and anything might come to Silverpool."

Silverpool held a hidden magical power that would cause supernatural trouble if it wasn't safeguarded. The Protectorate had done what it could to hide Silverpool's secret, but the fae knew it was here and congregated in large numbers. Demons were drawn to the fae, so a Protector was assigned to prevent any from getting too close. It was like a watering hole in the desert—it attracted prey and predator alike.

Willy's brown eyes widened with joy at my sorrel offering. "Oh no, I couldn't accept such a gift."

I tucked it under the lapel of his tiny jacket. The stem

was as thick around as his pipe. "Get it in some water before it wilts."

"You are too generous, Alma Bellrose. Four leaves. Such a gift." His eyes filled with tears. "How can I repay you?"

"Hide deep in your"—I almost said "hole" before I remembered he found that insulting—"home, and don't come out until it's safe."

Nodding, Willy kissed the edge of the leaf, his ruddy face flushing darker. "As you say. I have no interest in trouble."

"Squeeze a little lemon juice in the vase," I said. "It'll last longer that way."

Willy saluted me with the shamrock and then clambered up the root to a rectangular gap in the trunk, the entrance to the underground dwelling he'd been living in when I moved in. Probably since the Gold Rush, given his fashion choices. Young or indigenous gnomes thought red velvet coats were ridiculous, especially for creatures who lived under the earth. Impossible to clean properly, apparently. Only the oldest immigrant gnomes still wore them.

He snuffed out the candle and left me in the dark.

With Willy warned, I was ready to go inside. I got to my feet, brushing the bark chips off my knees, and tiptoed to the kitchen door that opened out onto a short step to my flag-stone patio.

I pressed my nose to the window, letting it steam with my breath. It was dark inside, but that didn't mean anything. A good spell could hide an elephant juggling blowtorches.

Putting my left hand on the bead necklace around my throat, I opened the door with my right, leaned over the threshold, sensing nothing, and stepped inside.

A blast of hot wind knocked me to the floor. Cursing, I rolled to one side. My own house! I'd been cautious, but not cautious enough. Heart pounding, I scrambled to my hands and knees but was struck down again. Face pressing into the

7

tile floor, gasping for breath, I clutched my necklace and sent out a stilling spell. I was working on overcoming my reliance on props, but I wasn't there yet, especially under stress.

Like when I was pinned to the kitchen floor in my pajamas and a dragon was dripping foamy spittle on my temple. Obviously not a real dragon, because that would be ridiculous.

I sucked in another breath and sent out a second stilling spell to the creature on my back. The dragon, its claws loosening over my shoulders, went limp. Pushing up to a plank position, I toppled over the miniature dragon to the floor and grabbed the rough-hewn staff next to my kitchen door. That I aimed at the source of power, a large man crouching next to the fridge.

With a yelp, the man fell to his side. Then silence.

I regarded his limp form with satisfaction. My abilities inside my house were exponentially greater than they were elsewhere, especially when I was upset. Never underestimate a witch in her own kitchen.

"Lights," I said. The overhead fixture flickered on. *That* nifty gadget had come from a hardware store. New magic could be as good as old.

When I saw the man's face, I became angrier than ever. I resisted the urge to kick him.

"Wake up," I said loudly, releasing my necklace. Then I used a word I usually avoided. "*Dad.*"

No wonder my spell had been so effective. Blood had greater power over blood.

His eyes popped open as if he'd been faking, which I knew he hadn't. "Hello, darling. I ate a slice of leftover pepperoni, hope you don't mind."

"What are you doing here?"

Blinking, he looked past me at the dragon. "Who hurt Ethan?"

"I didn't hurt him," I said, glancing at his pet. "He's sleeping. Just like you were. It's already wearing off." To maintain the spell, I would have to expend more energy than I had at the moment.

"I wasn't sleeping. I was— You don't have the power to put me to sleep."

I rubbed my face with both hands. My father had always underestimated me. "What brings you to Silverpool?"

The dragon sat up and began licking its front paws. I edged closer to the door so I could sweep my father and his pet outside if things got ugly. Uglier.

"You invited me," he said.

"When?"

"Well, you should invite me. Your own father."

"Technically," I said.

"That's all that matters, my dear." With the grace of a ballroom dancer, he bounced effortlessly to his feet.

"Why did you attack me?" I'd expected at least one magical being to make an appearance, but not my own father, and not inside the walls of my bewitched home.

He ignored my question. "Do you always sneak into your own home through the back door in the middle of the night?"

I crossed my arms over my chest. "Yes, as it happens."

"Well, I didn't know that. Which is another reason we should get to know each other better. I thought you were a… a burglar."

The little dragon folded his wings back and trotted over for a pat. Ethan was actually a golden retriever and reverted to the behaviors of one when my father wasn't commanding him. When not breaking and entering, my father used the golden retriever's classic, marketable looks for modeling work—dog food advertising, calendars, social media influencer.

"A burglar?" I asked. "What would anyone want to steal? My computer is ancient, and I don't have a TV."

He studied me for a moment, his crafty eyes narrowing, then shrugged. "Not that kind of thing."

"I don't have any significant amount of metal or gemstone." I didn't state the obvious, that I couldn't afford serious magic at the moment—and I wasn't going to follow in his footsteps.

"Never mind." He held out his arms, which confused me, especially when he moved closer, bumping his chest against mine.

Then I realized what he was doing. "Are you trying to hug me?"

"Am I doing it wrong?"

I sighed. I never could tell if he was kidding or not. Malcolm Bellrose was a liar and a cheat, a grifter and a thief, always on the make, never looking out for anyone but himself. But he wasn't all bad.

I hoped.

"No, you're doing all right." I pulled his wrists down and bumped against him for a moment. We drew back, both relieved it was over. My father pushed Ethan away—he'd jumped up on his hindquarters to join in, which neither of us wanted as long as he had three-inch claws and slimy green spit carried forth on his breath of fire.

"Why not let him be a dog all the time?" I asked. "Not just when he's got a camera pointed at him." I scratched Ethan behind the… earlike holes. "I think he'd be happier."

"But would I?" He waved a finger at Ethan, and the dragon bounded across the kitchen, flapping his wings until he was airborne. His fire breath set a kitchen towel blazing.

Saving my magical strength, I used my flesh-and-bone fingers to flick the towel into the sink. "It's not all about you." I extinguished the fire with a spray from the faucet.

But it was a waste of breath. Malcolm couldn't comprehend a universe without him at the center.

I peered out my kitchen window into the darkness. Last I'd seen him, he'd been dating a Freewitch. They were radicals who wanted to overthrow the Protectorate. Some even wanted to take over the entire nonmagical world. "Are you alone? Or did you drag that nut along with you?"

"Such ignorance," Malcolm said, clicking his tongue. "As it happens, the end of my last relationship has left me quite heartbroken. Not that you could see it, but Chantal was delightful. I thought you'd give up that kind of conventional thinking after the Protectorate fired you."

That was ironic. In spite of his criminal nature, my father had always held the Protectorate in higher esteem than I did. He was a notorious thief, but as the eldest male witch in the illustrious Bellrose family, he still held a bizarre respect for the ancient's Protectorate's status and power.

"They didn't fire me," I said. "It was an honorable discharge. It was officially recorded as an Incurable Inability."

"Believe that if that makes you feel better," he said.

I pulled open the door, determined not to show he had the power to affect me in any way whatsoever. Malcolm cast a spell over the threshold as he stepped outside. Right behind him, I immediately neutralized my father's attempt at breaking the barrier I'd set for dangerous creatures—such as himself—and inhaled the night air.

I could smell trouble. The fae's fearful singing still echoed through the river valley.

Why was my father here tonight? Tristan's death wouldn't affect him personally, but he might use it as a distraction. There could be something extremely valuable nearby. Something he thought I had in the house.

Not that kind of thing, he'd said.

I realized that I'd kicked him out of the house too soon.

He was going to get away without telling me why he'd come. "You weren't trying to steal my charms, were you?"

He paused on the steps and turned. "Your charms?"

I put my fingers on the warm wooden beads around my neck and sent out a small current. Nothing painful, just the witch equivalent of a tap on the shoulder. I didn't detect any of my fingerprints on him, nothing I'd made to sell. "My beaded focus strings are my livelihood now. I sell them on the magic market—the *legal* one. You might not know anything about that. To pay rent, buy groceries. Make an honest living." He'd never given me a thing, but I didn't think he'd actually steal the food out of my mouth.

"Only because you couldn't hold a real job."

I followed him around the house to the front yard. "What were you looking for, Dad?"

But he'd moved too far from the strongest source of my power in the kitchen and had broken into a jog. The dragon's breath was a blurry flashlight, leading the way.

"You, of course," he shouted. "But I'm intruding. Lovely to see you. Terribly sad you don't feel the same way."

"Oh, give me a break," I said. "You snuck into my house in the middle of the—"

A crackling sound cut me off. I spun away, squeezing my eyes shut as the white light flashed.

My father and his pet were gone.

Just like that.

Malcolm was rightly proud of his teleport spell. I myself hadn't mastered it. It wasn't the kind of spell you wanted to do without complete confidence. Unless you didn't care about your limbs, of course. One failed attempt at twenty had been enough to scare me away from those arts for a lifetime. I still had a scar on my left arm. The elbow wasn't quite as pointy as it had been.

Damn, he could be a mile away by now. Unlike the rest

of town, he wouldn't be blocked by the emergency vehicles on the bridge.

What was he looking for? It couldn't be a coincidence he'd appeared only hours after Tristan was killed. Whatever he was looking for, it had to be magical. Something he could sell or something he could use?

I blinked into the darkness, searching for any hint, any clue, of what he'd come for.

And found something—someone—else.

"Hello, Alma," he said.

I spun around. Unlike my father, this was a visitor I'd been expecting.

The demon who had cost me my job.

Chapter Three

✦

Seth Dumont stood in a beam of light from the house, grinning at me, darkly handsome as always. He looked thirty. I didn't know how old he really was; told myself I didn't care.

"Keep your voice down, SD," I said, crossing my arms over my chest. "It's the middle of the night." I cast out my senses to make sure Willy was all right. I didn't think Seth would hurt *me*, but demons were known to hunt fairies. Gnomes weren't as weak as little pixies, but they were part of the fae world. For all I knew, gnome kebab was Seth's favorite dish.

"Why are you wearing your pajamas?" He looked me over, frowning. "And were you swimming in them?"

"Busy night." I fingered my necklace, focused my senses. "As you must know."

"Shame about your ex," Seth said.

He bowed his head, but I knew he wasn't grieving. With Tristan gone, Seth was now free to explore Silverpool. Theoretically, he could invite other demons from all over the world to join him and overwhelm the Protectorate's resources to protect not only fae but nonmagical humanity. All demons were equally dangerous, and all needed to be destroyed.

Theoretically. That's what they'd taught me when I was an agent. But I'd developed doubts. What about due process? How could we execute somebody for a crime he or she *might* commit?

And how could we be certain that all demons were evil? Ancient mythology from all over the world had other theories about the varied nature of supernatural spirits.

My doubts had gnawed at me during my years of training, but I'd kept them to myself. Surely, I figured, I'd learn the answers with more experience. So I worked hard, practiced my spells, learned my lessons, and looked forward to my future as a prestigious demon killer. Finally, after a childhood of embarrassment as Malcolm Bellrose's daughter, I would be able to hold my head high.

But then Seth Dumont had showed up. I don't know what he'd done to draw attention to himself when he'd arrived in San Francisco, but my first big mission had been to track him down and drive a silver stake through his ribs.

I tried. I really did. I found him. I trapped him—and then, to the shame of my family name and my bank account, I let him walk away.

The upper-level witches who probed me afterward determined I was unable to kill not only this demon, but any creature. My heart was too soft. I was fundamentally too weak. A day later, my brief career as a Protectorate agent came to an end. The official dismissal report termed my weakness an Incurable Inability.

Only I knew that Seth had stayed in the area, apparently able to drop off the Protectorate's radar again. Sometimes when I drove out of town, he would appear and say hello, and we'd developed a bizarre almost-friendship. Once, he'd surprised me in the tampon aisle at a drugstore in Santa Rosa. It was usually something slightly embarrassing like that.

Honestly, I wasn't sure I'd done the right thing by letting him go. In fact, ever since I'd seen Tristan's body, I'd been wondering if I'd been an idiot, that Seth was just as evil as the Protectorate had said.

"I don't suppose you'll tell me who killed him?" I asked.

"Me? Why would I know anything?"

"Maybe because you killed him."

Seth's voice hardened. "You really think I'd do that?"

"Tristan wouldn't be the first witch you'd attacked."

He stepped closer. It was too dark to see his face, but I could feel the air around me get warmer. A living, breathing space heater. "I never attacked you."

As chilled as I was in the night air, I stepped away from his space-heater warmth. Seth had way too much sex appeal and the enthusiasm for wielding it to get what he wanted. "You threw my partner into the San Francisco Bay."

"He surprised me. It was a self-defense reflex." He moved closer, crowding me. His voice lowered. "But I apologize. As soon as you released me, I made sure he was all right."

"They found him sleeping in a day spa in Japantown."

"That was my doing. Warm and dry, smelling much better than before, am I right?"

Perhaps it was stupid, but I believed him. Darius did say he'd never felt so good. And we had attacked Seth from behind, unprovoked, as he walked across the Golden Gate Bridge.

"I'm freezing," I said with a sigh. "Let's go inside."

His white teeth flashed. "Thanks for the invite."

"Yeah, just this once." I had enough power inside my house to protect myself. As well as a silver stake I'd kept as a memento. But I knew the debt he owed me was more powerful than any witch's magic.

His chuckle trailed behind me as I walked around the house and through the door into the kitchen. Unlike my father, he didn't pause at the threshold to test the boundary spell. With his cockiness—and my spoken invitation—he marched right in.

"How's dear old Dad?" He bent over, swiped a blob of dragon slobber off the kitchen tile, made a face, and went to the sink to wash his hands. As he sudsed up, he didn't mention the embers of dish towel smoldering in the basin. "Still up to his tricks? No Bright witch would treat father-hood the way he does."

I began to protest, to defend "dear old Dad," but I agreed with him. "He was looking for something," I said. "Are you?"

"Am I what?"

"Are you looking for it too?"

"Looking for what?" Seth wiped his hands, his long nose sniffing the air, and before I could stop him, he'd wandered into the living room.

And from there, he disappeared somewhere else. I finally found him washing his hands in the bathroom.

I blocked the door before he made it into my bedroom. "Did you come here for whatever it was my father wanted?"

He looked at me with eyes as blue as a Sapphire witch's robes. "No," he said. And stupid me, I felt myself believing him again.

It really was an Incurable Inability.

I braced my hands on either side of the doorjamb and met his gaze. Then I stepped aside and let him out of the bathroom—but I followed him to the kitchen.

"Look, SD, I've had a rough night. What do you want?" I sighed a little so he could see a hint of my grief and exhaustion.

"The same thing I've always wanted." His gaze dropped to my chest.

Before I could react, the dish towel in the sink burst into flames again.

I rolled my eyes. "Fine." I walked over to put it out. I wasn't sure if the flames were real or magic, but I could use water on either one. "You don't want to tell me. Time for you to leave." I took the sprayer from the sink and aimed it at the blaze. The flame disappeared from the middle and then outward, leaving a shimmering, Hula Hoop–sized ring for a split second before completely going dark.

"It's the truth, Alma."

I picked up the charred remains of the dish towel and flung it at him.

"I like what you've done with your hair," he said, gracefully dancing out of the way. "The natural curls go with the wild-witch-in-the-forest thing."

"Just because I didn't kill you that night doesn't mean I won't hurt you now."

The smirk faded from his lips. "All right. I couldn't resist. I heard about the Protector's death and had to see if it was true. I came to see you because… it seemed polite."

I went over and cleaned up the remains of the towel, this time dumping it in the trash. "Courtesy accomplished, now you can go home and celebrate. Set your own towels on fire."

"I'm sorry you lost a friend," he said softly.

Delayed grief stung my eyelids. "Well, I can confirm he's dead. Very dead." I cleared my throat.

"Let me comfort you." He held out his arms in a display of faux paternal comfort that was even less convincing than my father's had been.

"Nice try." Wiping my eyes, I maneuvered out of reach. I'd had enough company for tonight. If Seth murdered a friend of mine, he wouldn't come to see me immediately afterward. Just because he was a demon didn't mean he was pure evil.

Of course, I was alone in thinking that.

"The invitation into my home is about to officially expire. Time to go."

"It's almost dawn. I'll make us breakfast."

"No, thank you. I'll be climbing into bed." I strode past him and opened the door, wrapping my fingers around my necklace for a quick burst of energy in case it was necessary.

He sauntered over to me, his full lips curving into a smile. "I won't joke about joining you there."

"You just did. Now out."

His grin widened. "If you say so, witch. I suspect you could make me if I put up a fight."

"You bet I could."

With a wink, he stepped outside. Just as I was closing the door between us, he asked, "Will there be a funeral?"

I was wondering the same thing. Tristan didn't have family, and the Protectorate kept their rites invitation only. "None of your business."

"I wish that were true, but the Protectorate has made itself my business," he said. "As you well know."

The chill in his voice was as sharp as the night breeze. As Protector, Tristan had merely blocked demons from entering Silverpool. His replacement might be more aggressive.

I met his gaze. Neither one of us wanted that to happen. "I imagine there will be a memorial service for nonmag people because he owned the winery and knew everybody. But I probably won't be involved in that. I'm too fringe."

"Shall I subtly encourage all his ex-girlfriends to attend?" His white teeth gleamed again. "Imagine what a crowd that could be. They'd have to hold it at the Oakland Coliseum."

My sympathy for him and his kind vanished. Seth just might be able to drop a few magical hints into a few—or a few dozen—unsuspecting human minds if he was feeling bored or vengeful.

"If you interfere in any way," I said in a low voice, "I'll drive a silver fork through your heart and feed you to my father's dragon."

Waving, he disappeared into the shadows, his rich laughter trailing away with him.

Chapter Four

The sound of howling woke me up.

I rolled to the edge of my bed and slapped the top of the nightstand for my phone.

Just before nine. At first I'd thought the noise was my alarm, but as my head cleared, I realized the noise was coming from the other room.

I clambered to my feet without a quarter of the grace my elegant father had, pushing the hair out of my face as I staggered through the house to find the source of the howling. My house was only nine hundred and fifty square feet, so it didn't take long. I found the creature in the living room trapped between my file cabinet, filled with beads, and the redwood staff, filled with magic, that leaned against it. Within the triangle of space between the two, wedged against the wall, a large black dog of mixed breed sat and howled.

"Hello there," I said.

The howling continued.

Where did he come from? I'd set up a second set of guarding spells before going to bed.

The curtain over the window above the file cabinet

rustled in the wind. Had he simply jumped in? My spells were only directed at enemies. Perhaps he wasn't dangerous and might not be magical at all, although some animal sixth sense had told him to stay away from the staff. Away from home, it was only slightly stronger than one of my redwood beads. But inside the house, because I'd carved it from a broken beam I'd found in the attic, it was quite powerful.

I walked over, watching the dog's dark eyes for any sign of intelligence or malice—too often the same thing—and picked up the staff. It warmed in my hand and vibrated slightly as it recognized its owner. I moved the staff behind my back, blocking its radiating power from the dog with my body.

The howl sank to a whimper, and then it was quiet.

The dog jumped up, tail wagging, tongue lolling, and bounded over to me, no sign of either intelligence or malice.

I reached out a hand, holding the staff behind me with the other one. "What are you doing here?"

Panting, he smiled a doggy smile.

"Are you going to eat me?" I asked.

He continued to smile.

I saw a collar around his neck, buried in the black fur, but I couldn't find any tags.

I looked into his eyes. His fur was soft, clean, freshly brushed. "Did the Protector send you to me?"

Too quickly for me to stop him, the dog's tongue shot out and licked my face, penetrating a nostril as it swiped past.

I wiped my face and used a quick spell to see if I could feel any hint of a human or magical fingerprint but sensed none. That didn't mean there wasn't any. I'd been kicked out of the Protectorate, after all—my powers were unreliable.

"So. Dog. We have a problem." The staff was awkward

behind my back, so I set it to one side, silently commanding it to relax for now. "You can't stay here."

He looked at me with the biggest, saddest eyes I'd ever seen and then tilted his head to one side. I felt actual pain in my chest, as if the needles I used to thread my beads were using my aorta as a pincushion.

"I don't have time to explain," I said. "I've got to go out, probably for the rest of the day." The shock of the night before was flooding back into my body, compelling me to take some kind of action. I wasn't sure what, which bothered me even more.

He trotted away from me and began exploring the house, his scraggly black tail wagging. I heard the sound of dog toenails against porcelain and hurried into the bathroom to find him in the tub, eagerly licking the dripping faucet.

Nurturing instincts kicked in. Whoever or whatever he was, I had to give him a proper drink. In the kitchen, I filled a bowl with water and set it on the floor. He loped in and immediately began lapping it up. Water droplets flew around his face and made a puddle on the tile. His pleasure was extreme, obvious, sincere.

I had been trained to identify the evil in demons and magic, both as a descendant of an ancient witch family and as an agent of the Protectorate, and I could sense nothing dangerous about the dog other than his thirst.

He finished drinking and sat back, panting and smiling.

I opened the back door and shooed him outside. Then I turned away from his sad eyes and went to the bathroom to take a shower. When I was dressed and ready to go out, I grabbed a can of cold coffee out of the fridge (the drink of the damned, Tristan had called it) and opened the back door. The dog was still there, right where I'd put him, acting thrilled to see me.

I rested my forehead on the door. If I let him back into

the house, I wouldn't be here to let him out. And under the circumstances, I couldn't leave the door open, even with a few spells. Too risky.

"You can't stay inside," I said.

He stared up at me.

I stared back. I thought about the forces gathering, the unknown ones that had already broken through. What else could I do? I stepped out, closed the door behind me, and jerked my head. "All right, come with me." He jumped up and trotted beside me to my Jeep in the driveway.

"I hope you don't get carsick," I said as I opened the back seat.

He jumped in and immediately scrambled forward into the passenger seat, where he sat upright and stared straight ahead. Tongue lolling out, obviously ready to rumble.

He seemed more sure of himself than I was. Once again, I put a hand on my necklace, buried the other in his fur, and stared at the dog with my third eye, the gift that even my father thought was a crock of sparkling fae scat.

My third eye didn't see anything but *canis familiaris*. The eagerness to please me and love me forever was indeed magic, but the kind of magic that all good dogs had.

So maybe… sometimes… a dog was just a dog.

But why me? Why today?

"You're so random," I said.

I got into the driver's seat and decided to find the one man left in Silverpool who might be able to help. Jasper was a fellow outsider, a witch who didn't work for the Protectorate. And he was the closest thing I had to a friend.

And if something was in town killing witches, he might need help looking after himself. I'd been kicked out of the Protectorate, but at least I'd been trained to kill.

Hadn't been able to do it, but killing was overrated.

As Tristan would surely agree.

TEN FEET PAST MY DRIVEWAY, a dark-haired, twentysomething woman in a cropped purple sweater and skinny jeans jumped out from behind the shrubs and ran in front of my Jeep, her arms flapping.

"Wait! Wait!"

I slammed on the brakes and flung out a hand to stop the dog from flying through the windshield. Although I hadn't been going very fast, it would've been fast enough to crush the legs of a nonmagical store clerk in her flip-flops.

"Birdie." It was my neighbor from across the street, Elizabeth Crow. Nickname, Birdie. I let out my breath, closed my eyes, and released my grip on Random's fur.

"Did you hear?" Birdie came around to the driver's side, her brown eyes wide with concern. "Tristan Price... on the bridge..."

"I heard," I said.

"Poor guy. So, so sad. I hope you're all right? Hi there, dog. Why do you have a dog in your car? Is that your dog? Or is it Tristan's? Somebody mentioned he was getting a dog. Not that I knew him, even though he came into the store a lot. Was in yesterday, actually, can you believe it? Now he's gone. Poor baby, your human is in heaven now, but don't worry, Alma will take care of you." She took a deep breath. "Listen, could you give me a ride to Livia's? My car battery is dead. I must've left the dome lights on or something. I'll find another ride back. Can you wait while I get my purse?"

I'd learned not to interrupt Birdie's flow of words. Talking only encouraged her, like shouting at a barking dog.

Speaking of dogs, Random was ignoring Birdie completely, staring straight ahead as if she weren't there. If I had to guess his mood, it was impatience. I could relate.

"I don't know, Birdie," I said. "Livia—"

But Birdie was already jogging away, looking over her shoulder and holding up an index finger. She wasn't a witch, but somehow that index finger had the power to keep me from driving away. I kept to myself, especially since I'd moved to Silverpool, and never got too close to normal people. But Birdie was a force of nature. There was no stopping her—not even with magic, and I was ashamed to admit I'd been tempted. We were about the same age, and she was painfully sweet; I felt guilty for not being more sociable with her.

"There! Thank you so much." Birdie climbed into the back seat behind Random, reaching forward to stroke and pat him. "Aren't you beautiful. What's your name?" She stroked his neck. "Nice collar. Did Tristan die before he had a chance to get him tags? No, he's not Tristan's dog, is he? Sorry, I got carried away. Everything makes me think of Tristan Price today."

"I know," I said. "Me too."

"He's a rescue, right? They say nobody likes to adopt black dogs from shelters, especially mixed breeds, because they're sinister or something, like bad luck in a fairy tale. Beast from hell," she said. "As if this sweet guy would ever hurt anyone. He's as gentle as a therapy dog. Will your cat have a problem with him? Obviously not or you wouldn't have gotten him. What's his name?"

I waited for a moment to make sure she was going to give me time to answer. "I think I'll call him Random."

"Great name! Do you like hiking, Random? I could take him hiking sometimes if you're not afraid of ticks. They were terrible last spring because we had so much rain over the winter. I got those clothes with the organic chemical stuff in it that is supposed to keep them away. I'm not sure it works, but I don't seem to attract ticks anyway. I think it's because I'm a vegetarian? Does that make sense?"

"Got your seat belt on?" I asked, hitting the gas.

Birdie yelped, laughing, and scooted back into her seat to put on the seat belt. The Jeep didn't have the smoothest ride, but it got me over the roads near the river when they flooded every winter.

The car fell silent as we drove down the hill into Silverpool's business district, which consisted of three quiet blocks of retail shops and small industry, and then up another road that led to the larger, wealthier homes overlooking the river.

People who didn't get to know Birdie—which, unfortunately for the socially starved Birdie, was most—never learned that the torrent of words faded away after the first few minutes of her company. It was as if the stress of first meeting triggered the word explosion, but as she relaxed, the talking slowed to a steady stream rather than a flash flood. I'd learned to let it flow before attempting a conversation.

"Thanks for the ride," Birdie said, reaching forward to pet Random. "I just couldn't deal with my car this morning. It's usually so reliable, you know? That's why I got a Toyota."

"Don't worry about it." I was a little worried about having to talk to Livia.

"Oh! I didn't realize! Livia is going to want you to tell her everything. You should've told me to find another ride."

I smiled faintly.

"You're right," Birdie said. "I would've blabbed on anyway. I get carried away and I just use words to hold on." Birdie sighed and turned her face to the window. "There I go again."

This was the time with Birdie that I dreaded—when she was beating herself up. Her shoulders slumped, the corners of her mouth turned down, the sparkle went out of her eyes.

After my rough night, I wasn't in the best place to cheer anyone up. Distraction might work though. "How did you hear about Tristan?"

Birdie reached forward to sink her fingers into Random's fur again. "On my run. The bridge was blocked off with police tape. I stopped and asked why. I can't believe anyone would run someone over and then just drive away. Didn't even call 911. I guess they figured it could be traced and they'd get in trouble." Some of the animation came back into her voice. "Cute cop though. I don't remember seeing him before."

The idea of a new, young cop made me nervous. The older ones tended to stay away from Silverpool or keep their visits short. Tristan had encouraged (and magically enhanced) that attitude.

"Lots of hotties out this morning, come to think of it," Birdie continued. "There was another cute guy selling apples out of his truck near Taco Perdido on Main Street. Gravensteins. I wanted to get some before they got mushy. You know how they're only crunchy for a week or two and then they get all waxy on the outside and they're like sourdough bread inside? I hate that. Anyway, these were good. He said to say hi."

I tightened my grip on the steering wheel. "Who did?"

"The apple guy. He mentioned you by name."

Chapter Five

❧❀❧

Birdie didn't seem to notice how her casual comment had upset me. Witches had ways of limiting any gossip about them. Too much casual chitchat about the woman with the messy garden or the guy with the chunky silver necklace could lead to disaster. That is, death.

"I figured you knew each other," Birdie said. "He didn't seem at all like a guy who'd be selling apples out of his truck."

That's because he hadn't been a guy selling apples out of his truck. More than one kind of magical being could've sensed Birdie's desire for apples and made it happen. Who was he?

"Describe the guy," I said.

"Cop or apple?"

"Apple."

"Agreed. Both were cute, but apple guy was cuter." Birdie smiled. "Dark hair, blue eyes, six foot one with lots of muscle, long nose with skinny nostrils, dimple in his chin, scar on his right cheek, pierced eyebrow, tattoo under his collar. The ink was orange. Fire maybe."

On the road outside Livia's house, I braked and stared at Birdie. She'd just described Seth Dumont perfectly. What was he up to? "Do you have a photographic memory?" I asked.

Birdie smiled. "I do if I want to take a picture of what I'm looking at."

With renewed appreciation, I asked, "How about the cop?"

"More like Luke than Han, you know what I mean? Blondish, boyish, guardian of goodness." Birdie leaned back into her seat and unfastened the seat belt. "We didn't talk. He was busy with the scene of the accident. Drivers were yelling at him to open the bridge. Looks like he did. It was open when we drove by just now, did you notice?"

"I noticed." When the bridge was closed, getting out of Silverpool meant a two-hour detour—out to the ocean, down to Highway 1, and then back east on a winding two-lane road through redwood forest, rolling grassland, orchards, off-the-grid homesteads, remote B & Bs, and dairy farms. Even with the bridge open, nonmagicals often had trouble finding Silverpool unless they'd been born there or were escorted by a resident. It was a spell Protectors had worked hard to maintain. With Tristan dead, not only supernatural threats but more and more human strangers, innocent and not-so-innocent, might start showing up.

"I hope it was quick," Birdie said. "I hate to think of him lying there."

"Me too." My voice wavered.

Birdie put a hand over her mouth. "I'm so sorry," she mumbled. "I just can't stop thinking about it."

"I know. Me neither."

I parked in the narrow circular driveway positioned below Livia's house, a luxury vacation-style home on a steep hill.

Right after moving in last year, Livia had cut down the original cedar, fir, and redwood around it to provide a panoramic view of the valley below from her wraparound deck. She'd pressured her neighbor downhill to do the same to improve her view. The neighbor, an elderly, irritable male witch, had refused.

Her next step had been to write him a letter on legal stationery, claiming the trees were a hazard. Soon after the letter, a family of skunks moved in under the planks of her deck, directly below the yoga mat where she did her sun salutations every morning. And then something annoyed the skunks, and her deck became unusable for months.

The trees were still there. It was a bad idea to make a witch your enemy. Even if you didn't believe in them.

"I'd rather drop you off," I muttered. "But I'd better say hi. She might see my car and be offended I didn't come in." I got out of the Jeep and went over to the passenger side.

Birdie climbed out next to me. "I forgot it would be awkward with you being Tristan's ex and Livia being in love with him."

Yes, it was always awkward. "I'll make it quick." I reached in and cracked the window. "I don't have a leash, so I'm going to have to leave him in the car." Even though he wasn't my dog, I felt responsible for him. With so many blind corners and hills, a dog could easily get run over.

I followed Birdie up the two dozen steep wooden steps that led to the deck and front door. Livia herself used a short driveway at the top of the hill behind the house, saving herself the climb she imposed on her guests.

When I got to the top, I looked back. Random sat rigidly in the front seat, watching me as if I'd commanded him to stand guard.

I watched the dog, and the dog watched me. Hairs stood up on the back of my neck.

Was he protecting me from someone? Or protecting someone else from *me*?

The door flung open. "Birdie, how nice of you to come," Livia said. Her tone cooled. "And you brought Alma."

Livia was the wealthy granddaughter of a boutique wine-maker in Napa. She'd only moved to Silverpool last year after meeting Tristan at a wine festival. In her late thirties and tall, dark, and beautiful, Livia wore the kind of clothes you'd see in a magazine feature about the wealthy granddaughter of a famous winemaker living in a luxury home in a rural Cali-fornian redwood forest. Lots of pale earth tones, silk scarves, handmade jewelry, expensive jeans that had been artificially distressed. Her white sneakers were as spotless as pillowcases at the Ritz.

"Alma brought me," Birdie said. "I asked her for a ride because…"

The gush of words began to flow. Birdie rambled on about her car battery and ticks and the cute guy selling apples, while Livia waited patiently for her to finish. When Birdie finally paused for breath, Livia turned to me.

"Why was he walking across the bridge in the middle of the night?" she demanded.

"He loved going for walks along there," I said. "Especially around harvest time."

Like other nonmagicals, Livia had known Tristan only as a rich guy with a winery. Who for some bizarre reason had befriended and briefly dated the broke, artsy nobody Alma Bellrose.

"It was a beautiful night," Birdie said.

Livia usually gave an impression of businesslike superior-ity, but now she crumpled, tears beginning to flow as she held out her arms to Birdie.

"Life is so unfair," Livia said, her voice hitching on a sob.

Birdie didn't hesitate to fling open her own arms. "It is," she said. Maybe the shortest sentence she'd ever spoken.

The two women embraced briefly. Livia sniffed, pulled back, and wiped her wet cheeks with the backs of her hands.

"Come on in." She opened the door. Just inside, three cats of various colors and sizes sat watching us.

Cats.

My skin began to itch. I'd never been inside Livia's house before. Becoming friends had never been on either one of our agendas.

"I didn't realize you had cats," I said.

"Of course," Livia said. "I have four. One of them always hides. Why, are you allergic?"

I took a step back. "I'm afraid so. I better not come in."

"But you have a cat," Birdie said. "Don't you?"

Both women stared at me, waiting for an explanation I couldn't give.

Chapter Six

This was one reason I didn't have friends. It was easier to avoid people than avoid lies. I took a moment to concoct a partial truth.

"Not full time," I said. "I have to get loaded up on antihistamines first before I let her in the house."

Livia gestured to a patio set of redwood furniture. "I suppose we can sit out here. The wind isn't too bad. It might be therapeutic to get out of the house. I've been crying nonstop since I got the news at three this morning." The chairs had yellow-and-white-striped cushions, which seemed impractical in a forest. "Should I make coffee?"

"Not for me," I said. "I can only stay a minute."

Although she obviously hadn't wanted my company in the first place, now she was offended I wouldn't stay. "Why not?" she asked. "What could you possibly be doing that's more important than grieving for a decent, generous man who was—who was—struck down at the prime of his life?"

I clenched my teeth together. Livia wasn't a witch, wasn't a demon, wasn't family or employer, but somehow the woman always got under my skin. Born to wealth and privilege, Livia instinctively judged everyone, especially people she thought weren't very smart or hardworking. Like me.

I shoved my hands in my pockets to stop myself from doing something I'd regret, such as inflicting a rash of posterior cystic acne. Livia was irritating, but she'd just lost the man she'd loved. Or her idea of the man, anyway.

"I have a dog in the car," I said. "And a friend's expecting me." Not quite true but close enough.

"A dog? Well, I suppose you would. It's not like you have a job." Livia closed her eyes and held up a hand. "Sorry, that sounded critical. All I meant was, you're home a lot."

That wasn't all she'd meant. Born with money, Livia was suspicious of people who seemed to survive without it. In some ways she was right to be suspicious—I must have *some* source of income to buy food and pay the rent on my house, however small. The beaded necklaces and bracelets I sold at the farmers' markets around Sonoma County and in the Bay Area shouldn't be enough to live on. Since she didn't know they were magical and therefore cost more than they looked, she assumed I must get my money from somebody else, somebody who wasn't as stupid and lazy as I was. Uncle Sam, perhaps, or—possibly her deepest, nastiest suspicion—the late, great, generous Tristan Price.

"Speaking of jobs," Birdie said. "That's where I met Tristan. I rang up the purchase order for the new kitchen he had put in last winter. Nice of him to shop local, don't you think? The boss always says that. She loves Tristan. Contractors come into the store all the time and put things on his account."

Birdie worked at Cypress Hardware, the biggest store in town, a general hardware, arts and crafts, agricultural and pet supply, and do-it-yourself retailer that managed to compete against the big-box chain stores in Riovaca. As if by magic, people said, which is exactly what it was. If you got lost driving out of town, you tended to shop local.

"You need to make sure everyone at the store is invited to the service," Livia said. "If nobody from the Price family steps forward, I'll arrange it myself."

I didn't think there would be any Prices showing up to throw a funeral in Silverpool. The only time Tristan had mentioned family had been in the past tense.

The Protectorate, on the other hand, would have some kind of gathering, but it would be private, and there wouldn't be any tears. The witches at the top of the Protectorate weren't the emotional type—another reason I didn't work there anymore. The witches at the bottom weren't supposed to have feelings—unless those feelings helped them murder demons.

Sorry. *Exterminate.* Like killing cockroaches. Just doing everyone a favor. The only person who had ever understood how I felt about that was Jasper. I wanted to talk to him now more than ever. Being with nonmagicals could be exhausting.

"I really do have to go," I said, glancing at Birdie.

She mouthed a silent apology: *Please forgive me. I never should've asked you for a ride here. I know what she's like. I'm so, so, so sorry. Can I make you muffins?*

It was much longer than any unvoiced message should ever be. Only my magic allowed me to understand it.

"Let me know if there's anything I can do for the memorial," I said as my first foot hit the stairs, just because I felt like I had to say something else before I could escape.

"Thank you, Alma," Livia said. "I will."

Tactical error. I didn't look back, just kept walking. In general, I'd be happy to help with a memorial service. But for Tristan? With Livia?

I shuddered and pulled out my car fob. When I climbed

into the Jeep, Random jumped at me, tongue extended for a kiss, his entire body quivering as if he'd given up hope of ever seeing me again.

"I know how you feel," I said. "It felt like a long time to me too."

Chapter Seven

Jasper lived in a bungalow a half mile west of town on an unmarked private road. Redwood and cedar surrounded the small olive-green house, hiding it from casual drive-bys. He grew apples and pears on a sunny slope behind the house and gave the harvest to the fairies. He'd learned to do that after his first winter solstice in town, when the Vago River had jumped its banks and flooded his home with high-tide sludge.

A gravel driveway curved around the back to a detached one-car garage. His old blue Prius wasn't the only car parked there. Behind it was a small white BMW I'd never seen before.

Who could that be? Jasper was almost as solitary as I was. Officially, he taught guitar, piano, digital music software. Secretly and more profitably, he taught magic. But on the morning after the Protector's murder? Unlikely.

With his little driveway already full, I had to park my Jeep on the road with my wheels in the drainage ditch. I looked at Random to see if he had an opinion about where

I'd brought us, but he panted and stared straight ahead, giving nothing away.

"We're at Jasper's house," I said, still hoping for a response.

He glanced at me and kept panting.

"Let me know if you think of anything," I muttered, getting out of the car. I held my door open for him to climb over and follow. He turned away and looked at the handle on the passenger side.

"If you insist." I slammed my door and had to walk down into the ditch to open the door he apparently preferred.

He jumped down to join me, furiously wagging his tail. I shut the door and watched for any sign of familiarity with Jasper's property, but he stood where he was, waiting for me to lead the way to Jasper's front door.

If he'd known Jasper, surely he would've rushed ahead on his own?

I studied the BMW as I walked past, saw the San Francisco dealer tags on the license plate frames. Although the city seemed light years away, it was only about seventy miles. A local person might make the trip to buy a luxury car if it was a really good deal.

I put my hand on the door, muttered a quick spell to probe the space inside, and detected a faint thrum of latent magic. Not Jasper's fingerprint, so his visitor's. A witch.

A witch with a BMW from San Francisco had to mean—

The door opened. Jasper stood there with a bright, unblinking look on his face that was trying to tell me something without saying it. "Alma. I'm so sorry about Tristan," he said. "We were just talking about him."

"We?" I asked.

A petite woman a little younger than me appeared behind him. If her face hadn't been red and splotchy from crying recently, she would've been stunning. With the tears and snot streaks, she was merely beautiful.

She held out a small hand. "Phoebe Day," she said softly. Bird-boned, golden-skinned, wavy-haired. Her almond-shaped eyes were the brown of black coffee.

"I'm Alma. Sorry, am I intruding? I can come back later—"

Jasper looked unsure, but Phoebe shook her head violently. "No, no," she said. "You have to stay. You have to. Please."

I glanced at Jasper, who smiled tightly and stepped away from the door to usher me in.

Then he saw Random, and his smile relaxed. "You got a dog?"

His question was warm and natural, as if the dog was just a dog, one unknown to him.

I paused, not wanting to say anything until I knew who Phoebe was. "Long story. Is he allowed inside?"

"Are you kidding? Of course," Jasper said. "Not safe for him otherwise. The fairies have driven away the feral cats I was feeding. Who knows what they'd do with a nice puppy like that. What's his name?"

"Random," I said.

The dog immediately sat down, rigid with attention.

"Come here, buddy," Jasper said, patting his thighs.

Random, eyes on me, didn't move.

"Go ahead," I said softly. He jumped up and trotted through the doorway, tail wagging, and went over to sniff Jasper and then the pretty, weepy Phoebe.

"You've done a great job training him," Jasper said.

I smiled faintly. "He was a natural."

"Oh, what a sweetheart," Phoebe said, stroking Random's head as he jumped up, trying to lick her face. "Dogs are so empathetic, aren't they? They really do sense distress."

"It's been a rough day," I said. "Were you close to Tristan?"

Jasper flung out a hand, gesturing at the sofa and chairs under the front window. "Let's sit. Phoebe was just telling me a story."

We filed into the room to sit. Unlike me, Jasper had new furniture. The sofa and chairs were a set. The area rug was color coordinated with the paintings and earth-toned walls. The two table lamps were identical twins. And everything was in all-natural, expensive materials: leather, oak, wool, jute, silk, hemp. When I'd first been over, I'd been surprised —he was messy and tended to wear thrift shop T-shirts and jeans—and he'd explained a former student of his had done the decorating in exchange for tutoring.

I took the chair closest to the door and tilted it to have a view of the street. I hadn't been an agent for over two years, but the training went deep. Well, the stuff that I liked. Phoebe sat on the couch and invited the dog to sit with her, but he broke away and sat at my feet. Jasper looked as if he'd rather stay standing but then took the other chair.

"It's a sign. Your showing up, I mean." Phoebe gave me a big-eyed, melting look. "I was just begging Jasper to intro-duce us."

"Us?" I asked. "You wanted to meet me?"

Phoebe nodded. She looked as if the tears were going to start falling again. "Yes," she whispered. She paused to take a handkerchief out of her pocket and dabbed her high cheek-bones. Thick silver and gold bangles rattled against each other on her wrists, marking her as a metal witch. Most agents were. "You have no idea what I've been going through. I don't know who to go to, who can help."

I shot Jasper a questioning look.

"Phoebe works at the Protectorate in San Francisco," he said, not giving me much.

"My sister's ex-boyfriend knew a guy who studied with Jasper," Phoebe said. "He said he was really nice. Really helpful. I'm sorry I can't remember his name. It's been so stressful. You have no idea."

"I've had a lot of students over the years," Jasper said. "I'm sure I can't remember their names either, and I knew them personally."

Phoebe gave him a grateful look, and Jasper flushed and sat up straighter, obviously not immune to her beauty. So far as I knew, Jasper hadn't had a date since I'd moved to Silverpool.

"You need a focus string?" I asked, trying to get to the point. "I do make them, usually out of redwood beads, but they're not powerful enough for solving big problems." Metal and stone witches usually held the less flashy botanical elements in contempt.

Phoebe shook her head and turned to Jasper again. "You can explain much better than I can."

Jasper looked as if he wanted to argue, but Phoebe blasted him with another gooey look. His gaze darted back to me. "She thinks you can help her," he said. "Something big was stolen from the Diamond Street office yesterday."

"It's actually rather small," Phoebe said.

"Something valuable." Jasper shifted in his seat, cleared his throat, and studied the tasteful colors of the rug under his feet. "The way it was stolen suggests a pro."

I dug my fingers into Random's thick fur, seeking comfort in his solid warmth. "Does this have anything to do with Tristan Price's death?"

"God, I hope not," Phoebe said. "That would… No, I'm sure it's just a horrible coincidence. Your—" She bit her lip.

An awkward silence filled the room.

Sounded like Malcolm had been busy yesterday. Sometimes he would go on a thieving rampage, like a pub crawl, hitting multiple victims in one night.

"You think my father stole it?" I asked. I kept my voice casual, like it had nothing to do with me because it didn't, not anymore. Even if he'd just been in my own home the night before trying to steal something. The only way I could survive with my criminal father walking the earth was to isolate myself from whatever he did.

"I am so, so sorry to come to you like this, but he doesn't realize what the torc can do. They barely explained it to me. It's a very powerful amulet." Phoebe leaned forward, delicate hands spread over her delicate knees. "If you could just tell him it's dangerous—"

"You don't know it was him. It could be"—I thought wildly—"Freewitches. For all you know."

Freewitches were the scapegoat for any witch-related activity the Protectorate didn't like: Shadow magic, crimes against nonmag populations, indigestion. I'd never actually met one. It seemed like the Protectorate called any witch they didn't like a Freewitch so they could claim authority over them.

Phoebe shook her head. "That was my first thought, but the way the torc was stolen…" Phoebe sounded as if she genuinely regretted having to say any of what she was saying. "I've been told it has his fingerprints all over it."

"Metaphorically, you mean," I said.

"Magically," Phoebe said, more sharply. "The spell signature reminded my boss of one he'd found when your father stole a book from the Berlin office."

"Let me guess." I moved my hand away from the dog, who might get injured if I kept using him as a stress ball. "Lorne. Thomas Lorne is your boss with the sharp detective instincts."

"Naturally, as his daughter, it would be hard for you to admit his guilt."

I concentrated on keeping my expression blank. If I told this ambitious young thing that Lorne was not only my father's enemy but also my own, she might not believe the lie I was going to have to say next.

While I silently prepared the spell to lie convincingly, Jasper clapped his hands and made kissing noises to Random, who bounded over and began barking.

Thanks to the distraction, I was able to keep myself from gagging when I said, "Lorne is a very powerful witch. A great man."

Phoebe's face lit up with a dazzling smile. "I'm *so* glad you agree. Yes, yes he is. A great, powerful *mage*."

Some of the metal and stone witches at the Protectorate called themselves mages, but most of us thought it was silly. Hard magic wasn't necessarily more powerful than soft magic like herbs and other biological materials, but those types liked to puff themselves up.

"You must be very proud to be working for him," I added.

"I am. I thought that with your own, you know, history, you might not appreciate him."

"How could I not?" I felt bile rising in the back of my throat. Lorne had been the one to fire me. "I'm sure he has excellent reasons to suspect Malcolm of taking this thing—what is it?"

"A torc."

"And what is that?" I asked.

Jasper frowned at me, probably wondering why I was playing dumb.

"A large, open ring you wear around your neck." Phoebe brushed her throat with a slender fingertip. Multiple shiny silver rings adorned each finger. "Most are a thick collar that's open at the bottom, under your chin. This one is gold."

"Then I doubt my father would want it," I said. "He's never liked wearing jewelry. It's too hard to teleport with. I guess the metal is a challenge."

Phoebe's upper lip twitched, an unhidden sneer. Her opinion of me, which was probably already low from whatever Lorne had told her, was sinking.

"He didn't want it to *wear*," Phoebe said slowly. "He wanted to sell it on the black market."

I made myself blush. "Of course. How silly of me." Let her think I was a failed agent, totally harmless; she might leave me alone. If the Protectorate went after my father, I could get caught up in the dragnet. Again. Honestly, what was the point of having a parent?

"Have you seen him recently?" Phoebe asked. "Jasper said you don't see him very often."

"I haven't seen him in over a year," I said.

When Phoebe's truth spell wafted around me, measuring my truthfulness, I let it swirl over my skin and return to its sender as pure and honest as it had arrived. I wasn't the most powerful witch in the world, but I had my talents. A Protectorate agent, even younger than I was, wasn't a match for me and my beads.

"And you haven't heard from him? A letter, an email, a phone call—nothing?"

"Nothing," I said.

Phoebe sent another spell. I deflected it easily as I had the first one. She would've benefited from one of my focus strings, not that I was going to offer her one.

Apparently confident in her truth-sniffing powers, Phoebe buried her face in her hands. "That's it then. I'm finished. You and Jasper were my only hope. I don't have any other way to track your father down." She looked up. The tears were falling again. "I had to come up here and ask."

"But why you?" I asked.

"I was in charge of security the night it was stolen."

"Really? You?"

Phoebe frowned, lifting her chin. "I'm unusually powerful for my age."

There were different kinds of powers, I thought. But maybe I was a little prejudiced against beautiful, younger-than-me women with high-paying, prestigious jobs. "Of course."

"Right after Lorne told me to make sure it was protected," Phoebe said, "I assigned the torc to two of our best agents. They were in the house with it the entire time. They say they saw nothing out of the ordinary, but when Lorne went to retrieve it from the box, it was gone."

"How could that be your fault?" Jasper asked. "Why not blame the two agents on duty?"

"I chose them myself. I'm responsible. If I don't find your father and convince him to return the torc, I'll have to resign. I could never walk into the Protectorate again if I'd failed in my primary duty."

I wondered if Phoebe intended to insult me with the mention of failure of primary duty, which was what had led to my discharge. Phoebe could simply be so self-centered other people's feelings didn't occur to her.

I struggled to keep a bland, sympathetic smile on my face.

"We can call you if we hear anything," Jasper said.

Phoebe turned to me with pleading eyes. "Would you do that?"

"Of course," I said. Lies were like pumping water. It could be hard to get them started, but once they started flowing, it was easy to keep going.

"Thank you." Phoebe stood and offered me her hand, rattling the bracelets again on her wrist. She shook my hand briefly in the limp-fingered way some women did, as if her bones would snap under the slightest pressure. And maybe hers would. She did look as if a canary could knock her over.

Jasper jumped up and walked to the door. "I'll see you out."

When Jasper came back into the house, he locked the door and paused for a moment before turning to me. Neither of us spoke.

Chapter Eight

Jasper squatted down to Random and rubbed his ears. "I'm so glad you got a dog."

"I don't suppose I could bother you for a cup of coffee?"

"Help yourself. I just made a pot." Perhaps noticing my evasion, he studied Random with renewed interest. I could sense him probing the dog with a spell of his own.

Because we were both witches of a similar age in a small, isolated community, he'd had me over for coffee every week or two since I moved to town. I went directly to the mugs, poured myself a cup, and plopped down at the kitchen table. The mug I'd chosen bore the logo of an estate lawyer in Santa Rosa, another one of Jasper's students. Teaching magic was a solid business.

Jasper pulled out a chair next to me. "I'm sorry about Tristan."

"Yeah." I was sad and a little afraid, although I hated to admit it. "He must've been hurt before they ran him over. He would've been able to deflect the car if he'd been in his full powers."

Jasper reached out and put a hand over mine. "They?"

"Figure of speech. He or she. Them. I don't know." I closed my eyes. "I felt magic on the bridge. The Protectorate will probably assume it was demon done, but I'm not convinced." Even though Seth had shown up so soon afterward.

"I put up an extra guard spell around my house," Jasper said.

"Good idea." I pulled my hand away to lift my cup. "I've already had company."

He looked up. "Really?"

"My father. I wasn't going to tell your visitor that, of course."

"You lied to a Protectorate agent?"

I hadn't expected him to disapprove. "They assume he's guilty."

"Don't you?"

I took a long swig of Jasper's coffee, the best in town. Instead of amulets and charms, he made brew. His talent with liquids included both magical and mundane. I savored the taste for a moment before saying, "Maybe. He was looking for something. Other than some pizza, he didn't take anything of mine. I think."

"So if he was at your house, he wasn't in San Francisco," Jasper said. "Right?"

"He's good at getting around." Out of old habit, I didn't like to share any of my father's secrets, even with friends. "He's always liked doing multiple jobs in one night. It's one reason he never gets caught."

"Still, I'm surprised you would try to protect him."

I preferred to see it as me protecting myself, not him. "I don't owe them anything."

He nodded, his gaze warming. "You definitely don't. The way they chucked you—"

"Hey. Not today."

"Sorry," he said quickly. "I didn't even know Tristan had died until I left the house to go to the bakery this morning," he said. "I felt something was wrong, but I didn't realize what until I overheard people talking."

"The Riovaca cops are investigating. They blocked the bridge."

"Nonmagicals will assume it was a hit-and-run drunk driver. Narrow bridge, no sidewalk, dark night, and a rich, local history of DUI." Jasper looked out his kitchen window onto the steep slope behind his house where he grew his fairy bribes. "But if he was dead before the car hit him…"

"It was a magical attack," I said. "Not an accident."

"Phoebe thought it was an accident."

"So she said."

"So she said," he agreed.

I was thinking about how Phoebe's distress felt genuine when Random sat at my feet and let out a loud sigh.

"This dog is a mystery too, by the way," I said. "He just showed up at my place this morning and won't leave me alone."

Jasper leaned over and studied Random under the table. "Could it be Tristan's doing?"

"I don't know. I thought if anyone might know, it would be you."

Jasper shook his head. "Not a clue. You'd need to find a good animal expert to be sure," he said. "I was just about to text you a warning that I had company. I had a feeling you might come over."

One great, ironic perk about technology: a nonmagical message was much harder for a witch to overhear than a spell.

"Do you think she's for real?" I asked.

"Let's find out." Jasper removed his laptop from a spell-protected backpack on the counter and opened it. Jasper had never worked at the Protectorate, but he had a knack with computers. Well, he had a knack for spelling apart password protections. Luckily for good and decent people everywhere, or even banks, governments, and corporations, he had no interest in committing crimes.

"She seemed awfully friendly with Lorne," I said. "Family connection?"

"Probably. Those old magic families stick together like demon spit on a Shadow witch's—" He glanced up from the keyboard, obviously remembering belatedly that I belonged to such a family, and made an apologetic face. "Sorry."

"None needed. It's true." I sipped my coffee. "If my father weren't a Bellrose, the Protectorate would've locked him up ages ago." Even without any evidence, which he'd brilliantly prevented. And they never would've risked hiring me, a known criminal's daughter, as an agent.

Jasper worked on the laptop for a few minutes and then said, "She's legit. At least she really works at the Protectorate. According to the current directory, she's got a desk on the top floor of the house on Diamond Street. Isn't that where you worked?"

The Protectorate had offices scattered around the world. Its local bureaucracy was in San Francisco, inside a large converted Victorian in the residential neighborhood of Noe Valley. A century ago, the local members of the Protectorate had been a small cooperative of witches living far from the action in New York, London, Paris, Tokyo. Now it wasn't much larger, but its location made it rich, and wealth made it powerful.

"Yes, I worked on Diamond." Although Jasper and I spent hours together chatting over coffee, I'd avoided talking about my time at the Protectorate. As I looked into my cup, I wondered if the talented Phoebe had my old desk. It was in the attic, facing west, which could get stuffy on sunny days but had a distracting view of a stunning sunset behind Sutro Tower every evening. "And I slept there, too. Most young agents can't afford San Francisco rent, and they work around the clock anyway, so most end up sleeping under their desks. It was like boarding school."

"Without beds."

"I got pretty good at making a soft-floor spell. And I learned how to close my ears so the snoring didn't bother me."

Jasper rolled his eyes. "Gee, too bad you got fired. Sounds like such a great job."

I poked him in the arm. "You're just jealous."

"Nope. I never saw the appeal. Never. Wealth, status, and power beyond measure? Pfft."

"Are you joking?"

"Of course I'm joking," he said. "I'd love wealth, fame, and power beyond measure. But they didn't even respond to my resume. Not once."

"How many times did you apply?"

"At least twice. Maybe three times."

I regarded the shallow pool of coffee at the bottom my cup, looking for hints of the future. But Jasper had spelled his house effectively; I didn't sense a thing. I couldn't tell him that I hadn't actually applied to the Protectorate on my eighteenth birthday, that they'd come to me. It might put a strain on our friendship, which I'd come to value, especially now. With Tristan dead, Jasper was the only witch left in town I could talk to.

"Your reputation is better for it," I said. "I'm a laughingstock."

Jasper frowned. "Nobody is supposed to know why you were let go."

"And therefore everybody does. Word gets around." I

pointed at his laptop. "But enough about me. What's Phoebe's level in the directory?"

"Quartz."

I whistled. Most witches hired by the Protectorate stayed at the Flint level, the entry-level tier, for at least a decade. I myself was still technically a Flint. "Either she's really good, really connected, or she's using an aging spell. What would you say she is, twenty, twenty-one?"

"At the most."

"Have you ever heard of any Quartz witches under twenty-five?"

"No," he said, "but they can spell themselves to look younger, right?"

"Somehow I don't think she's older than she looks," I said. "She acts young."

"Kind of emotional," he agreed.

"How about her family. Day. Do you know any Days?"

"Not that I remember. Could be an alias. To make her sound Bright and good."

"If it is an alias, Lorne would know it was fake," I said. "Unless she's so powerful he didn't unearth her secrets before he hired her." Every prospective hire at the Protectorate went through a months-long background check and magical brain scan.

"You told me Lorne wasn't very powerful himself, so maybe she fooled him."

"He wouldn't rely on his own powers to test her," I said. "He would pretend he did though. Most people still seem to think he's capable. Dude couldn't even get a sandwich out of a paper bag without his app's help."

An app was an apprentice. The term hadn't been nearly as confusing in the previous century before our neighbors down south in Silicon Valley had changed its meaning. Recently New York had commanded everyone to begin using the title "assistant" instead of "apprentice," but the abbreviation for *that* one had been too popular (in a bad way), and so most continued to say "app." (Although I'd been known to call my least favorite Protectorate people "Ass Mages," because how could I not?)

"I wish I had an app," Jasper said. "I'd have him feed the fairies every night when I go to bed so they won't sing outside my window and drive me crazy."

"I could come by sometime if you're really desperate," I said.

He got up and poured me more coffee. "I might take you up on that. You don't have to do anything, just sleep on the sofa. They'll be terrified of you."

"Me? I doubt that."

"You're the most powerful witch I know," he said.

"The most powerful witch you know with an Incurable Inability." I smiled. "You don't have to humor me. I've accepted—"

"One thing you can't do. One. The rest you can do better than anyone else."

I was too tired to argue. Besides, we'd had this discussion too many times already. "My father doesn't have the torc," I said. "At least he didn't have it when he came to see me last night. He wouldn't risk bringing something valuable into another witch's house. He might lose control of it."

"Phoebe had no right to come here trying to get to him through you."

"The Protectorate gives her the right. I don't like it, but I don't blame her for trying to do her job."

Jasper moved over to sit on the tile near Random, who was asleep, making faint, squeaky barking noises as he dreamed. "Maybe you should leave the dog here in case it's a spy."

"What about the fairies? If he's just a regular dog, they could hurt him."

"I'll hang a charm potion around his neck. The stray cats never let me get close enough to put them on. He seems friendly enough."

"He's very friendly." It would be sad to leave Random behind, but Jasper had a good point about spies. The dog showed up at my house for a reason, and secret reasons were usually bad. "You don't mind?"

Jasper stroked the sleeping dog with an arm that was tattooed with thin, black concentric arcs that radiated outward from a birthmark on his wrist, like rings on a tree. Each year he got a new one. The outermost ring, the twenty-ninth, now reached the curve of his bicep. "I love dogs. And maybe I'll be able to figure out where he came from."

"I'd appreciate that. I've never been very good with living things." I could make an excellent bead necklace or add a fourth leaf to a clover, but I'd never been interested in manip-ulating anything with a brain. I bent over and scratched Random's ears, already missing him.

I got to my feet. "I should get going. With Tristan gone, all kinds of trouble are going to get into town before they get a new Protector set up. I'd rather not be caught unprepared."

But before I went home, I had an errand to accomplish. A little something I wanted to collect before it became impossible.

"I don't get it," Jasper said. "Why Silverpool? Why does it need a Protector? It's the middle of nowhere."

Jasper leaned back, crossed his burly arms over his chest, and regarded me from under furrowed brows. "And don't repeat the official line about Tristan loving wine so much he had to have his own winery."

Chapter Nine

He's right, I thought. *I should tell him. I'll explain—*

A wave of pins and needles swept over my skin. The spell binding me to secrecy was strong, but after what had happened to Tristan, I thought Jasper should know. For his own safety, if nothing else. He might want to pack up and move.

When I opened my mouth to speak, the pins and needles became shards of glass slicing my skin, digging into flesh, piercing my organs. Nothing visible, nothing real, but my nerves didn't know it was an illusion. Gasping for breath, I grasped at my necklace and tried not to think about the spring deep beneath Silverpool, the spring that held the secret I'd been forbidden to share.

With effort that brought sweat to my forehead, I fought against the pins, the needles, the shards of glass. "Silverpool," I said tightly, doubling over in pain. "At the solstice. Winter."

I held my necklace, closed my eyes, and directed my inner vision to the onslaught of power coming at me from all sides. No, mostly to my left, where the Emerald witch had stood when he'd set the spell in San Francisco. I brought his image up in my mind: tall and strong with dark skin, a shaved head, and kind brown eyes.

He hadn't been the type to enjoy hurting anyone. Like me, he was an idealist, a friend, an artist. Twenty years older than me, with an excellent reputation, he'd had his own office with a view. He'd preferred gold over silver, and the bands of power I could feel snaking into my mind and around my tongue were also gold. Lovely and bright, warm as sunshine.

Tapping into the core of power I'd discovered as a small child, I followed the thread of power several feet in each direction. I gauged its size and shape and then, flinching at another wave of pain, drew deeply on my core. With the knife of my mind, I sliced at each shining band. They were handsome threads, but the witch's heart hadn't been in it. Inflicting pain just didn't come naturally to most good people, even witches. I could feel them shudder, break, fly away. And then suddenly there was no pressure, no resistance, and my tongue was free.

Jasper grabbed my shoulders. "Forget it. Alma. Forget it. I'm sorry I asked. Forget—"

"It's okay." I opened my eyes and smiled. "I broke it. I can tell you now."

He shook his head. "You can't be sure of that. It might have a second layer—"

"I'm sure. I felt it snap." I sank into a chair and let Random, who was jumping around my legs in distress, put his paws on my knees. I leaned forward, taking comfort in his soft fur, his cold, wet nose. "You should know about Silverpool. I should've tried to break it earlier."

"I'm not so sure about that." Jasper went over to a cupboard and reached up to the top shelf for a dark green bottle with a handwritten label. "You look like you need a drink."

I should've protested—time was short, and I didn't know what I was up against—but he had already begun pouring the black liquid into my coffee cup. White tendrils rose up in a spiral, reaching not directly upward but at an angle to Jasper's face. He waved it away.

"Drink," he said.

Reluctantly—all right, eagerly—I lifted the cup to my lips. Jasper's specialty was in potions, liquids of all kinds; he was a rare type of witch that had no routine job openings at the Protectorate. As I drank, the tendrils returned to the liquid and then filled my body with a soothing, restful glow. It regenerated the magic core inside me, the place old-fashioned hearth witches called the Witchwell.

All witches had some innate core of magic, of course, to set them apart from nonmagic humanity, but modern Protectorate teaching had a low opinion of the soft, invisible, mysterious powers of a person's inner self. A modern witch should instead develop the power that came from metal and stone. Such as a gold torc. It was power you could use, see, measure, nurture, collect, share—and steal.

The lingering pain vanished, the exhaustion fell away, and an urge to laugh overtook me.

"Demon's balls, Jasper," I said, fighting a giggle. "You sure know how to make a cocktail."

He nodded. "Finish it off. Don't want to waste a drop."

I did as I was told, knowing it took days of difficult magic to fill a small bottle. The buzz wouldn't last long, only a minute or two, but it would erase the ill feeling from the broken silence spell.

When I'd recovered my wits, I licked the rim of the glass and stood, handing it to him with a smile. "Thanks."

"Least I could do."

"So, Silverpool…" I paused to confirm the spell was

gone. Not a single needle jabbed me, so I took a deep breath and continued. "There's a wellspring here."

He stared. "What?"

"A wellspring. Here in Silverpool."

"No! Where?"

"It doesn't usually come to the surface. Not year round and not every year. Only when the conditions are right, around late December."

He exhaled slowly, shaking his head. "The floods."

"Silverpool's namesake," I said. "It's not too far from here, actually, which is probably why you have so many fairies bothering you all the time."

The town was named after the seasonal lake that formed during wet winters when the Vago River flooded. The business district, wisely, had been constructed a half mile up river, on higher ground. On the west side of town, however, where the river snaked toward the Pacific, a high tide and heavy rain changed the landscape. At the winter solstice, under a full moon, the contained waters jumped their banks and transformed a narrow, steep-banked ravine into a pool.

Silverpool.

"I feel like such an idiot," Jasper said. "I never suspected a thing."

"Lots of magic has been used to keep you in darkness," I said. "The Protectorate—" I stopped myself. I could break the minor spell of a kindhearted Emerald witch, but going against a major one and spilling the secrets of the Protectorate would trigger far worse. I gave him an apologetic shrug.

"Got it. Say no more," Jasper said. "Well, how about that. I thought the fae were attracted to me and my magic. Very humbling."

"I'm sure they're also attracted to your magic, Jasper." I

patted his arm. His homemade moonshine had left a lingering buzz on my mood. Tristan was dead, and it wasn't right to bounce around giggling. "And so is everyone else with any magic. I want to get home before anyone makes another visit."

"Would your father come back?"

"If he does, I need to make sure he can't get inside my house again," I said. "The Protectorate will think we're working together."

"Would he really do that to you? Risk incriminating you?"

With a snort, I got to my feet again. A wave of dizziness overtook me. "He wouldn't see it like that. I may be his biological child, but I'm not actually him. That's what matters. Besides, I worked at the Protectorate, so I'm one of them. And I'm a Bellrose, which makes me, as you pointed out, destined to receive certain privileges." I gave Random a pat on the head and moved to leave. With each step, my head cleared a little, and by the time I opened the front door, I was cold sober.

Random tried to follow me, but Jasper held him back.

"I wish I knew if and why somebody sent me a dog," I said, lingering in the doorway.

"I'll see what I can do. I might have better luck after I feed him." Jasper looked into the dog's soulful eyes. "Do you like cheese, Random? How about peanut butter?"

Random wagged his tail, but his gaze darted to me. *Don't go*, he seemed to say.

I squinted at the dog's jaws and long pink tongue. Had he actually said that? I touched the necklace at my throat, soothed by its weight against my chest, and looked out into the yard. A fairy mist was gathering on the hillside near the pear trees. Jasper might be able to make a charmed collar, but would it be strong enough if the fairies were truly motivated?

I just didn't feel right leaving him. "You know what?

Never mind," I said, reaching out my hand. "I'll take Random with me."

Jasper didn't release his grip on the dog's collar. "Are you sure? It might be dangerous to take him with you. Somebody sent him or he sent himself, and either way—"

"I'm sure."

After a pause, Jasper let go. Random trotted over to me and sat on my foot, gazing up at me adoringly.

"At least take this," Jasper said, opening a closet and taking out a leather leash.

"Where'd you get that?" I asked.

"Student left it behind."

"Are you sure? It looks new."

"The kid's long gone. I'll never see him again. Don't worry about it."

I took the leash from him, grateful I wouldn't have to buy one myself, although I'd have to get other supplies. "Thanks." I wasn't starving, but I didn't have many pennies to spare.

"If you need another drink later, if the pain comes back, just let me know," Jasper said.

"It won't come back," I said, "but thanks."

"You're the only witch I know who could just walk away from a broken Protectorate spell."

I'd always thought Jasper had an overrated opinion of the Protectorate's powers. "I owe it to your knack with potions, Jasper."

"Nothing I make is that strong."

I held out my arms. "Sure it is. Look at me." Before he could argue, I turned away and walked to my Jeep with Random at my heels, keeping so close you would've thought I had a pocketful of bacon.

Chapter Ten

R andom and I returned to my Jeep. Because the passenger side was tilted into the ditch, he waited for me to help lift him inside. And then, like before, he sat upright, staring straight ahead.

"What's your story, doggo?" I asked him.

Without breaking his gaze from the road ahead, he licked me on the mouth. I wiped it away, trying not to gag, and slammed the door shut. "Note to self. Watch out for the tongue."

I glanced up at the field behind Jasper's house and sent a silent greeting to the fairies. They didn't like witches very much, but I appreciated their company. Often I could hear them talking to each other, singing, sleeping, shouting. Sometimes they were loud enough to wake me from sleep. The tone of their voices could alert me to danger, warning me of incoming storms, powerful strangers (usually witches), human violence, wildfire—and death. Like last night.

I'd never told anyone about this little trick, mostly because it hinted at Shadow—something evil. A witch wasn't supposed to be able to hear the fae unless they wanted to be heard or had a specific magical amulet designed for the purpose, and even then most witches would need to team up and pool their resources. With my father, I'd had enough trouble developing a Bright reputation. I'd avoided admitting anything odd or suspicious about myself.

I started the Jeep and drove down the hill. Just before I hit the main road, I drove off the pavement and steered around a mound of blackberry brambles and into a smooth patch of dirt. Not quite a road but almost, and it hid my Jeep from any traffic.

I was going to visit the wellspring.

If Tristan had been killed because of the power beneath Silverpool, there might be a clue at the spring itself. Maybe some evidence of someone searching for it, upturned earth or broken branches, maybe even magic residue.

And I might be able to collect a little of the wellspring water while I was there. It was a valuable currency, although dangerous to keep around because of the unpredictable creatures it attracted. I kept a special kit in the car for collecting useful objects such as herbs, branches, bark, bones, fur, and liquids.

Even though I'd been to the wellspring several times before, it wouldn't be easy to find it again. Many forces worked to hide the spring from the world: nature, by keeping it dry most of the year; humans, by building fences and roads and property lines that diverted traffic away; witches, through the Protectorate; and the spring itself, inherently elusive as it rested deep below ground.

But the fae couldn't resist gathering around it like teenagers at a bonfire. The wood sprites that bothered Jasper so much would be there long after he was dead and gone—the wellspring was irresistible to them. Day and night, some of them would be camped out nearby, watching eagerly for the winter rains to begin and bring their party to the surface.

And party it would be. To fairies, the wellspring was the biggest kegger of the year. When the road flooded, Silverpool nonmagicals wrote letters to Caltrans and begged for highway funds, but the fairies came from miles around to drink the intoxicating water. When the pool was at its deepest and most powerful—late December, around the winter solstice—the fairies would camp out, drink, and party.

I tucked a few glass vials into my pocket and closed my eyes to listen for the fairies. I needn't have bothered—they were impossible to ignore. But they weren't celebrating; they were arguing. And loudly.

I turned to Random to see if he sensed them too. "Hear that?"

Random looked at me, panting and cheerful, giving nothing away. I attached the leash and guided him out the driver's side door. He jumped down into a patch of bare earth, still blackened from the wildfire last year. To find the pool, I had to puncture a blanket of spells that wanted me to forget the significance of a recent wildfire. To my right was the jagged stump of a charred tree. The fire had only burned a few acres, taking out the grass and trees halfway to Jasper's house.

But to the left, trees and brush grew wild and untouched. A straight line divided life from destruction.

That's where I needed to go. Along the fire line and then into the ravine that sloped behind the ancient oak with… I concentrated… all the fairies under it.

Lots of fairies, right there. There had to be a dozen of them, mostly the greenish-brown variety who lived rough, in fur loincloths and bark hats and that sort of thing. No velvet waistcoats for the little wood people.

Twelve. No wonder it was so loud. But that was a good sign—if a demon was around, they wouldn't be gathered now so openly and in such large numbers. They seemed to all be talking at once, waving their arms and stomping their bare feet. Most humans, even witches, would've seen the dust and assumed the wind had kicked up a dirt cloud. But I was looking for them.

Luckily, they weren't looking for a witch and a dog, and were too busy with each other to see me and Random sneak behind another mound of blackberries and climb down the steep slope into the ravine. I kept Random close, wanting to keep him away from the poison oak. That stuff was nasty. Didn't bother the fae, of course, which is why they planted so much of it.

The branches of the California buckeyes were already bare, but the many oak, fir, and redwood kept the ravine heavily shaded. A dry creek bed snaked through rocks, bare earth, fallen branches, grass, shrubs—and my mind failed me. *What am I doing here?*

I blinked and found myself staring into Random's warm brown eyes. *Who is this dog?*

For a moment I was hopeless and lost, but then I waited it out, listened to my breath going in, going out, going in, just gave myself time to catch up to reality, and it all came into focus.

The wellspring was just ahead under an eroding bank held together by the gnarled roots of the ancient buckeye growing overhead. I couldn't see the spring from where I stood, but I knew—with effort to overcome the magic twisting around me—it was there.

It seemed undisturbed. I sent out a spell and sensed nobody but the many fae.

Turning my attention to Random, I dropped the leash, wanting to see if he ran to the irresistible magic spring. If he was magic—part fae, possessed, or a bewitched creature—he wouldn't be able to stop himself from responding to it. But he trotted in the opposite direction and got busy peeing on some weeds.

Again, I was relieved. Sometimes a dog was just a dog.

I strode over the rocks and stones to the earthy patch under the eroding slope. I found a long branch and used it to push aside the mass of poison oak growing over an oval-shaped depression. As I got closer to the bank, the earth grew darker and wetter until there in the shadows was a shining puddle no larger than my palm.

After using a few heavy branches to pin down the twining poison oak out of range, I sank to my knees and dipped the three vials, one by one, into the water. Because of the magic, the liquid was perfectly clear, untouched by dirt, leaves, algae, or insects. Anywhere my fingers got wet, I felt a thrum of power, neither Bright nor Shadow, just raw energy.

I quickly tucked all three vials into the inside pocket of my jacket and got to my feet. I wasn't sure how I'd use my treasure, and I hoped I wouldn't have to, but I'd wanted to collect some before it was too late. With so many forces descending upon Silverpool, it was unlikely I'd be able return to the wellspring again without being detected.

The sudden sound of crunching, dry leaves made me fear it was already too late.

Chapter Eleven

Before my eyes, the poison oak began growing at a furious rate, pushing aside the branches I'd placed on top of it a minute ago, tendrils and leaves the color of old blood spreading like molten lava. The roots of the large buckeye tree on the bank came alive, twining over the wellspring in a thick net of gnarled wood. And the blackberry brambles began to expand, multiplying in every direction, long branches twisting and reaching like a monstrous, thorny octopus.

I spun around, careful not to draw attention to the vials in my pocket by doing something stupid, such as putting my hand on them to make sure they were safe.

I wasn't able to see who had joined me in the ravine. The sudden growth of vegetation blocked my view—and my escape.

Preferring to take my chances with the blackberry than the poison oak, I stepped on the thorny vines and began stomping my way out. Thorns caught on the legs of my jeans, the hem of my jacket, the delicate skin of my sad, bare hands, but I kept going, too afraid of whatever lurked nearby to attempt any spell.

"Alma, are you all right?"

Jasper's voice reached me just as I tripped. I stumbled out of the branches onto my hands and knees. Stones and jagged sticks from the dry creek bed dug into my palms, and my left foot was stuck in a thorny cluster behind me, but the rest of me was free.

As I kicked and tugged my leg out of the brambles, Random, the leash dragging behind him, jogged over and licked my face.

I ducked to escape the tongue and rolled toward Jasper, who was making his way through the poison oak. He was one of those lucky creatures who was immune to the nasty stuff.

"You followed me?" I asked him.

He smiled apologetically. "Not exactly. I came looking for the wellspring and saw your car. Figured it must be down here somewhere since you said it was close."

I wasn't sure why I hadn't told him where I was going. Maybe because I'd already broken the rules and told him it was there. Maybe because I was embarrassed to admit I'd been looking for clues, chasing demons again as if the Protectorate hadn't fired me.

"Sorry," I said. "I thought— I was curious to see if Random had any interest in the wellspring."

"And?"

"Nothing," I said. "Not before the spells kicked in anyway."

I got to my feet and wiped myself off. My hands and ankles were scratched, but I was basically fine.

"Too bad the Protectorate didn't teach you the spell to break through." When I didn't say anything, he added, "I wonder if Phoebe knows it."

I heard the longing in his voice—and not for Phoebe. Wellsprings could be irresistible for witches as well as fairies. Like poison oak, some were more sensitive than others. I hadn't noticed any effects myself and had never been distracted by its pull—but I could see by the wild look in Jasper's eye that he wouldn't be so indifferent if given the opportunity.

I decided not to tell him about the small stash I had in my pocket. In fact, I began to regret telling him about the spring in the first place. It might become a problem to keep him away from it. Witches were drawn to the springwater for its power over fae, the difficult, mysterious creatures who didn't use magic like us; they *were* magic. Unpredictable and dangerous, fae broke spells and ruined potions with the blink of a small, golden eye.

"I'm not sure it's the Protectorate who's guarding the spring," I said. "It feels… wrong."

"Shadow?"

"I don't know. Maybe it's something Tristan cooked up." Random sniffed my hands and then began licking the blood from my torn-up skin. Pulling away, I picked up his leash and began to walk toward the Jeep. "Let's get out of here. I have a bad feeling about this."

We climbed back out of the ravine, skirting the tree where I'd seen the fairies, although now they were silent, hidden, or gone. Or I was too stressed to concentrate properly.

I looked around. "You came on foot?"

"You said it wasn't far. My bike is over there." He gestured to the other side of the road from the Jeep.

"Listen, I'm sorry I didn't tell you where I was going. I've gotten used to keeping it a secret and—"

He held up a hand to stop me. "I don't want you to tell me any more secrets. I've hurt you enough already."

"You didn't hurt me. It was my decision to break the secrecy binding—"

"For my sake. And I appreciate it. But I think it would be better if you didn't tell me any more."

"Why not?"

"You're already under suspicion. Breaking more oaths to talk to me isn't going to help your case," he said. "I'd feel bad if you got in trouble because of me."

I'd been trying to protect him by telling him about the wellspring, but maybe he was right; we could be a danger to each other. When the Protectorate witches began coming to Silverpool to investigate Tristan's death as well as the loss of the torc, I would be in the spotlight. He might get caught up in the dragnet with me just as I would get caught up with my father. Guilt by association.

"All right," I said. "I won't say another word."

"I'd better get back." He patted Random on the head and began walking away. "I have a feeling the fairies are gathering. I want to go home and get the crystal out, see if I can figure out where they are. Last year they got into my water heater, and it cost me a month's rent to replace it."

I glanced over my shoulder, searching the grass for any hint of the missing fae. The only sound was a flock of quail darting through the woods. "Good idea," I said. "It does feel… restless around here."

Jasper pedaled away, and I got into the Jeep with Random and drove the opposite direction. An offshore fog had crept in from the west, blanketing the town in dim, gray light, making noon feel more like dusk. When we reached the stoplight near the bridge, I looked to my right, over the bank and down to the river, feeling a shudder run through me.

Tristan. I could feel his spirit lingering nearby, weightless but shackled in place. He wasn't the type of man to walk away from unfinished business. Or float away.

The dead didn't talk, but they could haunt you. Mindless and bodiless, only their emotions remained, and those were in a concentrated state that I'd never liked to get too close to. Every cemetery, city street, hospital, old house held the unfinished emotional remains of the dead. Most were harmless, even beautiful. But a witch murdered at the height of his powers would have unfinished business, and I worried about how long it would keep his soul trapped here, ephemeral but miserable.

The Protectorate will investigate, I told myself. *They'll find who did it.*

I made a quick stop at Cypress Hardware to get dog food, glad the store was militantly dog-friendly, and sped home.

For a few minutes I waited in the Jeep in front of my cottage, feeling for any hint of danger or unwanted visitors. When I was as sure as I could be—my father had tricked me just the night before—I prepared a defensive spell and then took Random and his dinner inside.

Quiet, empty. Safe.

"Hungry?" I locked the door behind me and poured his kibble into a bowl. I hoped he wasn't going to be finicky, because I couldn't afford raw, organic, grass-fed—

Before I could finish the thought, the food was gone. He'd inhaled it as quickly as my father vanishing from a burglary.

"Not picky, I see." I patted him approvingly as I walked to my file cabinet in the other room.

It looked like a secondhand secretarial file cabinet from the late twentieth century—beige-painted steel, massively heavy, scratched and dented from decades of abuse.

But inside…

I put my hand over the beads around my neck and sent out a thrust of power. The canister lock twisted and popped. The top drawer began to shake as if a large truck had rumbled by.

I sent out another dash of power. This time the middle drawer shook. You'd think a gnome was inside trying to kick his way out.

For the third drawer, I closed my eyes and muttered a few words that meant nothing to anyone but me. Keywords. Passwords.

"Crispy crème brûlée," I said softly. "Icy-cold chocolate eclair."

The folks in Silicon Valley weren't the only ones with security tricks. When I was done, the bottom drawer began smoking not with heat but with cold tendrils of dry ice. I took a deep breath, exhausted from the use of power, and sat on the floor.

I reached inside my jacket pocket and took out the three vials as I pulled the drawer open. Inside were my most valuable treasures, only a few of them dangerous. I set the vials next to my old baby blanket and locked the drawer and cabinet again.

Relief washed over me. It was a risk to bring springwater into my house. But riskier not to.

If it weren't for their interest in my father, I would've been relieved to see Protectorate agents in town. Unlike me, they didn't mind killing things.

Because I had a sickening feeling that something in Silverpool would need killing.

Soon.

Chapter Twelve

A round two in the morning, Random's furious barking woke me from a shallow sleep.

Other than my eyelids, which sprang open, I didn't move a muscle.

Somebody was trying to break into the house. They might already be in my bedroom—

No. I felt nobody that close. And Random was still barking in the other room.

I heard a crash from the kitchen, something wooden and heavy falling over, rattling to the floor. Gathering my power in my hands, I jumped out of bed and sent out a blast of sleep, the same I'd used on my father the night before.

I paused, heart pounding, trying to hear any hint of what was in the other room.

Had my guarding spells failed? I would need to brush up on my technique. I'd been trained to hunt and destroy my prey, usually prowling the grimy streets of urban California, not to defend a tiny house in a rural village nestled in a redwood forest.

I crept into the kitchen and saw a chair on its side in

front of Random, who glared at the back door like a trained police dog, although his body was beginning to slump, a reaction to my sleep spell.

The kitchen was filled with the aroma of cedar and woodsmoke, a neighbor's chickens, my compost heap. All the scents of the Silverpool outdoors, now blowing into the house through the open door that shouldn't have been open.

Before I moved into the room, I put my back to the wall and listened for the sound of fae or human footsteps or magic from anyone. Everything unfamiliar came from that door, a muddy haze of energy spilling in from outside.

"Thank you, Random," I said quietly.

I patted him gently as I walked to the door and looked outside. Birdie's house was around the corner through the woods. Behind her, the couple with the chickens. I held up my hands and sent out another blast of sleep, then listened for thudding bodies. Nothing.

I closed the door, replaced the chair and the dead bolt, and went to the living room. Before bed I'd fitted my staff through the drawer handles of the file cabinet, and now I pulled it out like the sword from the stone and returned to the kitchen. I removed the chair from under the door, unlocked it, and went out to the backyard to look for intruders.

The spell around Willy's tree was fine, untouched; I saw no sign of him. If a demon had come near, he or she would've attacked the gnome first. Although Willy was not my servant, other witches over the centuries had enslaved domestic fae, forcing them to use their magic for human purpose, and a hostile demon would've tried to take him out before going for me.

I rubbed my face, trying to clear my head. Sending out the sleep spells was exhausting even when I was awake; doing them when I'd just been dreaming myself was like drinking a bottle of cold medicine.

I went inside, replaced the chair and dead bolt again, and took a long, deep breath. My heart was still beating too fast, and I was worried about what might've happened if Random hadn't woken me. The fact that somebody had been able to open that door was a problem. A big problem.

I found Random curled up at the foot of my bed with his nose tucked under a crocheted yellow blanket.

"Hey, I owe you a steak," I said, stroking his back.

He opened one eye a millimeter, gave the staff a suspicious look, stretched apart his jaws in a yawn, tongue curling the way yawning dog tongues do, dropped his head back to the mattress, and returned to sleep with a sigh.

Leaving him to the bed, I took an old comforter out of the closet and returned to the living room, where I plopped on the couch that had its back to the wall. Trying to stay upright, I propped myself up with some pillows, and I balanced the staff, warm to the touch, across my thighs, wrapping both my hands around the bumpy-but-polished shaft.

I tried to stay awake the rest of the night. Between my yawns and moments of dozing, I tried to focus on the doors, the windows, the vents, on the alert for anything unusual. Finally the dawn came, and I fell into a deeper sleep, interrupted only by the clucking of the neighbor's chickens, a distant leaf blower roaring and whining, Willy singing to the dew on the grass, all the sounds I would expect on a normal day.

"Alma, are you up?"

That sound was not normal. It sounded like Livia. Why would Livia be in my—

Was she *inside*? I jumped to my feet, the staff ready to

strike. No. She wasn't inside. "Livia?" I asked carefully, an edge in my voice.

Then I heard knocking on the door—the front door I never used because the front yard was a wilderness of shrubs, wildflowers, herbs, redwood saplings, and weeds. I walked over, reluctantly set the staff in the umbrella stand near the door, paused, then opened it a crack and peered out. "Livia?"

Random came up from behind me and began barking at the new intruder.

"Hello," she said, recoiling slightly. "I thought you'd be awake by now."

Putting a leg out to block Random, I glanced down at my sleeping uniform of pull-on shorts and a nightshirt. "What time is it?"

"Almost ten," she said as if it meant something.

"I was up late," I replied, stroking Random's head. He settled down and sat at my feet to stare at Livia with me. "What do you want?"

She swatted away the tall branches of overgrown oleander poking her in the side. "May I come in? I'm organizing the memorial service."

"Sure, of course, right." But I hesitated. I didn't really want Livia in my house. She didn't approve of my lifestyle, and I didn't approve of her personality. But what choice did I have? Tristan needed memorializing.

I kicked aside a moving box I'd never unpacked to open the door wide enough for her to enter. She had the grace to say nothing about being forced to step over an aggressive rosemary bush.

I stopped myself from apologizing or using the excuse that I only used the kitchen door in the back. The truth was I used the front garden as a living moat of passive magical protection, not that I could tell her that. Besides, it was kind of fun to have her assume the worst about me. I couldn't wait to offer her canned coffee. Reheated in the microwave, if she was particular.

"We need volunteers for the service," she said, taking off her puffy suede boots and setting them near the umbrella stand. Her socks were black with little red and white wine bottles on them. "There's a list of things you could help us with."

"Us?"

"It's a communal effort." She took a tablet out of an orange leather purse and looked around the living and attached dining room, at its mismatched old furniture, unpacked boxes, plastic storage bins of craft supplies stacked six feet high, the old file cabinet, my makeshift bedding on the couch. "I have a friend who's a clutter consultant. Would you like her number?"

"I don't need any more clutter right now," I said, "but you can give me her name and I'll keep it handy in case I find a little more room in the future."

Livia gave me a sharp look. She was annoying but not stupid. "I was only trying to be helpful."

I had to remind myself it was bad luck to be rude to a guest, even an uninvited one. "Sorry. I didn't sleep well. Coffee?"

Shaking her head, Livia began walking around the house on her own. "I don't have time to stay." Her voice trailed off as she poked her head into my bedroom, the bathroom, the spare room. "The house has good bones. You could really make something out of it."

"I rent," I said.

She joined me in the kitchen, her eyes still looking at everything but me, her gaze drifting over the vintage enamel sink, the crown molding, the built-in ironing board, the original backsplash tile. "Where's the laundry? The garage is detached."

"In the old pantry." At first I'd thought Livia was just being a curious snob, but now I wondered if there was another reason she was taking such an interest in the minutiae of my living quarters.

"But there wasn't a litter box in there, was there? I'm always trying to find a good spot for the litter box, and I didn't smell yours so I thought you knew some magic I didn't."

I did indeed. "I don't keep her inside," I said. "I'm allergic."

"So you don't really *have* a cat," she said, "so much as feed a stray. Did you have her neutered? The explosive feral cat population is bad for their own health as well as songbirds—"

Her invasion had gone on long enough. "You had a list of jobs for the memorial service?"

She pursed her lips together, lifted her tablet, and ran her finger over the screen, her thin eyebrows drawing together. "I want it to be tasteful and civilized, just as he was."

I was reminded of the time Tristan, practicing a new spell, had bitten the head off a squirming, freshly bathed mouse, hoping the animal instinct would rise up in him, commune with his innate magic and the amulet around his neck, and transform him into a red-tailed hawk, his favorite living thing.

"I was thinking you would collect the photographs, make a slideshow that would run continuously on the flat-screen at the tasting room," Livia continued. "You've lived in Silver pool longer than I have, know the people I don't, and you had your own... brief friendship with him, and of course you're artistic. Can you do that? Please let me know now if you can't do it so I can find somebody else."

"Of course I'll do it," I said. "When's the funeral?"

"Not a funeral. A memorial. We want to celebrate his

life. That's why I chose the event space at the winery. I can't stop people from wearing black, but I can set the tone with the setting, the food, the drink. I've convinced the winery manager to open up the reserve bottles from last year. We can drink it in his honor."

I didn't like Livia, but I thought she had the right idea about what would've pleased Tristan. He'd loved his vineyard and playing at being a professional winemaker; like Livia, he'd adored the trappings of wealth: handsome property, expensive furnishings, collectible statues and paintings, custom-made shoes. Bling.

"He'd like that," I said quietly. "When?"

"Saturday at one. The tasting room."

"I'll do the slideshow. Anything else?"

"Some prints would be nice. Old school. A flattering image of him in a classic pose, enlarged and framed. There might already be an easel at the winery for visitors—with the hours and menu, that sort of thing."

"I'll go up there and check it out."

"I'll tell Donna what you're doing so she lets you in."

Although I was confident I would be able to walk inside without any help—now that Tristan was gone, his spells would be useless—it would probably be better for me to avoid doing magic until I knew who had killed him and why. Now that I was out of the Protectorate, I could hide my nature with a triple strand of beads around my left wrist, a trick that had been forbidden to me when I'd worked for them. The rules and regulations for an agent were longer than the US federal tax code. But the beads only hid my powers if I wasn't actually using them, like concealing a handgun. The moment I cast a spell, my camouflage would disappear.

I thanked Livia, assured her I would follow up on the slideshow, the framed portrait, the easel, and walked her back to the front of the house. Next to her boots, my staff was humming inside the umbrella stand; it was still attuned to me from the night before and sensed my eagerness for Livia to leave. I hoped she didn't notice the slight rattle, though if she did, she'd assume it was a mouse.

Which made me think of Tristan again, the way the rodent gore had trickled down his short beard and dripped on the celadon polo shirt with its Silverpool Vineyards logo, looking like spilled pinot noir.

"Saturday," Livia repeated as she pushed out the door and climbed over the shrubs in the front yard. "But you should have it done by Friday night so we can prepare." She walked through the overgrown oleander and disappeared. A moment later I heard the hum of her Tesla drift away.

I shut the door and locked it before grabbing the staff and waving it at the entire front of the house. What else did I have to do to keep people away? Did I need an actual moat? With flesh-eating spiders and a poison oak hedge maze without an exit?

This was ridiculous. I needed to up my game on my self-defense spells. What I already knew was obviously not enough. I would have to ask an expert.

I would have to ask Helen Mendoza.

Chapter Thirteen

The drive to San Francisco took almost two hours and reminded me of why I'd moved to the boonies. Seems like another million people moved to the Bay Area every Wednesday. Each with three cars. Once again I thought of my father and his gift for apparition, but even he couldn't travel seventy miles through empty space and expect to survive. I didn't know how far he could travel now, but when I'd been growing up, it had been less than two miles. That's why we'd always had to rent a room fairly close to his target; if the heist went bad, he could escape to his safe spot in a hurry.

The Golden Gate Bridge was fogged in, the visibility so limited I could barely see the people walking and cycling on either side of the lanes. The rust-red beams faded into white over my head, and the sea below was a blurry gray. I felt as if I were passing into a dream world.

The weather was good luck for me; Helen loved the fog, and it would put her in a good mood, possibly good enough to answer her front door.

My Jeep rolled up and down the steep hills from the

bridge to the cozy family neighborhood of Noe Valley where both Helen and the Protectorate had homes. Side by side, as it turned out—which was ironic because they despised one another.

I parked at the top of a steep hill three blocks away from both houses and took a moment to put on heavy-rimmed plastic glasses and an Oracle baseball cap and a GoPro sweatshirt. Magical disguise would've been more effective under close scrutiny but would also be more likely to draw casual Protectorate attention. A dog-walking twentysomething woman in local regalia—I got the branded tech swag at a Goodwill in Silicon Valley—was as invisible as a wood sprite in Muir Woods.

Helen's house was a tall, narrow Queen Anne painted pink, purple, and white with aqua trim. Next door, the Protectorate house was a cheerful but generic yellow. Keeping my head down, I pulled Random with me up the dozen slightly uneven wooden steps into the portico and waited in front of the double doors. Helen didn't have a knocker or doorbell.

The left door swung open with a loud screech.

"Get inside, are you crazy?" Helen grabbed my arm and hauled me inside. After glaring at Random as he trotted in with me, she kicked the door shut behind us. Although the front doors still had their original stained glass windows, the entry hall was dim. Helen didn't use a lot of electricity, and on a foggy day, the old house didn't get much sunlight.

"Nobody saw me," I said.

"Of course they saw you. They don't know why you're here, but they saw you and now they're going to come bother me."

"Sorry."

She let out a sigh that was more like a growl. "You brought a dog."

"Did I?"

"Are you suggesting he brought you?"

"I don't know." I waited without saying anything else. My best bet for getting help from Helen was to tempt her with a mystery.

"Huh." Helen frowned at Random. "How long has he been hanging around?"

"Since Tristan died."

"Well, he's not Tristan, I can tell you that. If Tristan were to turn himself into a canine, it would be some kind of pedigreed show dog. Which that mutt ain't."

"Is he a dog?"

"Sure looks like a dog," she said, "but I've always leaned to flora over fauna."

"I call him Random."

"He stinks."

"He likes cheese," I said, hoping that would soften her opinion of him. Helen loved anything with cheese in it.

"And it obviously doesn't agree with him," she said, wrinkling her nose. "I hope you don't expect me to adopt him. I don't want a dog. They mess up the garden."

"I had a break-in. Two, actually. I need help learning a few new spells."

"What will you give me in exchange?"

I paused. I'd hoped she would be in a better mood than to demand payment upfront. At least she'd opened the door. "I don't know how they're breaking in, so I don't know how expensive what I'm looking for might be."

"Who's breaking in?"

"I don't know that either," I said. "Once was my father. I don't know about the other time."

"Only one other time?"

"That I know of."

She pulled her lip between thumb and forefinger, the

nails short, the skin discolored with ink or dirt. Not, I hoped, blood. "What kind of herbs were you using?"

I hesitated. I was hoping we could find another way. "I used redwood to reinforce my spells."

"You planted redwood around the perimeter? A bit large to be called an herb, but the saplings have charm, so to speak—"

"No, I used redwood beads on a silver chain to focus myself when I cast the spell."

She rolled her eyes. "You people. You're too lazy to learn the old ways." She poked me in the stomach, which, being relaxed and unprepared, compressed like rising dough.

"I know I need help," I said. "That's why I'm here."

"You know you need my plants."

"Or whatever you've got."

"I've got plants," she said, shaking her head and walking deeper into the gloomy house. A threadbare runner, once red and now pink, absorbed her heavy footsteps. "Come on, let's get your animal outside before he pees on the hardwood floor. I haven't had them refinished in eons, and any urine will get sucked up like a sponge."

She walked me past the first parlor, the second parlor, a staircase, a dining room, a second staircase, the family room, the kitchen, and finally the deck with her prized glass-roofed conservatory. Everything was crammed with Victorian knick-knacks and antiques in velvet, brass, mahogany, stained glass. Below us was the basement I knew well from my days at the Protectorate—for a small fee, she would let novice agents sleep in a storage room and do laundry. Upstairs were the bedrooms, I presumed, though I'd never been invited to see them.

"You caught me at a bad time," Helen said, gesturing at the deck beyond a pair of sliding glass doors. "I was just digging up the garlic."

The closeness of the kitchen to the outdoors was like my own house, which was no coincidence. Hearth witches needed easy access to their gardens. Unlike my plot of overgrown weeds, however, Helen's was a nursery, a well-run commercial enterprise with glassed-in conservatory and potting shed, providing her with the income to support her expensive San Francisco lifestyle. Although to hear her tell it, she was on the verge of destitution at all times, which was why she had to charge Protectorate novices her standard fee of ten bucks a night to sleep on the cold, damp concrete slab in her basement.

"How did you know I was coming?" I asked. "That's the magic I need. I could deal with unwanted visitors if I had advance notice."

She paused with her hand on the door, not opening it. "There's nothing tricky about it. It's called paying attention."

I remembered how Helen was as particular about precise language as a tutor at the Protectorate. "All right then, would you please teach me how to pay attention?"

She grimaced. "Listen to you. So polite. Back when you were a newbie at the Protectorate, you never would've let me bully you so easily."

Sadly, it was true. I would come over and give her hell, arguing with her and calling her names, and she lapped it up like a sprite with a bucket of springwater. "I crashed and burned, that's what happened."

"They squashed your confidence." She clucked her tongue. "Such a shame. Just because you can't kill demons doesn't mean you should be walking around with your tail between your legs."

"Just because I'm being polite doesn't mean I'm afraid of you."

"That's good. You shouldn't be afraid of me. I'm one of the Bright. Your buddies over there"—she pointed at the

Protectorate house next door—"need help remembering we're on the same side. I can tell that Lorne would love to accuse me of being a Freewitch. Just because I don't fall to my knees and grovel when he walks by, he thinks I'm a radical separatist plotting his downfall."

"Have they been bothering you again?"

"No more than usual," she said. "You're the one in their sights now, Alma. They talk about you."

The hairs rose on the back of my neck. "How do you know that?"

"Same way I knew you were coming. Same way I heard about Tristan and that ugly necklace that went missing." She glanced at the house next door again. "I could use a secrecy spell on you, but I'd rather just ask you to keep my methods to yourself." Then she added under her breath, "And it would probably be more effective in the long run."

"I promise to keep it to myself," I said.

She ran her hand through her short white hair, plucking at the strands to make them stick straight up, a mannerism some novices thought was a cognitive binding spell but I suspected was just a compulsive habit. "I'll show you. You'll understand. And please keep your mouth shut." She gave Random the side-eye. "You too, dog."

He hung his head.

Helen opened the sliding glass door and walked us across the deck to the narrow entrance to her conservatory. The air inside was thick, warm, humid, smelling of rich earth, fertilizer, nectar, life. She closed us inside and walked past a row of tables heavy with flats of seedlings and pointed at a padded patio chair, a footstool, and a small table with a magazine, box of chocolates, coffee cup, and a short segment of white PVC pipe about a foot long and two inches in diameter.

She gestured for me to sit and took Random's leash from me. I sat, felt myself sink low into the cushions of the obviously well-used seat, and leaned back. I could see she was waiting for me to figure it out, and I did have a pretty good idea, so I looked at the objects on the table, picked up the pipe, and held it to my ear. Just to my left was the glass wall of the conservatory. I leaned the pipe against it and listened.

Rolling her eyes, she reached over me and slid the window to one side, dislodging the pipe from my ear.

Ah. Beyond a narrow gap between the houses was another window, painted black and tightly shut. Old houses in San Francisco were built inches from one another. I leaned over with the pipe and rested it gently against the blacked-out glass of the neighbor house's window.

"I asked for black beans, not refried," a man was complaining, his voice low and hoarse from decades of smoking.

My eyebrows shot up into my head. Helen grinned at me.

Lorne, I mouthed at her. My old supervisor's voice was unforgettable.

Helen crossed her arms over her chest, smirking.

"You'll pay for a new one yourself," Lorne continued. "And don't ask anyone to transform it for you. I want the real thing from the taqueria. I'll know the difference."

A mumbled reply, a slamming door, and then, "They get more confused about their place in the world with each cycle of the earth around the sun. It's a new century, a new millennium, but it's not a new world. It's the same world. Witches today are wrong to think anything's different today than it was a thousand years ago."

A woman's voice, faintly audible, said something about California.

"It's just as bad in New York. Even Tokyo, Cape Town, Berlin, Santiago. They've forgotten our mission, our purpose, and their place in the world, which is not a democracy and never can be."

Helen tapped the pipe, eyebrows raised inquisitively. I put it in my lap, closed the window, and stood up while Helen took a sage-green leaf from a wreath tied around her wrist and sprinkled it in the air between the houses.

"It never would've worked with the witch who had that office before him," Helen said.

"Why not?"

"She was smart," Helen said. "This guy hasn't added anything to the spells the Protectorate has on the building, which don't stop me from a little harmless information gathering."

"I'm not sure he would know how. The rumor is he's got very limited power, utterly dependent on a few pieces he wears under his suit. Thick silver, a few stones, some piercings."

"Relying on hard magic has atrophied whatever natural gifts he was born with." Helen pointed at the white pipe. "What did you overhear? Your face lit up with some of that bad attitude I remember you had before they squeezed it out of you."

"He's complaining about novice agents wanting to be treated with kindness and respect," I said. "I heard that speech many times."

"He does go on." Helen pulled at her hair again and gestured for me to follow her back inside. She didn't lock Random outside, instead bringing him with us into the kitchen, where she dropped the leash and walked over to the antique stove. "Hearing that blowhard blathering is enough to turn one's stomach. I'll make us ginger tea."

"I still don't understand how you knew I was coming," I said. "Were they talking about me? Are they having me followed?"

Not answering, she filled the kettle with liquid—I hope it was water—from a large mason jar on the counter, placed two handmade earthenware mugs on the counter, then came over to me and set her hand over mine. "Yes, they've got their eye on you because of the torc. But I've already given you enough for nothing. What are you going to give me to tell you more?"

A warm current of power buzzed between our knuckles. She was touching my thoughts the way a pickpocket brushes against a well-dressed tourist in a crowded market, not sure what she'll find but always looking for something she could use, with no compunction about taking what wasn't hers.

I made a point of not touching my redwood necklace as I sent out a virtual knife and sliced off her probing psychic fingers. Her eyes went wide.

"Nice," she said, then laughed.

"I did give you something. I told you about Lorne being a weak witch."

"You said it was a rumor. The boss is bound to have jealous, unhappy critics telling nasty stories about him."

"All right," I said, "it's not just a rumor. I felt it for myself when I worked for him."

With a nod, she opened a canister, scooped out a spoonful of dried ginger, and dumped it in a teapot before pouring the boiling water over it. "I suspected but wasn't sure. His carelessness with guarding spells could've been his overconfidence."

"He relies on his apps for everything," I said, "and uses nonmag tech to hide it."

"Figures. I bet he'll be promoted." A moment later she set a lumpy brown mug, no handle, in front of me. "Drink up."

"Is it safe?"

"Funny of you to ask. If it isn't, you'll never know. Isn't that why you're here?"

Chapter Fourteen

I picked up the mug, this time wrapping my left hand around the beads at my throat, and probed the liquid for danger. "This is a test, isn't it? One sip and I turn into a frog."

"A newt would be more useful. You could eat the snails in the garden that eat my basil. And then lick up all the little ants on my kitchen counter."

"Your tea parties are just as fun as ever," I said, bringing the mug to my lips.

She stuck out her tongue and made slurping noises.

I waited a moment to make sure my body didn't morph into something slimy before taking a second sip. It seemed to be ginger tea, sweetened with a little honey, nothing else. "I should pity you for having to listen to Lorne all day."

"I neither do so nor have to do so," she said. "I have better things to occupy my time."

"You heard about Tristan though?"

She lifted the second mug and blew the steam into a spiral pattern that swirled to the ceiling in impossible symmetry. "I was sorry to hear about Tristan and especially disgusted when Lorne seemed to be more upset about the theft of some trinket than a Protector getting run over."

"Why do they care about the torc so much?"

"Because they always care about trinkets too much. It's all stone and metal with those witches. They've forgotten the flora, the fauna, the elements. They're as bad as nonmagical humanity, obsessed with their machines, always copying and stealing from one another."

"I've heard your speech before, so you can save your breath," I said. "What does this particular trinket do?"

"Don't know. Don't care."

"They think my father stole it."

"*I* think your father stole it."

I set down my tea and turned away. "I think I'd rather be a newt than have to defend him again."

"You're screwed, that's for sure. Families stick together, especially magical ones, and they'll expect him to involve you somehow, which he always does."

"At the very least I need to keep him out of my house."

"As I said before, I'm just a poor old lady here and can't be working for free."

"You're loaded. I'm unemployed." I held out my arm and shook my wrist, surrounded by a triple strand of carved wood charms. "But I did bring one of my best pieces for you. Redwood, cedar, blue—"

"Give me the vials," Helen said.

I avoided her gaze, which might see more than I wanted her to see, looking instead down at Random, who was using my foot as a pillow. "Whatever you can give me will be worth far less than even one drop of what might be in one of those vials I may or may not have with me."

"One vial and I'll give you five items that should repel any witch, fae, or demon with ill intent."

"What about nonmag humans with ill intent?" I asked.

"That goes without saying."

"Say it anyway."

She shrugged. "It might work on them."

"Might? For all I know the last break-in was a nonmag transient looking to score some food."

"Then put out a few snacks and lock your doors."

"You're impossible."

"You're impractical," she said.

"What about animals? This dog walked right in through an open window."

"I would worry if he'd walked through a closed one."

I stifled the urge to inflict her with a butt-pimple spell. "Will you be able to help me with animals of ill intent?"

She pursed her lips. "Depends how you define ill intent. If it's in their nature, like a mouse or spider, I doubt it. But if they're twisted by fae or Shadow to do you harm, then my items should help." She paused, then added, "I'm sure they will. So you can give me two vials."

"One vial," I said. "Which is way more than enough."

"I'll take the one vial. Little old ladies have no hope of acquiring wellspring water on their own. Think of it as an act of charity."

I had feared she would demand both—I'd brought two, just in case, as she'd divined—but I would've preferred giving her the bracelet. Knowing blue was her favorite color, I'd threaded lapis beads in with the redwood ones, but nothing could compete with springwater.

I took one of the vials out of my bra and set it on the counter.

"Doesn't that jacket have pockets?" she asked.

"I needed to put it somewhere I'd be sure to notice if it went missing. You've got a reputation for lifting things that don't belong to you."

"Says the daughter of the most infamous magic bandit of

our age." Eyes shining, she swept the vial into her palm and held it to her forehead for a moment before tucking it into her own bra. "Don't get fresh," she said, patting her breasts with a chuckle.

"Five items, you said."

"You're going to feel cheated, but that's not my fault. These are everyday items you probably already have or could easily get, but like your Protectorate overlords—"

"Please. Just give me the goods."

She flung up her hands. "Fine. You're missing out on so much of the fun though when you give up on the drama. It's really part of the magic." She went over to a cupboard and took out an enormous black cast-iron frying pan, an object so heavy she used both hands and held it unsteadily.

She set it on a padded cushion in the window seat overlooking the garden. "First item," she said. "Iron."

"What do I do with it?"

"Didn't they teach you anything at that fancy school your father sent you to?"

I'd spent most of my adolescence parked in boarding schools up and down the West Coast. Some were for witches, most weren't. "The culinary arts teacher used nonstick."

"Iron. You need iron. Malevolent spirits can't stand it."

"I hope I don't have to hit them with it, because it looks hard to lift."

"You'll use it as a cauldron. With a few other things." She went over to an antique cabinet painted bright blue and opened the pair of the doors over a shelf of decorative plates. Inside was a row of ceramic canisters, each marked with runes I didn't recognize. "I assume you already have lavender and rosemary in your garden."

"Yes."

"Yarrow?"

"Probably," I said.

"How can you not know if you have yarrow?"

"I may have deadheaded all the flowers when they got messy. Will the roots do?"

"Not in this case," she said, popping the cork from a canister and reaching inside. "I'll give you a palmful of the dried petals. Next year you should save your own. You've got a garden. Why aren't you storing the harvest? I thought you liked botanicals."

"I do." Trees were botanical, and wood came from trees.

"Other than trees."

I didn't want to offend her, but modern witches weren't as fond of plant and animal magic as they'd been in the past. There was more emphasis now on using metal and stone to amplify the mysterious and unpredictable magic that came from inside one's own body. Relying on a cornucopia of dried herbs, bodily fluids, lucky coins, seashells, black velvet bags, fingernails, colored ribbons, moon-shaped stones, whatever —was old school, old-fashioned, old *wife*.

When I told my former coworkers at the Protectorate that I now made my living selling wood bead necklaces, carved and threaded by hand, they gave me pitying looks or rolled their eyes or laughed in my face. It was the witch equivalent of announcing I was living on a commune without electricity and making my own granola out of oats and raisins I'd harvested myself.

"I also have cedar, buckeye, oak, pine, and manzanita," I said.

"You like trees," she said.

"I like trees. And so do my customers. Wood has a wider market than yarrow petals or burnt acacia leaves, and it makes better jewelry."

"You're responding to the market," she said.

"I have to make a living."

She lifted one shoulder in a shrug. "I suppose I can relate to that. You need to make a living."

"Yes. I do."

She leaned closer to me, pointing one stained index finger into my face. "But this is more than making a living. This is about being a witch, the best you can be." Her voice dropped, and she held my gaze with hard eyes. "This is about your ultimate purpose. The gathering, the acquisition, the storing, protecting, and categorizing of the one most important thing of all."

I glanced at her canisters. "Herbs?"

She slammed her hands on the counter. "Knowledge. Your purpose, every witch's purpose, is to acquire knowledge."

"Yes, yes, I know—"

"You don't know. You're taking magic for granted. It revealed itself to you, and you have a duty to learn as much as you can. Most of humanity is blind. Most witches today are myopic, hoarding their amulets and wands and chalices and pendants as if those objects were the treasure. No. Knowledge is the treasure."

I'd heard her complaints about the Protectorate many times before—she shared them with all the novices sleeping in her basement—but I'd never heard her talk like this before. Her tone was personal, intense, sincere.

"Why are you telling me this?"

"You have brains," Helen said. "So many don't. You need to use it. Really use it."

"I just want to stay out of trouble. Tristan is dead. The Protectorate wants to blame me for whatever my father has done—"

"You don't have the luxury of staying out of trouble. You need to seek it out. You must be brave, unearth secrets, find answers. You can't just draw a protective circle around your-self and hide like a gnome."

I cleared my throat. "Why not?"

She turned aside, snorting in disgust. No. Anger. Her hands were clenched at her sides, her entire body tensed and shaking.

Suddenly she shoved her hand down her shirt, pulled out the vial, and came at me, forcing it into my hands, closing my fingers around it so tightly I cried out.

"Keep it," she said.

"No, please—"

"You want to be safe? With enough vials of this you could pay a dozen highway goblins or an army of bridge trolls to stand guard around your house for as long as your mortal form walks this earth," she said. "Nobody will be able to hurt you. You won't be able to leave, of course, but no matter—you're not interested in freedom."

"Hey," I said.

She picked up her mug of ginger tea and dumped it into the sink. Random got off my foot and walked over to a colorful rag rug near a heating vent, then slumped down again with his back to me.

I felt very unpopular.

"What can I do, Helen? I got kicked out of the Protec-torate because I don't have what it takes to fight Shadow. I keep to myself and don't hurt anybody. Why isn't that enough?"

"You slept with that man, did you not?"

"Who didn't?" At the time I'd been flattered, only later learning Tristan had had a reputation for flattering every woman he'd met.

"His sleeping around isn't the point. You liked him enough to share yourself with him, and now he's dead, probably at the hand of somebody you know, witch or fae or demon, maybe even nonmag human. If I were you—"

"You're not. You've got herbs and money and a house and a lot more experience than I do."

"I'll give you the herbs. And a few other things, including the benefit of my experience, to protect yourself," she said. "But you have to put your own desires into the spells, or they aren't going to work any better than a love potion would work on a corpse."

I looked at the vial of springwater in my hands. I knew she was right. I had to know what had happened to Tristan, not only for my own safety but for his hurt, lingering soul.

I set the vial on the counter and stepped back, acknowledging I'd lost. She'd been right all along. I had no choice. I had to know; the compulsion to know had gotten me out of bed that night and had propelled me to her door.

"All right," I said. "Teach me everything. I'll be ready to fight if I have to."

She clapped her hands together and laughed. "Hah! Ginger tea. Works every time."

Chapter Fifteen

I t was dark when I got home. Random was curled up on the seat next to me, his rear legs hanging off the edge and bouncing with each bump in the road. I parked and put my hand on his soft, warm fur, invisible in the darkness, and stroked his ears. Now his collar held a jade disk with a square hole in the center. Also a cheap aluminum tag from a pet store off the freeway in Petaluma, engraved with RANDOM in block letters and my phone number. The jade was to protect him from malevolent spirits, but when I'd strung it around his neck, I'd watched carefully to see if he recoiled, even slightly, but he'd seemed to take the collar and its charm in stride.

Helen had given me a Trader Joe's shopping bag filled with the objects she promised would help me repel evil and pursue truth. I hoped she was right. The Protectorate favored the hard magic of metal and stone for a reason: it was consistently more powerful, more reliable, more measurable. The old herbal concoctions were like supplements from the vitamin aisle of a grocery store, mostly likely to work if I believed in them and just as likely to cause unpleasant side effects.

But I'd gone to Helen because I'd used up the limits of my own magic and knowledge. I had no regrets and was eager to get started.

On my way into the backyard, I picked the tiny dried leaves off my blueberry plant at the side of the house, a pitiful skeleton of twigs that had given me about seven blueberries all summer, and shoved the harvest in my jacket pocket—she'd said I'd only need a few because they were powerful—before I stopped by Willy's tree.

"Good evening to you, fine gnome," I said.

He appeared the way spirits can if they're in the mood, immediately, without following the rules of physics, flashing into view like a lamp turning on. "Welcome home, Alma Bellrose. Were your travels arduous?" In one hand he held the acorn cap he used as a cocktail glass; in the other was an old-fashioned lantern that shone with fairy light.

"Can't complain," I said. "Have you seen any activity around the house while I was gone?"

He ducked his head, looking embarrassed. "I'm afraid I've been drinking the springwater," he said, holding up his acorn cap. "The solstice approaches soon enough. I no longer have to be so stingy with it."

He journeyed to the wellspring in December and collected a tiny bottle that he made last all year.

"Enjoy yourself," I said. "Glad nobody's bothered you."

He saluted me with the cap eyes twinkling and faded into the hole at the bottom of the tree trunk.

Random was relieving himself in the grass, and as soon as I opened the kitchen door, he galloped inside to his food and water bowls. He stared at me until I filled them both.

I liked having a dog. I did wonder how he got along with cats.

The house was dark and quiet for once. I'd left the goods inside the Jeep so I'd have my hands free to defend myself and Willy if necessary, but after assuring myself it was safe, I went back to get the bag and heavy cast-iron skillet.

Now the fun could begin.

In spite of the circumstances, I was smiling. I loved learning new things. Helen was right about that—knowledge fulfilled me more than anything else ever had. The Phoebe Days of the world wanted wealth, power, and prestige, but I was happy with knowing more than was necessary. In fact, I was miserable if I didn't know. When the Protectorate had refused to give me a good reason to kill Seth, it had begun the unraveling of my career.

"All right, let's do this." I set the heavy skillet on the stove and cranked the electric burner to high. A gas stove would've been better, but I got what the landlord provided and couldn't afford more. When the burner ring was glowing red, I sprinkled the blueberry bush leaves into the iron frying pan and watched them curl, brown, and then smoke. When the first tendril reached my nostrils, I spat into the pan and jumped back as it sizzled.

I took a gulp of water from the bottle Helen had given me and spit into the pan again. More sizzling and a stink I couldn't describe in words, like burning hair and fried chicken and orange juice. When the bottom of the pan was covered with the simmering liquid, I turned the heat off and sent out my first spell.

My own spells are usually silent. I don't chant or sing anything. I just, as Helen accused, use my beads to focus my thoughts. Like praying. I visualized my desire for safety and protection and sent it into the liquid with a push of my mind —although technically its center was near my throat, halfway between head and heart.

Now I'd have to wait for it to cool.

"Random, how about a nice brushing?" I asked him.

He was asleep on the floor and didn't respond. I took out the dog brush I'd gotten at the pet store and squatted near him, hoping he was the type of dog to like grooming. I hoped there was such a dog, because I needed a lot of his fur for this spell to work.

"Dogs are protective," Helen had said. "But they can't be everywhere you need them to be, so you've got to spread them around."

After I'd freaked out a little, telling her that I wasn't going to be doing anything violent or nasty to my volunteer companion animal, no matter what he was or who had sent him, she comforted me with the news I'd only need his fur.

And he had a lot of that. In just the brief period he'd been at my house, he'd shed tumbleweeds of black fluff that were now bouncing around the floors. I would collect those too, but I needed more.

With the first touch of the brush on his back, Random jumped off the floor like a rocket and began licking me furiously. I tried to brush him while he moved around, lunging and chasing after him, but he was too fast. I tried again and again. I offered him turkey and peanut butter, but he wouldn't allow it. I was able to yank one large matted chunk of black fur out of his tail as he danced around, but it wasn't enough.

I didn't want to use a sleep spell on him because it would reflect back on me, and I needed as much alertness as possible to stay up doing the rest of my spells.

It was almost a half hour before he finally settled down and fell asleep again. With a quiet spell, I crept up on him with a pair of scissors and hacked the hair off his tail in three quick snips. There hadn't been much fluff to begin with and now there was even less. I regretted the visible dent, as did he, but it would grow back eventually.

"Sorry, friend," I said.

He ran to the other side of the kitchen and curled up in a corner, one eye cracked open to watch for further assaults.

The black dog hair went into the black frying pan until it was a soggy wad, which I then scooped into a black velvet bag and tied with a black drawstring. As it dripped on the floor, which was the point, I strode across the kitchen to the back door, sprinkled it along the threshold, and continued outside.

Willy stood on my deck, watching me, as far from his tree as I'd ever seen him. I knew he traveled but hadn't witnessed it myself.

"Strong magic you're brewing, Alma Bellrose," he said, hands clasped in front of him.

"I'm afraid of trouble coming to town with the Protector dead," I told him, a little spooked by his closeness. "A witch in San Francisco is guiding me. Have I offended you?"

"I must ask you the same thing, for the magic you use is aimed at the fae and would be useless on the man who calls himself your father or the unspeakable one who visits and makes you forget your love for your recently departed."

Willy seemed to have a particular antipathy for Seth Dumont. "I am using many spells the other witch gave me," I said, "in case the enemy is a malevolent spirit."

"So you do not fear me then?"

"Of course not, Willy. In fact, I hope these spells will help protect you as well."

He pulled his lips into a grimace. "That one will only do so because its odor is so offensive to me I must move myself deep into the ground to escape it, where none but the gophers and earthworms will find me."

"Sorry," I said, but I was more hopeful now that its nastiness would work even better on evil spirits.

He vanished, and I continued my march around the

outside of the house, dodging the overgrown shrubs and weeds as I sprinkled drops of wet dog fur and toasted blueberry leaves around the perimeter.

Willy's behavior had supported Helen's claim that the first spell would repel the fae. Now I needed to block the other dangers.

I got to work collecting twigs from my acacia tree.

Chapter Sixteen

I was on my hands and knees in the kitchen when I was startled by a knock on my back door. It was past midnight—who would be visiting this late?

And how disappointing that all the spells I'd enacted so far were obviously ineffective. I squeezed out my sponge, got to my feet, shrugging off the idea of washing my hands, and went to the door. Instead of opening it, I waited, listening and feeling for danger.

"Alma? It's Birdie," said the voice on the other side. "Are you there? I'm sorry if you're not. I'll come back tomorrow. It's just I saw your light and I know you can be a night owl like me, but maybe you don't want company, totally understand that's—"

I opened the door. "Birdie."

She waved a few fingers at me. Wedged beneath her arm was a golden-orange shipping envelope. "I know it's late. I'm so sorry, but I saw your light and I know you can be a night owl like me, but maybe you don't—"

"It's fine, no problem. Is anything wrong?" I didn't invite her in because—well. Because.

"What's that smell?" she asked. "Oh no, did your puppy have an accident?"

Realizing that was a perfect excuse for why the kitchen floor reeked of urine and why I was on my knees with wet rags, I stepped aside and invited her in. "You know how it is," I said with a shrug.

Birdie cupped her hand over her nose and mouth. "Wow, I didn't realize dogs could, you know, make so much."

The dog hadn't. A witch's own urine was supposed to be an effective protective spell. Not effective enough, apparently, because Birdie walked deeper into my kitchen, looking around.

"Where's the guilty party?" she asked.

Poor dog. "Sleeping on my bed." In the end, I'd had to send him to dreamland with a sleep spell, and I'd just finished my third can of coffee to compensate.

Birdie laughed. "Oh, you're smitten, aren't you? He peed all over, and you still let him sleep on your bed."

"I know, right?" I glanced at the clock. "So, what brings you by? I kind of need to get back to cleaning up this mess."

"Sure, sure, of course." She grabbed the envelope from under her arm and held it up. "I have pictures of Tristan. Livia said you were collecting pictures for the memorial, and I had a few I thought you might look at. They're probably not good enough but—"

"Great, thanks. I'll scan them in. I haven't even started working on that yet." I washed and dried my hands before I took the envelope from her. "Why did you have pictures of Tristan?"

"You might not want them. You'll probably find better ones. Somebody dropped them off at the store."

"Somebody just dropped them off? Why there?"

Birdie shrugged. "We're kind of like the unofficial community center. Biggest building and business in town, right on Main Street. Everyone uses our bulletin board. I figured Livia put the word out that the memorial would need pictures."

I pulled out a glossy eight-by-ten portrait of Tristan in full glamour, clean-shaven and well-dressed, smiling at the camera. Just like last week, he was blond and handsome with perfect teeth and held a wineglass in his hand. Bottles of Silverpool's finest vintage were artfully arranged beside him.

"It looks like an old head shot," I said, peering more closely at the bottles. "Those labels aren't in production anymore. I think that one is from twenty, maybe twenty-five years ago."

"Huh. He ages well, doesn't he?" Birdie asked. "Until he died, I mean."

"Until then, yeah." I realized I shouldn't have dated the photograph, drawing attention to the fact that Tristan hadn't visibly aged five years since then. "Maybe he took old bottles out of storage for the shot. Anyway, this is great. Thank you so much."

"There's another one," she said. "A candid."

I reached under the eight-by-ten and found a strip of black-and-white pictures from a photo booth. Tristan's companion was a giant stuffed teddy bear with plastic saucer eyes and a glittery bow tie, like the kind they gave away at carnivals. He and the bear were both smiling, as if the date was going really well.

In this one Tristan looked more ordinary and relaxed in just a T-shirt. He was unshaven, a little scruffy.

"I wonder who took this one," I said. "She must've hidden it from him."

"Why do you say that? How do you know it was a she?"

"Look at his face," I said. "He doesn't look like that when he's with other guys. That's a man who just got some, probably more than once and only got out of bed to make her happy."

Birdie took the picture from me and stared at it. "Oh," she said.

"He looks like he just rolled out of bed and hasn't shaved or had a shower yet. He hated to be caught unprepared." I thought about his ugly death on the bridge, how much it would've bothered him, how much it surely did bother him, and felt tears well in my eyes.

I turned aside, clearing my throat. "Thanks again. I'll stop by the store myself and see if anything else gets dropped off."

Birdie hesitated. "I have some floor cleaner that's got a nice lemon scent…"

"It's late. You go home. Don't worry yourself about my stinky house." I ushered her to the door. "I've got it under control. Thanks again!"

I closed the door before she could argue and got back to work. After I coated the floors with pee, I had some acacia branches that needed boiling and shaping.

Chapter Seventeen

A text message from Jasper just after dawn woke me from a deep sleep. Random was still groggy at the foot of the bed, although he did peek at me out from under one heavy eyelid when I jumped up to get my phone.

Jasper knew I wasn't a morning person and would only send a text this early if it was urgent.

Phoebe and older guy on their way to your house right now.

Older guy? My first thought was that it had to be Thomas Lorne. But surely the big cheese himself wouldn't make the trip to Silverpool...

Sure he would. A precious amulet was missing, and Tristan was dead. Even an incompetent director of a minor Protectorate satellite would step out of his office and travel a few miles for that.

I jogged to the bathroom to wash up, then threw on some clothes and raced around the house, locking up my beads, hiding my staff, cleaning up my dirty clothes, putting out guest towels and fresh soap.

Thank Brightness I'd already put away all my spell ingredients from the night before. After Birdie had dropped by, I'd gotten paranoid about other surprise visitors asking me about my unusual floor wash or the nasty-smelling incense with its faint hint of prickly pear, so I'd tidied up a little.

The smell lingered, however, so I set out bowls of lavender and gardenia blossoms and stuck a loaf of bread in the oven. It seemed to help. I didn't want Lorne to think I lazed about, wallowing in my own filth, peeing on myself.

Then again, why not? What did I care what that jerk thought of me? After they canned me, why would I still be trying to impress that overpaid windbag?

Because I couldn't help it. I was still human. Magically gifted, but human.

I opened the back door, sent a warm, safe thought to Willy, and walked across the yard to find one of the last suggestions Helen had made before sending me home. It had been too dark to find one last night, but in daylight it was easy. I was just tucking the oak leaf into my bra, smoothing it over my left breast, when I heard them arrive.

I closed my eyes and reached out to the new spells I'd cast around my hearth and home. I sensed the power humming along like an electric engine, quiet but strong, steady. It had been worth giving Helen a vial of springwater for what she'd taught me. My defenses were at least twice what they had been. And now I felt a sizzle of active, aggressive energy that hadn't been there before.

I smiled. *Come and get it.*

"She doesn't use the front door," Phoebe was saying from the front yard. "We'll have to walk around to the back."

Standing in the middle of my patio with the oak leaf over my heart, I waited for them to appear and wondered how Phoebe knew which door I used.

"Hi, Tommy," I said. "Phoebe. So nice of you to drop by."

Thomas Lorne, my former boss, stopped walking and shot an annoyed glance at Phoebe. "I didn't think she would be expecting us."

"I didn't tell her." Phoebe didn't look as surprised as Lorne to find me waiting for them, and I wondered if she'd told Jasper and if he'd get in trouble with her for texting me. For all his sarcasm, I thought he'd love to be included more in Protectorate business.

"Won't you come in?" I gestured to the kitchen door. If it still smelled like a subway station elevator, I'd blame it on the dog again.

"We have important matters to discuss," Lorne said.

Because I would be even more powerful inside the house —and them weaker for being under my roof—I invited them into my kitchen.

"Canned coffee?" I asked. "I can warm it up if you like."

"We don't have time for that," Phoebe snapped. "Answer Mage Lorne's questions."

"He hasn't asked any yet," I said.

Lorne turned to me and gazed at me with the hard, tense-jawed look that suggested he was attempting a verity spell. "Did you know the Protector Tristan Price was dead before the car hit him?"

"No," I said. The power in my body matched the notes of the spells singing in my floorboards. I could've told him I was Genghis Kahn, and he would've believed me.

"The nonmag police have lost interest," Lorne said. "They've ruled the cause of death a heart attack. He was run over later. The only crime, they believe, was in not reporting the collision. They're not looking for a murderer, just whoever fled the scene. They're convinced he was walking at night near his home, collapsed on a dark road. A small SUV, possibly a Jeep, ran over his corpse."

"We've noticed what you drive," Phoebe said.

"Half the town drives compact SUVs," I said. "Probably more."

"The Protectorate is trying to get nonmag officials to forget everything," Lorne said, "but they have the body, so the wisest step is to let procedure run its course. Police have too much to do to chase down a car that ran over a dead body in the middle of nowhere."

"Then again," Phoebe said, "if the person driving the car was also the only known living relative of an infamous thief on the same night a precious object was stolen, then the accidental death seems not so accidental."

"Your father is talented with telekinesis, is he not?" Lorne tried to use his verity spell on me again, and the effort was making his eyes bug out. "A simple matter of aorta manipulation would look like natural causes."

"My father is not a murderer," I said. The hairs on my arms stood at attention, drawing from the magic laced through the wood frame of my house, the earth around my property, the oak leaf over my heart. "If you suspect my Jeep of running him over, then you should suspect me, not him."

Phoebe smiled. "Come now. We know better than anyone you're *incapable* of that. You were let go for a reason."

"You don't have to take the blame for that man any longer," Lorne said. "You're obviously a soft, gentle soul, and he's been able to bend you to his Shadows since the day you were born. We don't blame you."

"We pity you, but we don't blame you," Phoebe added.

"Gee, thanks," I said.

"The timing of the theft of the torc on the night of Tristan's death is too perfect," Lorne said. "It cannot be a coincidence."

"My father is not a murderer," I repeated, this time lacing my words with the force of my new protective spells. "If you suggest such a thing again, you'll be forced to leave."

Did they hear the crackling in the air as I spoke? It was like the sound of thin ice breaking.

"Your father has committed more crimes than you know," Lorne said. "For the torc I'm sure he'd commit another—"

Suddenly he clasped his throat, unable to speak. I heard another sliver of ice break. My hands began to shake.

"Out," I said. "Get out."

The door flew open of its own accord and sucked Lorne through it, as if the vacuum of space had claimed an astronaut from a broken space ship.

"You can't—" Phoebe began, but then she was tipped onto her side and propelled headfirst through the doorway, a dainty cannonball with her mouth spread open in a silent scream.

Crackling with power, I followed them outside, walking slowly, not in any hurry because this was my home. I didn't owe anyone a thing, least of all two officious witches who didn't respect me.

I allowed their bodies to land near Phoebe's BMW. As fun as it would be to watch them float out of sight, I didn't want her car left in my driveway, blocking my Jeep. And with each inch they floated away from my house, my power weakened; they were lucky I didn't drop them from ten feet in the air.

Phoebe got to her feet first and was as red as Willy's velvet coat. "How did— How could you— You don't have the— You—you're not what you seem," she sputtered. "Uncle Thomas, see? See what I told you? She's powerful. She's hiding it! I tried to get in to look for the torc, and there is no way she should've been able to stop me, but she did. She's powerful, Thomas. You don't believe me but—"

"Her father must be helping her," Lorne—Uncle Thomas, which explained everything—said, staggering over to the passenger side of the car. "Alma couldn't possibly do this on her own. That criminal is more dangerous than you realize." He pounded the roof of the car. "Open the door, damn it!"

Phoebe fumbled with her purse, and the doors opened. They both fell inside.

"So nice of you to drop by," I said, trembling with the drain on my strength. Then added, "Don't come back."

"We could've done this nicely," Lorne said.

"Too bad you didn't," I said.

I used the last burst of my power to slam both doors shut. It was Phoebe's foot on the pedal that sent the car spinning into the road and down the hill, away, away from me and my home.

Where I was, finally, safe.

Chapter Eighteen

※❦※

A full day later, after sleeping around the clock to recover from the confrontation with Phoebe and Lorne, I drove to Tristan's house at the winery.

Silverpool Vineyards was a boutique winery perched on the rolling hills on the east side of town. The coastal fog and cool temperatures made the climate ideal for pinot noir, and Tristan had worked hard to make the best bottles he could— but not too good, which would draw unwanted attention and visitors to Silverpool. He'd told me once that most of his wine was sold private label, but he couldn't resist making a few with his own logo on the bottles.

Such as in that photograph Birdie had brought me.

Thinking about that old picture, I got out of the Jeep and went to the side door Tristan had used for his friends and neighbors. The main entrance led to the tasting room, banquet hall, and little shop where he'd sold wholesale bottles, T-shirts, branded glassware, corkscrews, that sort of thing.

The man had been a busy witch, protecting the town, loving women, making wine, running a business. He'd gotten away with sleeping around so much because he'd also been a good friend. Being his ex hadn't changed that, and I didn't regret our brief fling together. Not usually.

I'd phoned ahead to let the housekeeper, Donna, know I was coming, and she answered the door on the third ring.

"You didn't bring the dog?" Donna asked, peering around me as if it were hiding behind my legs. I'd met Donna a few times, but she was only part-time, not live-in.

As she'd requested when I'd called and mentioned Random, I had left him at my house. "I didn't bring the dog." And I felt guilty about it. He'd been locked inside the house with me while I slept and was stuck there again after only a brief walk around the neighborhood.

"I didn't want to have to clean it again," Donna said, stepping aside to let me in. "The police were here."

"They probably won't be back," I said. "They think he had a heart attack."

"Terrible," Donna said. "Who would run over somebody having a heart attack?"

"I think it happened later," I said. "At least that's the theory."

Donna smoothed her hands over her violet tracksuit. I'd never seen her wear anything other than athletic workout gear, usually in bright colors. She wasn't a witch but knew about us.

"I don't have any pictures," Donna said. "Livia Caruso asked me for some, but why would I have any pictures? He didn't like cameras."

"I know, but do you mind if I look around, see if I can find anything?"

"You have as much right as anybody," Donna said. "Did he tell you who he was leaving it to?"

"What, the winery?"

"The house, the winery, everything," she said, raising an

eyebrow. "There are things here he didn't want anybody to touch, not even me cleaning it. Now what's going to happen to it?"

"I don't know." I'd assumed the Protectorate owned the winery, and Tristan was just stationed here as a front, but maybe not. If Phoebe and Lorne weren't here already, maybe it had been Tristan's personal property and they were laying low until the police lost interest. "What kind of things?"

"I don't know what they are. He had them in a cabinet, and he wouldn't even let me dust it."

Like Tristan, I had cabinets filled with objects I wouldn't want anyone to touch, not even with a feather duster. Even if I could afford a housekeeper, I probably wouldn't have one because of the risk. "It was probably safer that way," I said.

"Yes, you're like him. I've been waiting to ask you about the cabinet because nobody else here knows what he was and I'm worried they might get hurt poking around."

"Good point," I said quietly. "But I'm not really authorized to take anything—"

"No, you can't take this. It's huge."

"Would you show me?"

"You'll… turn it off or whatever? Make sure it doesn't… explode? Turn me into a toad or something?"

"I don't know," I said, looking around to make sure nobody else was in the house to overhear me going along with the housekeeper's crazy talk. "I'll see what I can do."

Nodding, Donna played with the zipper on her jacket. "Thank you. I almost wondered if I should tell the police "

"No. They don't know anything. They'd think you were crazy."

Donna sighed, shaking her head as if she thought the same thing, and led me down the hallway to the other end of the house.

As we walked past his private office, I noticed a framed

picture of Tristan on the wall. Like Birdie's portrait, it wasn't a recent photo, but he looked almost the same as last week. The hair and fashions of the people next to him looked mid-1980s, but his ageless face matched the man I'd met a few years ago.

"It's in there," Donna called out ahead of me, pointing into one of the guest bedrooms.

No, not a guest bedroom. It gave the illusion of a guest bedroom. He must've used some stationary magic to keep the spells working after his death. I had to squint past a boring front of cream embroidered bedspread and wrought iron bed to see the massive armoire taking up most of the room. It was as big as my Jeep, a block of hand-carved wood with dozens of doors and drawers, bronze latches and hinges.

Donna stood behind me. I turned and asked her, "Can you see it?"

"Damn near broke my toe on it once," she said. "I could see it after that. But not before."

Sometimes the nonmagical could tap into what little powers they had by getting hurt. Survival was the greatest motivator.

"Give me a few minutes," I told her. "I'll see if I can, uh…"

"Neutralize it?"

I knew I couldn't do that without knowing what was inside—and maybe not even then—but I said, "Yeah. Exactly."

"I'll be in the kitchen."

"All right."

"You really don't know who's going to take over this place? I'm not the only one who needs to know if we still have a job. Oscar—he's the landscaper—he was asking me. Everyone else works for the winery, but Tristan paid us directly."

"I don't know. I'm sorry."

She let out a long sigh and left me to the invisible toe-breaking cabinet.

Which turned out to be better guarded than I'd expected. I couldn't even get into the room. With my first step, a wave of nausea swept over me, making me double over. Hands on knees, I gasped, trying not to cast up my coffee and toast on the bamboo plank flooring as I struggled to concentrate on Tristan's protective spell.

Sweat coated my body, and I began to shake from head to toe. My abdomen spasmed around what felt like a ball of barbed wire, reminding me of the time everyone got food poisoning at boarding school.

Donna was lucky to have only stubbed a toe.

I fell on my ass and flung a hand up to grab my necklace. The beads had a highly personal power, and it rushed into my body like fuel, tearing down my skin like wildfire, cutting the bonds between me and the...

The guarding spell was coming from an invisible wall at the threshold. I rolled over and put my face near the floor, inhaling as I searched for a visible line on the wood planks.

There. A row of tarnished silver dots. The heads of pins that had been driven into the... rowan. The bamboo floor in the hallway ended at the doorway and became witch wood. No wonder I felt sick, but Donna had walked right in.

Tristan hadn't feared the nonmagical finding his cabinet. This was for people like me. Witch people.

I was more curious than ever about the cabinet. Donna was right—it could be dangerous for normal people to get their hands on anything he guarded so carefully.

Clutching my stomach, I forced myself to sit up, bracing my back against the hallway wall with my legs sprawling out in front of me.

Rowan and silver would be a challenge for me to break. The wood alone was doable, but bound with metal—

I got to my feet, having to keep my hand on the wall for balance, and lurched down the hall to the kitchen, where Donna was mopping the floor.

Her floor wash smelled a lot better than mine.

"Hi," I said to get her attention.

"Oh my God, what happened? Should I call somebody?" She rested the mop against the refrigerator and began to come over, although she stopped with several feet between us. "You don't look so good."

"I don't feel so good. Would you mind getting me a glass of water?"

"Sure, sure." She turned and opened the fridge, but I stopped her from taking out a plastic bottle.

"Just tap water," I said. "Please. From the faucet."

"But he—Tristan won't be drinking this—I'm sure he wouldn't mind—"

"Tap. Please." I smiled at her until she shrugged and got a glass.

As she filled it at the sink, I concentrated on my desires that the hint of wellspring magic that made its way into Silverpool tap water would help me recover.

"I think it tastes bad," Donna said, handing it to me.

I gulped it down without comment. It was faint, but I felt a thread of magic dissolved in the water and now seeping into me, my lips and mouth and esophagus and finally my stomach…

The cramping ceased. I let out a long breath and moved to get more, but she stopped me, pointing at the wet floor and my boots, and refilled it for me.

After I'd finished that one, I felt good enough to smile sincerely. "Thank you so much, Donna. It has a little something in it, you know? You might want to drink it sometimes."

Her eyes narrowed. "What's in it?"

"You know. Something." I held up my thumb and forefinger about a millimeter apart. "Just a little."

"Tristan never drank water out of the faucet," she said. "He didn't even want me cooking with it."

That surprised me. I'd thought Tristan wasn't as hostile to wellspring magic as the mainstream Protectorate witches who would've buried every spring under mountains of rock and mud if they'd had the power. In fact, they'd tried just over a century ago, down the coast in Big Sur, but fairies had immediately redirected the water to the surface nearby. Probably laughing while they did it, triggering a few earthquakes in revenge.

I handed her the empty glass with my thanks and went to look at the cabinet again. From the mantle I grabbed a framed photograph of him standing in front of the Silverpool Vineyard sign at the bottom of the drive, the rows of vines rolling up the hill behind him in bright, golden autumn light. It was a recent picture, or at least timeless. He looked happy.

Being in his house was bringing up a lot of memories, making me depressed. Living in Silverpool was going to be lonely without him. He'd been a womanizer, but he'd found me the rental house, encouraged me to sell my beads, and then found me wealthy witch customers to buy them, usually for much more than I'd priced them. When the Protectorate had dumped me, he'd helped me get back on my feet when I'd felt completely alone in the world.

I lifted the photograph and looked him in the eye. "I owe you."

I waited a moment to see if he'd reply (you never know)

before hugging the frame to my chest and returning to the hexed guest room.

Holding Tristan in my thoughts, and his picture over my heart, I studied the cabinet again from the safety of the hallway. In many of its visible compartments, I could see keyholes. It was certainly locked in more than one way.

"It wasn't always here, you know," Donna said behind me, making me jump.

"Where was it?" I asked, then caught myself. "You mean he got it recently?"

"Last year. It used to be a guest room. People slept in here. But then a guy from town came in with the cabinet in pieces on a dolly, and then I didn't see it again until I stubbed my toe on it."

"What guy?"

"I've seen him around. Contractor type. Handyman, remodeling, that sort of thing," Donna said. "He was at the deli last week in his work clothes. I was standing behind him in line, and he was covered with dust. Even his hair. If you're going out to a restaurant, even a takeout place, don't you think you should brush yourself off first?"

"Do you remember his name?" The man who made it would know what kind of mechanical locks the cabinet had. Even after I figured out the magic protections, I'd still have to get it open.

"Sorry. Local, that's all I know."

I thanked her, got her permission to take the photo, and hurried out to my Jeep. I would have to ask Birdie at the hardware store if she knew about a cabinetmaker working on an elaborate piece of furniture for Tristan.

Chapter Nineteen

꧁꧂

Cypress Hardware was the biggest building in the business district, with a full-sized parking lot that set it back from the street, pushing it against the river's edge. Cypress not only provided sand bags to the community every winter, it relied on them to form a dam along its property line, when the river turned into a brown, flowing lake every December. The town, like so much of California, had a tendency to build in floodplains. Unlike the rest of the state, however, having the Protector as a close neighbor meant the store floor remained dry, even when the river broke its banks and took out the bridge.

I parked and found Birdie at the customer service counter near the front door. It was a small-town hardware store but was oddly enormous, with ten registers, big-box warehouse architecture, and dozens of aisles stacked high with do-it-yourself merchandise. When the UPS truck usually got lost, you stopped ordering online.

"Where's your dog?" Birdie asked me. She wore a green Cypress apron and a bulky canvas coat over it to stay warm.

It got cold next to the door, even in late summer. "You know you're allowed to bring him in here?"

"Thanks, I know. He's home," I said. "I need to get back and take him for a walk."

"I'll take him anytime," Birdie said. "If you trust me."

"Of course I trust you." It was true. She wasn't a witch, but now that Tristan was gone, I felt closer to her than anyone else in town, even Jasper. "Did anyone else drop off any pictures?"

"Oh. No. That is, maybe. I don't know." Rubbing her eyes, she bent down to look under the counter.

I realized how tired she looked, as if she'd spent all night washing her floors with her own urine and then had to drive Protectorate witches away. "Are you all right?"

Busy with a pile of plastic bins under the counter, she didn't answer.

"Birdie?"

"What? Yes?" She stood up, clutching a bin to her chest. "Am I all right?"

"You seem tired." Now I noticed the dark circles under her eyes, the dullness of her complexion.

"Oh, I'm fine. But I don't see any more pictures." She pushed the bin back beneath the counter. "You could ask Carolyn. She worked on his kitchen remodel."

"Sure. Thanks." I started to walk away, then turned. Maybe a happy dog would cheer her up. "Would you be interested in taking Random for a walk later? I don't know if you'd be willing to have him in your house—"

"Sure! I'd love it." Her face fell. "But I'm working until eight. And then I can't."

"Maybe tomorrow then. He seemed to really like you."

"I'm really sorry. I said I could take him anytime and then the first time you ask, I'm like, no, busy."

"Totally fine," I said. "Listen, do you know any wood-worker or crafty guy who made a custom cabinet for Tristan, at least a year ago? It's a big thing, lots of nooks and crannies—"

She shook her head. "Carolyn might know. Ask her that too."

"OK, thanks," I said. "Are you sure you're all right?"

"Totally. It's not like a stroke or cancer. I'm fine." She smiled faintly and then began to laugh.

Concerned, I lingered at the counter until I realized a customer holding an air conditioner was standing behind me, waiting for Birdie, and I hurried away.

I found Carolyn behind an office desk in the Designer Showroom area, where several mock kitchens and bathrooms had been set up in the back corner of the building. She was in her thirties, highlighted gold-and-copper hair, lots of makeup, flattering black pantsuit, pretty but unhappy. I'd seen her around, but she was the type of person I avoided—smart and observant but aggressively conventional, a bad companion for a witch trying to live under the radar.

I introduced myself and explained I was looking for pictures of Tristan for the memorial.

"Livia told me you were making a slideshow," she said, wiping her nose with a tissue. I noticed she might be wearing so much makeup to cover a recent bout of crying; her eyes were bloodshot and puffy, her nose red. "Such a tragedy."

"You knew Tristan?"

Her voice dropped. "I knew Tristan." She sighed and looked off into space before offering me a chair. "I do have pictures. Tons of them. I'm not sure how many you can use, though."

"I only need a few."

She looked past me again, then leaned over the desk. "Can you be, you know, discreet? I want to honor his memory, but…"

"Whatever you feel comfortable sharing."

"What I mean is, do you have to say you got them from me?" Licking her lips, she glanced at the ceiling. "You see, although I did work with Tristan on the remodel, these pictures aren't exactly from the project itself, if you know what I mean."

"I don't want anything, you know, inappropriate—"

She recoiled in horror. "No, of course not. It's just these are obviously, uh, casual shots. He's at the beach."

"Fully clothed?"

"Of course! You think I'd offer naked shots of him for his memorial?"

"But then why are you so afraid to give them to me?"

Carolyn sat up straighter but didn't meet my eyes. "Look, it's Livia. She— You know how— She really admired Tristan, but things never—"

"She doesn't know that you... knew... Tristan pretty well."

"She thinks our relationship was strictly professional."

I almost felt sorry for Livia. The only woman in town he hadn't slept with. "I don't need to tell her you gave me the pictures. I already have a couple that were dropped off anonymously at the store."

"You do? Oh, that's great." She let out a long sigh and smiled. "Livia and I have been friends a long time. Since we were both living in Napa. I had a bad divorce and came out here, told her how nice it was, and one day she just showed up."

"But if you knew Tristan from before, then she could hardly mind—"

"I knew him but didn't know him, if you know what I mean. Until a few months ago." Flushing, she arranged some folders on her desk and shoved them into a binder. "She'd kill me if she knew. She'd made no secret of her feelings for him."

No, she hadn't, I thought. "It's just a little slideshow," I said. "Do you want to email them to me?"

She shook her head. "I'll make prints and… give them to Birdie. Anonymously. Will that work? You never know with email what's going to get forwarded, and I don't want my name attached."

"No problem. I'll come by the store… say, tomorrow? The memorial is on Saturday."

"They'll be ready first thing in the morning." She stood up as if she was going to send me away, but I stayed in my chair.

"Listen, do you know anything about a handyman Tristan bought a cabinet from?" I asked. "A local guy?"

"You mean Nick?" She sank into her chair, smiling more easily now. "Don't let him hear you call him a handyman. He's a *craftsman*. His pieces cost a fortune, and they should. Gorgeous work."

"Do you have his number? Last name?"

"Takata. Nick Takata. Sure, why?"

I hesitated. "I saw the cabinet he made Tristan and was interested in talking to him, one woodworker to another." I cast a quick convincing spell to help her believe me.

"Oh right," she said, eyes dropping to my necklace. "You're kind of an artist."

"Kind of," I said. "I'm learning."

She jotted down a number from her phone onto a yellow notepad. "Well, he's amazing. Not easy to talk to though. Don't say I didn't warn you."

I took the note, thanked her again, and headed for the parking lot. Birdie was busy with another customer as I approached the front doors. I waved, but she didn't see me. Was she ill? A cold was going around. Working hourly, she probably couldn't afford to take time off.

As I walked to the car, I vowed to check up on her later.

Chapter Twenty

After a few rounds of phone tag, Nick agreed to meet me at Taco Perdido at four that afternoon on his way home from work. He'd explained that he was working on a job in Marin and might get stuck in traffic. I took the opportunity to go home and take Random out for a long walk.

Willy came out of his tree as I was leaving again. "Your animal misses you when you're gone. He cries."

"I hate to leave him," I said, "but I have no choice."

Willy put a hand over his heart. "I will sing to him."

"Thank you. I won't be gone long."

A short drive later and I was at the taqueria. Based on Donna's description of a working man coated in sawdust, I was pretty sure I recognized Nick Takata the moment he walked in. Tall, broadly built guy with black hair cut short, wearing paint-splattered jeans, a black T-shirt, and a brown canvas jacket that looked as if it had been dragged behind a truck doing ninety in a muddy field.

"Nick?" I asked.

He took off a pair of sunglasses to look me over, which

he did slowly, his face blank. Then he walked past me and placed an order at the register without looking at the menu.

He was a little older than me, good-looking but, as Carolyn had warned, obviously not the friendliest guy in the world.

When he had his drink and a bowl of chips, he came over and took the chair across from me. "Aren't you eating?"

"Looks like it's ready now," I said, getting up for my burrito, which waited for me in a red plastic basket at the counter. "Thanks for agreeing to meet me. Salsa?"

"All right."

I got the burrito and two bowls of salsa and returned to the table. He'd taken off his coat, revealing broad shoulders and a silver chain around his neck. I could feel the power coming off it in slow waves, a sign it hadn't been used for a while. Maybe he didn't know what it was.

"I could've emailed you the picture," he said, holding up his phone. On the screen was a shot of Tristan, the cabinet behind him, not yet put under enchantment.

I peered at the screen. I'd crop out the cabinet, which might interest the wrong people. "Could you do it now?"

He nodded and hit a button. "You got my name from Carolyn?"

"I saw that cabinet at Tristan's this morning."

"Thought so," he said, rolling his eyes. "This isn't about his memorial."

"I came across your cabinet while I was getting ready for the memorial."

"And now you want the key," he said.

"Do you have the key?" I'd been afraid Tristan had hidden it somewhere I'd never find it.

He made a face and stood up to get his own burrito. When he returned, he turned his attention completely to his food, sawing through the aluminum foil with a plastic knife and scooping black beans into his mouth without speaking.

I watched him chew for a full minute. "Have I offended you somehow?"

He tore open a white paper salt packet and sprinkled it over the chips. The chain around his throat continued to hum, but no differently than before. "I know what you are," he said.

I took a bite of my burrito and tried to chew as silently yet aggressively as he had. "Fine. That makes it easier."

"How so?"

"I can explain my motives," I said. "Donna's worried that with Tristan gone, somebody might get hurt by that cabinet you built. Somebody who doesn't know what Tristan was."

"Liar," he said. "You want it for yourself."

"It's much too heavy. And my house is cramped as it is."

"You want what's inside it."

I couldn't help myself. I leaned closer and asked, "Do you know what's inside it?"

He shook his head and commenced passive-aggressive chewing.

Eventually I asked, "How do you know what I am?"

His gaze dropped to my necklace. "That."

"Lots of people wear necklaces. You're wearing one."

His lips curved in a brief smile. "Yeah, I knew you'd notice that. My ex gave it to me."

"Your ex was like me?"

"My ex was a witch. I'm not afraid to say it. Normal people don't quite understand what I mean when I do." He snowplowed his beans together on his plate. "At first I thought she was normal, staging houses. A real estate agent friend introduced us. But then I found out she was nuts, even for your kind. She hated normal people being in charge of things, but she hated other witches even more."

"Sounds like a Freewitch."

"Yeah, that's what she—" He broke off and stared into space, the fork dropping out of his fingers.

I sensed magic at work. "Nick?"

His gaze slowly returned to mine. "What?"

"She was a Freewitch?"

"Who?"

"Your ex-girlfriend," I said.

He retrieved his fork. "I don't know and I don't care."

The puff of magic I'd sensed had faded away, leaving only the disgruntled expression on Nick's face.

"Why do you still wear the necklace if you're mad at her?" I asked.

"I'm not mad." He stabbed the swollen center of his burrito. "Besides, it won't come off."

Seeing an opening, I said, "I could help you with that."

"I don't need your help."

"OK, but do you have the key? You don't have to give it to me, obviously, but I'd like to know. There are other people—"

"Witches."

"Yes, witches, who would like to have what's inside."

"Tristan explained that to me when I built the cabinet," he said. "That's why it's locked." He spoke slowly and deliberately, as if to an idiot.

"I'm not a thief," I said.

Nick snorted. "That's what Tristan said."

"Excuse me?"

"*He* called himself a collector. I've known a lot of rich guys in my life, and I recognize somebody who's got things he shouldn't have but doesn't want to admit it or give them up. And for one of you people, who knows what that might be." He pointed over my shoulder with his plastic fork. "The dude down in Belvedere where I've been installing a whole house full of custom built-ins, for instance. Same story. Gray market, black market, who knows, but he wants his booty and he's not going to share it with a museum."

"I'm not like that. For instance, I don't collect things unless I use them for my art." I tapped my necklace.

"Then why do you want to get in the cabinet? And don't tell me you're worried about normal people getting hurt. The safest thing is to leave that cabinet and whatever he put in it alone."

"I'm curious," I said.

"Uh-huh."

"The magic around it is unusual. I don't know why he would feel the need to do something like that in his own home."

He scoffed. "So what makes it your business?"

I thought about what Helen had said. "I'm driven to know. It's what I do. He was a friend and he was—" I started to say *murdered*, but the official cause of death was a heart attack. "Cut short in the prime of his life."

"Not as prime as he looked," Nick said. "My ex was like that. I found out she was pushing fifty. That creeped me out. Not that I don't appreciate older women, but I don't like liars." He gave me a level stare.

"I'm not lying to you."

"It doesn't matter if I believe you. That's just your magic making me believe you."

"I'm not using any magic right now."

"Sure."

"All right," I said, "there's something missing, something that was stolen the night he died, and the—authorities—"

"The Protectorate?"

"Yes. They think I have it. I know I don't. So if I find it, I can clear my name."

"Why would they think you have it?"

"Because my father has a reputation for taking things that don't belong to him."

"Does he deserve this reputation?"

"Definitely."

He smiled his first real smile. "I see. Bad luck for you."

"Very."

"OK, I feel like you're being open with me, which is probably all a trick, but what the hell."

"So you'll give me the key?"

"I'm not saying I have it," he said. "I'll have to think about it."

"You've got my number—"

"I sure do." He wiped his lips with a paper napkin, soiled but neatly folded. A craftsman in love with right angles, or maybe it was compulsive. "I swore I'd never get involved with witches again. All of you are trying to destroy one another. As if the world wasn't in enough trouble."

"It's understandable you might carry a grudge."

"I don't carry anything except this chain around my neck."

"The one she put there," I said.

He set down the napkin. "Time for me to go."

"It's not just witches you have to look out for," I said. "That's what Tristan's job really was, protecting Silverpool from those other things. With him gone—"

"Stop right there. I know what you're talking about. *Demons.*" He made air quotes with his big hands, his voice heavy with scorn. "Mankind is the monster here, always has, always will be. With or without magic." He gave my necklace another pointed look.

"There are all kinds of monsters." I was starting to lose my temper. "And more are on the way. When other people—and other things—learn Tristan had a secret cabinet under heavy disguise, they're going to go looking for it, wherever it is, whoever has it. Whether that's Donna or some estate agent or you."

"I'm sure Tristan thought of that before he died. He seemed like a very careful guy. Nobody's going to hear about it unless you tell them."

"They'll hear about it from somebody. It's guarded and invisible, not really hidden. Somebody else is going to stub their toe on it and start poking around."

"Let them. It's locked."

I didn't know how to get through to him. I understood his point of view—what claim did I have? I was just some stranger wanting the dead guy's loot for myself.

Just then I realized that Nick must believe the official story, that Tristan died of natural causes, though tragic.

I had to give him more reason to believe me.

"Tristan was murdered," I said. "And the reason might be in that cabinet."

He got to his feet and cleared the table. "All the more reason to leave it alone."

Chapter Twenty-One

I returned home to find Willy singing to Random through the kitchen window. The dog had climbed up on a chair and was fogging up the glass, panting desperately at the gnome on the other side.

"He enjoys the old songs," Willy told me as I unlocked the door. He jumped off the window ledge, his red cap bobbing on his head like a quail's feather plume.

I set the package I'd brought the gnome on the patio tiles. "Thank you for keeping him company. I've brought you some horchata and flan." Knowing how much he loved sweets, I always got dessert to go. It wasn't just cynical manipulation on my part; I liked to make him happy. He always returned the favor.

"My pleasure." Willy picked up the bag, almost as big as he was, and dragged it behind him to his tree.

After Random got the love, kibble, and potty time he needed, I went to my file cabinet, lifted my staff, and sat on the floor with it balanced on my knees.

I took several deep breaths and calmed my mind as best I could.

Nick Takata hadn't believed me about the murder, hadn't given me the key. As I got more frustrated, I wondered if he was right, if I only wanted to get inside to satisfy my own greedy urges, either possession or knowledge. What right did I have? The Protectorate would deal with it.

The torc wasn't inside the cabinet. Why would it be inside the cabinet?

I kept telling myself that, fingers wrapped around my staff for focus, strength, calm.

It didn't work.

Nick had said Tristan reminded him of black market collectors he'd known. If the Protectorate opened the cabinet next week, after Tristan was buried and they'd seized his property, and found the torc inside, would they tell me? Would they absolve my father, apologize to me?

No. I'd be left worrying forever. They'd use it as an excuse to spy on me in the future, and the Bellrose name would never be redeemed.

But how could Tristan have the torc?

Because he stole it, a voice inside me whispered. Had my father tried to steal it from Tristan, and then—

None of it made sense. I had to know more.

I reached up to my desk for my phone and scrolled through it until I found one of my father's phone numbers. He'd used a lot of burner phones and went through email addresses like an internet scammer, but this one usually reached him eventually.

I hadn't expected him to pick up, but his voice answered on the second ring. "Alma, so nice to hear from you."

"Hi. Quick question. Need the truth. Ready?"

"Lovely weather we're having."

"Where are you?"

"Home, of course. Where else would an old man like me be after dark?"

"I can think of a few places," I said. "A few of them in Europe, closely guarded."

"I've retired, honey. How many times do I have to tell you?"

"The Protectorate has been here, looking for something they think you stole from the Diamond Street office. I need to know if you have it."

"*You* think *I* have it?"

I'd expected him to be incredulous, but I didn't expect for his act to convince me. But he had managed to fool me countless times before, even since I'd been an adult. He knew I was an honest person, and people like us are easy marks. He was my father but had no morals whatsoever about lying to me again. At a fundamental level, Malcolm Bellrose would always be a cheat.

"Do you?" I asked.

"Turn all your verity spells on me and hear the truth, my daughter. I do not have it."

If verity spells worked on my father, he'd be in a Protectorate jail by now. "Did you ever have it?"

"Of course not."

This was a waste of time. He'd swear the sky was a flat-screen TV from the future if he'd get something out of it. For me to get information from him, I'd have to offer something valuable in exchange. But not too valuable. I couldn't tell him about the cabinet—he'd be at Tristan's house in five minutes, key or no, rowan or no—but I could fish a little.

"I'm helping out with the memorial," I said.

"The what?"

"Tristan Price. Protector of Silverpool. He died."

"You slept with him," my father said.

"That's not why he died."

"I was simply attempting to clarify that we were discussing the same individual," he said.

"Yes. Same individual, as you well know," I said. "Anyway, I've been collecting photographs of him for the memorial, and an interesting quirk about him has come to my attention."

"I hope you're not shocked to learn you're not the only woman he slept with."

I closed my eyes for a moment. "No, I was aware of that."

"What kind of quirk are you talking about then? Rich witch like him probably had a few interesting kinks."

"Rich people like to buy things," I said, "things my father might know about because they're not totally legit."

The line went silent.

"Dad, please," I said, softening my tone. "Is it possible Tristan had the torc before he died? You don't have to admit anything, just yes or no. Is it possible?"

After a long pause, Malcolm said, "I wasn't a good father to you, was I?"

"Just—please, answer the question. Is it possible?"

"If I answer, are we cool? You'll forgive and forget?"

I decided that his question referred to only recent crimes, not a lifetime of them. "All right," I said.

"Lovely," he said. "Doesn't that feel good? I bet your heart is lighter now."

"Answer the question."

After a pause so long I thought he'd thrown the phone in the San Francisco Bay, I heard a single, quiet word.

"Yes."

And then the line went dead.

THE NEXT MORNING I called Nick again to ask him if he'd reconsider giving me the key, but he didn't pick up, and my texts went unanswered.

It only strengthened my resolve to find another way. Besides, the physical key was the least of my problems with a cabinet so heavily spelled. Breaking through the magical protections would take time. And knowledge. And who knew what else.

After sucking down a can of cold coffee, I sat outside under Willy's tree, cross-legged in the dirt with Random curled beside me, and got to work. Thinking. So much of magic was just figuring things out. My father had taught me how effective a well-planned invasion could be, even against what seemed insurmountable.

The key. Maybe that would be the least of my problems.

The rowan. It could either work for you or against you and was always powerful. With the right tools, I could turn it to my side.

The silver. Like the rowan, it could repel evil or perceived evil intent. With a pure heart, I would be able to enter. Since I didn't have a pure heart, I'd have to trick it—by taking it down an exhausting, twisted path. A knot snare.

The unknown. What glamour had Tristan used that had survived his death? Something physical, embedded in the ceiling or the floor, perhaps the cabinet itself. Metal? Another botanical? Old magic or new?

And stone. Tristan had loved precious gems. He'd worn sapphire cuff links on fancy occasions. Numerous jade sculptures from Chinatown adorned the living room—had there been any in the room with the cabinet? I'd been too busy trying not to throw up to notice.

I cast my mind back, trying to remember. I couldn't see it in my mind's eye, but I could feel it. A guardian spirit, green, stone, watching me from across the threshold. A monster with five eyes, tiny but deadly, claws digging into his perch on the top of the—I strained to remember—on top of the cabinet itself. No bigger than my fist.

Covered with sweat, I opened my eyes and let myself fall onto my back on the ground, sucking in deep breaths. Random wiggled out from under me and began licking my face.

"I think I'm ready," I told him.

Chapter Twenty-Two

D onna greeted me on Tristan's doorstep. She'd been
in Santa Rosa when I'd called but had agreed to
meet me at the house.

"Thanks for letting me in," I said. A bag slung over my
shoulder was heavier than it looked, digging a painful groove
into my collar bone.

Donna, still wearing her coat, stepped aside to let me in
the house. "I can't stay," she said. "I've got another job."

I held up a box of pastries from the Riverside Café. "I got
these for you, if you're interested. I really do appreciate your
making the trip."

Frowning, she took it from me. "Donuts are bad for my
blood sugar, but I'll see if Oscar wants any."

"There's a gluten-free keto vegan nut bar in there too," I
said. As unusual as Silverpool was, it was still California. "If
that appeals to you."

"Maybe. Thanks." She tucked the box under her arm and
stepped outside. "Pull this door shut when you leave. It'll
lock behind you. I'll be back in a few hours to make sure
you're OK."

I swung my heavy bag to the floor, where it landed with a thud. "You don't have to come back." I didn't want her to interrupt me while I was casting my spells.

"You don't know what that thing might do," she said. "Who should I call if you… you know…"

"Drop dead?"

She nodded.

"The police, I suppose." If something killed me, the Protectorate deserved to have the nonmag officials asking questions. "But I'll be fine."

She shuddered. "That's what Tristan said," she said as she left.

A few moments later, as I was dragging my bag down the hallway, I thought about her choice of words. I dropped the bag and caught up to her in the driveway.

"Did he say that the night he died?" I asked. "That he'd be fine?"

"He said that every night." Donna covered her mouth as she spoke. She held the nut bar in the other hand.

"OK, thanks again."

For a part-time housekeeper, Donna seemed awfully familiar with Tristan and his secrets. She'd been working for him as long as I'd known him. Had they slept together? Did it matter?

I went back inside to my bag in the hallway. The first thing I removed was a long necklace of carefully knotted red yarn, which I pulled over my head and looped around three times. My eyes still ached from focusing on the tiny knots, making sure the spacing was right (clustering them in fives, nines, and sevens). It rested on top of my favorite redwood beads.

I was a witch, but I did wonder if some of this stuff was superstitious nonsense. My wood beads gave off a power I could feel, a power I'd carved and polished into each piece. But would five knots in a strand of red yarn really help me any more than would six knots in yellow yarn? Really?

"Don't scare away the magic by doubting it," Helen had told me.

"Maybe magic that's so easily scared away isn't very powerful," I'd countered. "A spell tied with a chain of ancient silver isn't so easy to break."

"You got a chain of ancient silver lying around?" she'd asked me.

I'd had to admit I did not.

"Yarn is cheap and doesn't raise questions," she'd said. "Everyone thinks you're just a harmless old lady. They don't look twice."

With just the yarn, maybe, but after I'd darkened my eyes with kohl and sat cross-legged in front of the guest room's doorway—wearing a skirt but no underwear—I appreciated my solitude. Wielding the power of the feminine felt ridiculous, and I'd rather not have an audience.

The cabinet flickered into view in the room in front of me. Now that I was looking for it, I could see the small gargoyle perched on the top, facing the door and me, his grotesque features twisted into a snarl. He was green as jade but no longer stone; his form was rippling, alive, with strands of slime hanging from his fangs and wet stains puddling under his feet. It slid down the outside of the cabinet to the floor, its landing an audible drip, drip, drip.

Wordless terror struck me like a hot wind. The creature specialized in fear, triggering the latent survival instincts in every living thing. Prepared, I drew a simple circle in the air between us, a shield of safety.

It took me a moment to calm down enough to concentrate on the familiar well of magic inside me, the warm glow of strength and power, like a small sun, that I'd felt as long as

I could remember. There. That was real; that was power I could count on.

The gargoyle would have to wait. The first hurdle was the spell Tristan had set in the rowan doorway with the silver pins. I really would've preferred the ancient silver chain to counteract his metal, or maybe copper, but Helen had promised the fancy knots in the yarn would function as a trap. The magic would be drawn to the twists and turns, strive to get closer, fall into my maze of wool.

I put both hands on my necklaces, and easy as picking dandelions, I used my mind to lift each pin out of the wood, one by one, and move them aside. Disarmed, they fell into a harmless pile next to my bag.

Thank you, Helen.

Without the silver, the rowan could be bent to my will, and my years of working with wood served me now as I turned the spell away from me into the room, toward the little green monster. An invisible current of ice struck him in the face.

The creature yelped, then froze into stone. Once again he was the smooth and immobile carving he'd been when Tristan had enchanted him.

I stood, brushing my skirt over my thighs, and retrieved my bag for the remaining items. The frying pan hadn't gotten any lighter when I'd filled it with a bag of pennies. About time those things came in useful. I'd kept meaning to roll them or bring them to the coin machine at the grocery store in Sebastopol. Now I'd use the metal coins for luck.

Because I didn't know what the next protective spell around the cabinet would be. I could feel something hot, red, blazing... somewhere inside the room. I held the frying pan as if it were a breakfast tray and stepped over the threshold.

"Room service," I muttered.

The iron under my fingers began to get warm, uncomfortably warm, then hot, scalding. I held on. My skin began to blister and smoke, and a nauseating smell—my own cooking flesh—filled the room, but I held on and took another step.

Oh my God. This was bad. Very bad.

Don't panic. Just hold on.

The fire stretched up above my wrists, seeming to catch the hem of my sweater on fire. Yellow flames danced up to my elbows, and my skin bubbled under the blaze. My hands were raw, white finger bones visible under the blackened flesh that fell in small, crispy chunks to the floor.

Nausea roiled within me. I was grossing myself out.

I closed my eyes and took another step. The fire wasn't real, the pain wasn't real, nothing in our world was real, existence was an illusion, we were nothing more than the paintings of fairies, the nightmares of demons, the daydreams of angels—

I screamed. It felt real. Something Tristan had left behind had set my hands on fire—for real—and I was just walking into it like an idiot, and then how would I make a living carving and stringing beads if I didn't have any arms?

To hell with arms—what if my heart stopped? The burning had raced beyond my elbows, over my shoulders, pierced my sternum, and was attacking my heart, surrounding it with heat, breaking its cell walls, melting...

Melting my heart?

Oh, Tristan, such a ladies' man, even now. I lifted the burning pan to my lips and kissed it. If I was wrong, my face would fall off. But if I was right...

Hah. I was right. I still had a face, with eyes that could see the source of the fire, a small box in the corner to my left. Ignoring the feeling I was a living candle and not living much longer from the feel of my chest, I staggered over to the box and swung the pan. It struck the wall, missing the box. I stuck my foot—what was left of it—into the corner and swept the box out with my charred, stumpy toes and then dropped the pan on it again, this time crushing it completely.

I was still on fire. Crap. I reached through the blaze to grab the box—an old-fashioned matchbox, palm-sized, cardboard—and shake out the contents into the frying pan.

A red and black powder scattered over the coins, sizzling like steaks on a grill—or was that my flesh?—and finally, slowly, the fire went out.

As the heat cooled, I forced myself to look at my hands as they regrew their muscle, flesh, veins, skin, tiny hairs, each freckle. My sweater knitted back into view. My heart returned to its healthy, stony state.

Damn. Whatever spell that had been, I wanted Helen to teach it to me. Keeping my eye on the cabinet for further horrors, I rested against the wall as I caught my breath.

No wonder Donna hadn't forgotten this cabinet. If I were the housekeeper, I'd be out of here pronto no matter what Tristan paid me.

I put my hand on my necklace and rubbed my thumb along the largest bead as much for habitual comfort as for power. Casting out my awareness to the cabinet, I felt for more gargoyles, boxes of pepper and camphor, silver, anything at all—but found nothing else blocking me.

I got to my feet and forced myself to approach. It was a lovely piece of furniture, not that I knew about woodworking, but it looked artistic, unique, complicated. Dozens of cubbies, doors, slots, and drawers on three of four sides. The back was smooth and plain, designed to go against the wall, although it stood in the center of the room.

My gaze was drawn immediately to the keyholes, of which there were seven, lucky seven, on each of the three usable sides of the cabinet.

Nick Takata had never changed his mind about sharing any keys with me. Fortunately, however, I'd been raised by a thief. Well, we'd spent vacations together.

I pulled a mass of keys out from under my shirt. I'd hung the silver ring on a black ribbon like I'd done in the old days, back when I would risk anything to be with my father, even my own future. It's hard to care about your future when you're only eight.

They might not work. They were old, some of my earliest, clumsiest magic, the witch equivalent of a crayon family portrait in kindergarten.

They didn't look like keys, but they should function as them. They were pieces of elements, minerals, metals, botanicals, anything that could unlock the power of the universe. I had a soft chunk of redwood, my first love; a stainless steel measuring spoon; old coins from around the world, drilled with holes; a rabbit's foot I still felt guilty about, although I loved to rub its silky toes; a gold-plated bracelet; an angrily discarded platinum wedding band; more broken jewelry containing assorted metals and gems; a vial of witch's spit (my own); a single juniper berry…

I flipped through the collection, feeling for a reaction from any of the pieces, deciding to go with my favorite, the redwood. I held it up to the largest keyhole on the side facing the door and sent my wish through the wood into the opening.

It rattled and popped open. Inside was a black velvet bag, and inside that was…

I pulled out a black onyx bracelet. I recognized the hum of power, the flavor of Protectorate magic surrounding it, similar to licorice, and slipped it back inside.

There were good reasons Tristan might have Protectorate artifacts in his house, such as guardianship, self-protection, compensation for services rendered. I would reserve judgment.

The next door didn't respond to the redwood key, so I used the rabbit foot, offering my millionth apology to the bunny who would never bounce again. The door popped open, this time revealing a small green bottle, unmarked and uncorked.

I didn't pick it up. The stench was warning enough. Whatever small monster had died hadn't wanted its heart to end up pickled in cat urine and left in a cabinet, no matter how skilled the craftsmanship.

I pushed the door shut until it clicked.

The next six compartments were much the same, filled with some magical treasure or horror, beautiful art or disgusting trophy, some things powerful, others simply unique.

My understanding of Tristan was rapidly evolving. He'd been a Protector, a respected leader in the ruling magical bureaucracy, but now I saw evidence he'd dipped his toes into Shadow.

And he'd never told me, never hinted at it. In fact, he'd frequently consoled me for having a father who had made my life so difficult by staining the family name with his antics. With noblesse oblige, Tristan had seemed to have the grace to console me, the pathetic child of an infamous thief, a woman who herself had been sacked by his employer for not being quite good enough. A woman he'd slept with. But that almost went without saying.

Teeth gritted, I opened the rest of the cabinet, each door and drawer, cursing his unhappy, murdered soul under my breath.

He could live under a bridge with trolls for as long as the earth rotated around the sun, for all I cared. The hypocrite.

There were books, amulets, rings. There were sculptures,

icons, dried herbs, carvings, snakeskins, animal teeth of all types and sizes, gems, stones, liquids, powders. And lots of gold, lots of silver, some copper, old and new, all of it magically crafted into jewelry, buckles, buttons, and pins, all of it usable, buzzing with available power.

He wasn't a collector; he was a pirate. My father stole things but didn't keep them, the ultimate explanation for his continuing freedom. Nobody ever caught him with the goods. The thrill of the hunt inspired him to sneak and steal, and he was quick to unload and run away from any traceable treasure.

Unlike Tristan. Why would he be so crazy to keep all this stuff? It was dangerous to have one or two of these things in your possession, but to have all of it together was suicidal.

And now he was dead.

Angrier with each moment, I searched the cabinet for any corner or crevice I'd missed, but for all the loot I discovered, big and small, vegetable or mineral, visible and invisible, none of it could be the torc that Phoebe had described.

Had Malcolm been trying to trick me into blaming Tristan for the theft? Or had Tristan had it when he was killed, and my father knew about it because he'd taken it from him when he'd—

No. My father could not be a murderer. I wouldn't believe it.

Not yet.

The objects in the cabinet needed to be disarmed by Protectorate officials who did this sort of thing for a living. I neither had the skills nor the inclination to spend any more time breathing in the lingering odor of barbecued me.

The doors relocked themselves, as I'd hoped, and I slid my hands over the cabinet to make sure I hadn't left anything ajar. Nick's face flashed before my eyes for a moment, the residue of his soul in the handiwork. Nice face, although I was tempted to laugh in it, gloat about not needing his help after all, maybe tease him about the necklace his ex had glued to his throat.

I picked up my frying pan, no hint of the earlier fire, although the black pepper was still visible over the mound of old pennies, and brought it to the hallway, where I put it in my bag with the rest of my things. Before I left, I used my fingers to return the silver pins to the rowan threshold where I'd found them, fascinated to see how easily they slid into place. Herbs were nice, but metal… metal was gorgeous. Modern witches loved it for a reason.

I turned back one last time to glance at the cabinet, fading behind the illusion of a guest bed, and caught the eye of a small but furious figure, green and ugly, as he pointed at me.

It was the last thing I saw before everything went dark.

Chapter Twenty-Three

The next thing I saw was Livia. She looked as if she'd just come from the salon; her hair was helmet-smooth and perfectly streaked with copper and gold. It hung down around her face, toward me, where I lay on the floor.

"Nice haircut," I said. "Did you get that done in Silverpool?"

Livia scowled, which was a funny look from below. Very unflattering. "What happened to you?" she demanded.

For several long, awkward seconds, I couldn't remember where I was. To prevent myself from saying something incriminating or embarrassing, I closed my eyes. When in doubt, play dead.

Without Livia's face to distract me, I remembered Tristan, the cabinet, its contents, and the gargoyle's parting shot.

I was going to have to find a jade monster like that for my house. Impressive. I had totally underestimated it.

"I must've fainted," I said, pushing up onto my elbows. A quick glance told me my backpack was beside me in the hallway, safely zipped up. "Allergy meds. Or low blood sugar. I'm fine now."

"How did you get in? Did you still have your own key from when you were... when..." Livia shook her head. "You should've returned it. Somebody needs to get the locks changed on this place. God knows how many keys Tristan gave to... people."

"He did like"—I paused for emphasis—"people."

A man's voice caught my attention. "Are you sure you're all right?"

To my surprise, Jasper stood above me on my other side. "What are you doing here?"

He glanced at Livia. "I've volunteered to help with the memorial." The way he said it suggested he'd been drafted against his will. Tristan had been establishment Protectorate, with none of the cute damsel-in-distress charm that Phoebe had going for her, and Jasper hadn't been a fan. Men didn't have much use for Tristan, who seduced women so easily, so frequently.

"I know you two are friends," Livia said. "I got the impression you might need some help. I was in the tasting room yesterday, and they said you hadn't even come by yet to ask about the easel."

That was so typical of Livia to imply I wouldn't get my work done in time. Just because I didn't even remember what work I was doing for her, what day it was, or why I would need an easel.

"I was just headed there now," I said. I'd remember eventually.

"Before you fainted," Jasper said, holding out a hand.

I accepted his hand and pulled myself up to my feet. Gravity wavered for a second, but he held my arm and—nice of him—sent me a quick recovery spell, as welcome as that first sip of coffee on a cold, dark morning.

More of my memories returned. "Donna let me in. I was going to look for another picture or two." I pulled my phone out of my front pocket. "And get a few shots of the house and winery for the slideshow."

"I'll help you," Jasper said.

I gave him a grateful smile. "That would be nice." My strength was returning, but slowly. Over Livia's shoulder, I could glimpse the gargoyle strutting back and forth on top of the cabinet, a green, angry sentry. It was time for me to get away from him and Tristan's horde.

"Livia thought we might want to get his portrait enlarged as soon as possible," he said.

"It'll have to be a rush job if you haven't already requested it," Livia said.

"I'll take care of it," I said, carefully picking up my back-pack. If Livia noticed how heavy the bag was, she'd probably assume I'd nicked something. As if I would risk taking anything out of the house after what I'd seen in the cabinet and what the gargoyle had done to me. "After I look for the easel in the tasting room."

"I already found one," Livia said, "but it's broken. We need another one. As well as few poster boards and frames and a few smaller display stands."

"I'll take care of it," I repeated, although I was less enthusiastic about memorializing Tristan after seeing evidence of his hypocrisy. "I'll see what Birdie has at the store."

"A hardware store isn't going to have anything nice enough. And you need the enlargements, so you should drive—"

"We'll take care of it," Jasper said.

Livia seemed to hear him in a way she hadn't heard me. With a satisfied nod, she gestured down the hallway. "If you're done in here, I'll lock up. We don't want anyone breaking in."

I looked at the small, ordinary key in her hand and thought how useless such a thing was when Tristan had booby-trapped the place with spells that survived his death. Who knows what else he'd left behind?

Eager to get out of the house, I moved past Livia, Jasper at my side, and went out to my car. There I saw a familiar bike resting against a bench. "Birdie's here too?" I asked.

"She was going to help me plan the reception." Livia stopped and tucked the key to Tristan's house in her purse, shaking her head. "But there's nobody here to talk to. Did you know Tristan didn't run the kitchen himself? There's no permanent cooking staff. Any event at the winery was catered."

"I never asked him how he ran the business," I said.

"I'm just so surprised," she said. "He seemed so smart, but that was a serious waste of opportunity. The winery has so much potential. I was always telling him."

Birdie came out of the door to the tasting room in baggy sweater and leggings, her hair buried under a baseball cap, her eyes dull. When she saw Jasper and me, she flinched the way people do when they don't feel sociable.

I wondered if she was sick. Livia had always been able to boss her around, and I wouldn't put it past her to drag Birdie out of bed even if she had the flu.

"Are you still having car trouble?" I asked Birdie, gesturing to the bike.

"Yeah," she said with a sigh. "It won't start, and I don't have the money to have it towed right now. Until the winter rains start, I can use the bike."

"Let me give you a ride. I'm going to Cypress on my way home."

Birdie glanced at Livia. "Um—"

"Go ahead," Livia said with a loud exhale. "There's nothing we can do here. I'll have to call around. Friends of mine in

Napa have a restaurant, but I don't know if they can help out with such short notice." She walked off to her car and got in.

When Livia was driving out of sight, I turned to Birdie. "Are you feeling all right?"

"Sure. I mean, of course. Yes, I'm great." She gave Jasper a nervous smile, and I realized they didn't know each other.

After quickly introducing them, I put my bag in the Jeep's back seat and opened the hatch. "You can fit your bike in here. You look like you should be in bed."

"No, no, it's nothing like that," Birdie said.

"Would you like me to deal with the enlargements?" Jasper asked. "I'm going to the dentist in Santa Rosa anyway. There's got to be a place near there where I could get it done quickly."

"You don't have to do that," I said, overriding Birdie's objections about the ride by lifting her bike into the Jeep. "I've got a picture of him here that I thought would be good, but I haven't scanned it yet—"

"Give it to me," he said. "I'll bring it in. They can do all that. You want a poster board, right? Something you can set on an easel?"

I nodded. "The rest will be a digital presentation. Hold on, I'll get it for you." The folder of pictures was in the Jeep, and I got it and pulled out the one of Tristan in front of the winery.

"You sure you only want one?" he asked. "I could get more done. Get Livia off your back."

"You sure you don't mind?"

"What else are friends for?" he asked, offering a lopsided smile.

I took a few more out of the folder and handed them to him, and soon he was driving away in his car, and Birdie and I in mine.

"He's kind of cute," Birdie said. "Cool tattoos. I've seen him around, but I didn't know you were, you know."

"We're just friends," I said.

She smiled, a hint of her usual sparkle flashing to life. "He wouldn't mind if you jumped him. It's written all over him."

"No, I really don't think so," I said. "It's not like that."

"That's probably why he's so depressed. And why he let Livia talk him into coming up here with her. Any excuse to get closer to you."

I laughed aloud. "It's really, really not like that." I tried to imagine myself in bed with Jasper; it was about as sexy as imagining a gnome in a Speedo. I laughed harder.

Birdie sighed. "Poor guy."

"Don't feel sorry for him. He's never once suggested he's interested in me in that way."

"Well no wonder," she said. "Men would rather die than be laughed at."

"I wouldn't laugh at him if—"

"I know. You're too nice," she said. "But he can feel it, and it's bumming him out."

I fell silent. There was nothing I could say to convince her. If she saw Jasper when Phoebe Day was around, she'd see I wasn't his type.

I continued chuckling to myself, unable to stop myself from imagining Willy running around the garden in nothing but a postage stamp of tight Spandex, and Birdie sighed again with misplaced compassion.

I PARKED in front of Cypress Hardware and asked Birdie where I could find the poster board. "You can wait here," I said. "You really don't look like you're up for visiting work on your day off."

She looked miserably out the window and then opened the door. "It's OK. You'll never find it. They put that kind of stuff near pet supplies. Picture frames, cat food, storage bins, kitchenware. All the stuff they think women come in for."

Inside, Birdie led me past the cash registers and summer clearance patio furniture to a far corner of the store. I picked out a few hard poster boards, some decorative lettering and tape, a large presentation easel, as well as several smaller stands that Livia would never suspect came from a neighborhood hardware store.

"This place is amazing," I said, setting my goodies in a cart. "I always find what I want when I come in here."

"Like magic," Birdie said.

I glanced up sharply. She was chewing a fingernail, standing behind a vertical pole that held a stack of plastic watering cans in all colors of the rainbow.

"Magic?" I repeated carefully.

She met my gaze. "That's what people say. It's kind of a joke when you work here. I've never met the store buyer, but he does seem to know what people want before they know it themselves."

Skin prickling, I felt around me with renewed attention. As far as I knew, the store wasn't run by witches. I couldn't feel any familiar magic around me, although that itself was unusual. I'd never thought about it before. I was unusually sensitive, but I couldn't find a hint of magic anywhere, even on the handle of the shopping cart, which should've been contaminated with not only the usual bacteria but also the residue of the many magical beings in the area.

"I could really use a photo duplication and enlargement service," I said in a loud, clear voice.

"You don't need it anymore," Birdie said. "Jasper is going to do it in Santa Rosa."

I cursed inwardly. I had been attempting to see if I could make the photo department, which had not existed when we walked in, suddenly appear and fulfill my need.

But Birdie had spoiled my test. "You're right," I said. "Forgot."

A woman turned the corner and waved at us. It was Carolyn, the woman who had given me Nick's number. She held a stack of glossy kitchen design brochures.

"Hi, are you still looking for pictures for Tristan Price's memorial?" Carolyn asked.

"I am," I said.

Glancing from side to side, Carolyn pulled out a manila folder from the stack of brochures. "These were dropped off at the store." She cleared her throat. "Anonymously."

I took the folder from her, wishing I'd run into her before Jasper had left for Santa Rosa. Maybe I could scan them in and email them to him. "Thank you."

"My pleasure." Carolyn sighed, visibly relieved to have handed over the contraband, and turned to Birdie. "Sorry to hear you're leaving us."

"What?" I asked.

Birdie avoided my gaze. "Thanks," she muttered.

"Leaving?" I asked.

"I'm sorry. Wasn't it common knowledge?" Carolyn asked. "They told us at the morning meeting."

Birdie shrunk another inch. "I gave notice. I've got two more weeks."

"But why? I thought—" I stopped, realizing I'd put Birdie in an awkward position. She'd seemed to love working at Cypress, and there weren't many steady jobs in Silverpool. I turned to Carolyn. "By the way, thanks for this," I said, holding up the envelope.

"I apologize, Birdie," Carolyn said. "I didn't realize everyone didn't know."

"Everybody knows or should know," Birdie said. "What's in the envelope? More pictures? Is it from when you and Tristan were spending all that time together on that project?"

Frowning, Carolyn clutched her brochures against her chest. "Oh, no, these were just dropped off by somebody. I didn't see who." Her expression morphed into a professional smile. "Excuse me, I need to get back to work. It was nice running into you both. See you, Birdie."

"See you," Birdie said.

I didn't say anything else to Birdie until I'd gone through checkout and we were out in my Jeep again. "I didn't mean to put you in an awkward spot," I said.

"It's not awkward, not awkward at all. Don't worry about it. My fault. I should've said something. I forgot. I just get so used to walking in there, you know? It totally slipped my mind. That I won't be there anymore. Soon. Eventually."

I started the engine but didn't back up. "Birdie?"

She sank into her seat, head down.

After a moment, I threw the Jeep in reverse and headed for our neighborhood. "Hey, forget it," I said. "You don't have to explain anything to me."

She looked out the window and said nothing. For the first time since I'd met her, I wished she would talk more.

A few quiet minutes later, my Jeep pulled up in front of her house. She opened the door and jumped out before I could think of anything else to say.

"Birdie—"

"I'm really sorry. I'm really sorry," she said, waving as she turned away.

"Your bike," I said, climbing out.

"Oh! Right. I forgot. Thanks."

As we worked together to haul it out of the back, she

continued to avoid meeting my gaze. I watched her lift it up the steps to roll it into the front door of her cottage, a spare, one-story structure similar to my own, not much larger than a three-car garage in a suburban McMansion.

She waved at me and closed the door.

I drove the short distance to my own driveway, glancing at her house in my rearview mirror, wondering.

I didn't know if I should be worried, suspicious, or both. Or why.

Chapter Twenty-Four

The morning of the memorial service was cold and hazy with a low, damp fog that was worse than rain. This moisture was useful only for the redwood trees, which pulled it out of the air but not enough to fill the rivers—or the wellspring.

I parked my Jeep in the visitor parking in front of the winery and carried the easel and as much as I could carry of the other visual displays into the tasting room. Livia was already there, rearranging the flowers. When she saw me walk in, she rushed over and grabbed the easel.

"Finally," she said.

"The service is in an hour," I said.

"People are already arriving. Jasper brought me the portrait last night."

I'd spent the day before making a collage of the photos I'd received from friends, neighbors, and those who wanted to be anonymous. Carolyn's pictures caught Tristan in his bathrobe, which explained why she didn't want to be identified with them. The photo booth shots Birdie had given me seemed too small and precious to glue to a board, so I'd scanned, enlarged, and printed them myself at home on glossy paper I used for advertising my beadwork. Something about Tristan's face in those photos from Birdie looked more like him, the real man behind the glamour, than any of the other pictures or even my memory of him. Layers of deception, I thought of it now. Not just vanity, not just magic, but lies. He was hiding his crimes.

Even after a day or two, I was still feeling bitter about how he'd been as greedy as my father—simply less honest about it. Mostly, though, I was mad at myself for being taken in. Malcolm Bellrose's daughter shouldn't have been such an easy mark.

Livia put the easel next to the biggest bouquet of flowers and set the enlarged portrait from Jasper on it. His artificially young face smiled at them, handsome as always, but now I saw a sneaky shadow in his eyes.

"Do you think it's big enough?" Livia asked.

I swallowed a retort that it would never be big enough to capture Tristan's ego or insatiable appetites. "It's perfect. And the TV will be playing the slideshow."

On the wall above the tasting bar was a large flat-screen that had been used for marketing and informational videos. Now I went over with my bag and set up the video, about five minutes of fade-in, fade-out images of the dearly departed and the picturesque scenery of Silverpool: the vineyard in each season, the Vago River, the little downtown, the old redwood grove. I did not include a picture of Silverpool Bridge, thinking that would be too evocative of his death.

"What music did you choose?" Livia asked me from across the room. While Jasper arranged chairs, she set a single white rose on each one.

At that moment, I realized there were three fairies behind the bar with me, all green-skinned, one twice as tall as the other two. With the tall one's help, they were drinking the wine through the still-corked bottles, which were about the same size as the short fairies.

I looked around the room. Jasper and Livia didn't seem to notice them.

Of course they didn't. Fairies were invisible. I'd had this problem before—even witches weren't supposed to be able to see fae who didn't want to be seen.

"Music?" Livia repeated.

I stepped out of the way of the tall one, who was staggering around the floor near my feet. "Music?" I asked, trying to focus on Livia.

"For the slideshow," she snapped.

"I didn't put any music in it. Just pictures."

Livia looked as if she might cry. I almost felt sorry for her. My grief had been softened with disillusionment, but hers was still full strength.

"I can hook up my phone," Jasper said. "Did you have anything in mind? Classical, modern, any old favorites of his?"

"I should've realized she wouldn't think to do the music," Livia muttered, turning away from me.

I wanted to push aside the two small fairies who were huddled in front of my laptop like moths around a porch light, but then they'd know I could see them and might cause trouble. Some fairies loved to screw with technology. I wouldn't be surprised if they short-circuited the motherboard just for fun. Ignoring Livia for a moment, I set up a quick protective spell around my laptop, TV, cables, and cords.

All three of the fairies shook their heads in disgust and went back to the bottles of Silverpool chardonnay on the shelf under the bar. I thought about setting up a boundary spell around the wine, too, but other people were arriving and I didn't want to be seen drawing circles in empty air, sprinkling something from a black pouch on the refreshments.

I left the bar, went out to my Jeep, and made two more trips to bring in the other displays. As I set them around the room, Livia followed me, correcting my aesthetic choices, but I was too distracted by the fairy party behind the bar to care. The scent of magic from so many witches gathering—there were several locals as well as Jasper and me—could be a powerful draw for the spirit people. Three wasn't too bad.

I went up to Jasper, who was attaching his phone to the audio system, also behind the bar. The fairies were ignoring him, a small mercy.

"Set up a protective you-know-what around your phone," I said quietly.

"You think somebody would steal it here? In the middle of a funeral?"

I shook my head and glanced at the fairies he couldn't see. The tall one was right at his elbow, smirking and playing with his vape pipe.

"Fae," I said in Jasper's ear.

"You can see them?"

Even to friends, I didn't like to admit it. "Strong feeling," I said.

He nodded and cast a quick spell around his phone. I left him to find a seat by myself near the back.

Then I saw Nick Takata already sitting there, scrolling through his phone. Cleaned up for the service, he wore black jeans, a black long-sleeved T-shirt, and clean gray-and-black running shoes.

I walked over to him but didn't sit down. "Hi," I said. "Nice of you to come."

He didn't look up from his phone. "I didn't come for you."

Annoyed by his rudeness, I took the seat right next to

him and gave him a friendly smile. "Such a good-looking chain," I said, dropping my gaze briefly to his neck.

"I'm not going to give you the key."

"All right," I said.

He gave me a suspicious look. "Even if I had it, which I'm not saying I do."

"Why would you?" I asked. "Tristan wouldn't have wanted you to keep one."

Nick crossed his legs away from me. "He was happy with my work."

"I'm sure he was. It's a beautiful cabinet."

Suddenly he turned and leaned toward me. "Leave me alone," he snarled into my face. "You and your... Just leave me alone."

I recoiled, embarrassed at how several people in the room turned to see what was the matter. Knowing how he felt about witches, I shouldn't have approached him at Tristan's service. "I'm sorry," I said, standing up. "I shouldn't have bothered you." I moved to the other side of the room and found a seat in a middle row.

Over the next half hour, several dozen more people arrived to pay their respects, mostly people I didn't recognize, about half of them witches. Birdie and Carolyn walked in together and sat in a middle row. At some point I noticed Phoebe Day had already arrived; wearing head-to-toe black, she stood to one side by herself.

When I saw she didn't have Lorne with her, I relaxed into my seat.

"Boo," said a voice in my ear.

I jumped and turned to see my father standing behind my chair. "I wish you wouldn't do that," I said. He enjoyed sneaking up on people as well as treasures. "Why are you here?"

"Emotional support." He rested a hand on my shoulder. "For you."

I pushed it off, noticing the heavy gold watch on his wrist. "I don't want it. Since when do you wear a Rolex?"

"Just holding it for a friend of mine," he said.

"Is that what you're calling it these days? Holding?" I asked, turning away from him.

He didn't move away from my seat. I could smell the hint of magic on him as he leaned down, breathing into my ear. He must've used it to get here.

"Did you find what you were looking for?" he asked.

"Not quite."

"Shame," he said.

I said nothing.

After a moment, he said, "Don't hate him. He was in a difficult position." He cleared his throat. "And now even more so."

"I'm not going to talk about this with you."

"He appreciated uniqueness. He was intoxicated by it. In many ways, it controlled him. He couldn't stop himself from wanting what he didn't have. I'm sure he tried."

"He should've tried harder," I muttered.

"I thought you said you'd forgive me."

"I'm sure I tried," I said.

With a sigh, my father straightened and took a step away from my seat. The reek of magic lingered. The fairies were probably here because of teleporting Malcolm Bellrose's chemtrail.

I let my gaze fall on Tristan's portrait at the front of the room. There was no casket or urn here, only memories and people to share them. Livia was talking to an unfamiliar woman in a burgundy dress who held a folder. She was attaching a microphone under her chin, fiddling with the controls. A moment later she smiled at us and introduced herself as the official "celebrant" who would be leading the service.

I looked at Phoebe Day, sitting near the back to my left, wondering when the Protectorate would have their ceremony or if they'd had it already. Witches liked to hold important rituals at liminal times and places—boundaries such as midnight, solstice, dawn, a seashore, a clearing in a forest. An obscure vineyard's tasting room on an ordinary Saturday morning, filled with nonmagical nobodies, wouldn't command the same supernatural heft.

Birdie sat with Jasper in the middle of the room, directly in front of me, and I thought they looked cute together. If I could convince Birdie there was no hint of attraction between Jasper and me, on either end, maybe she'd ask him out on a date. It seemed unlikely he would make the move himself.

The officiant began the service, and I listened to the cover story Tristan had established for himself be presented as fact: raised by international businesspeople, orphaned at twenty, a career in San Francisco as a corporate accountant followed by an early retirement and new start as boutique winery owner. Never married. Lots of friends. Generous with charities, loved travel, gourmet cooking, walks in the moonlight...

Thinking that last bit of trivia was unfortunate, given his death, I looked at the fairies sitting on the bar. They could drink through the bottles without opening them but not enough to drain them. Just a sip here and there was enough to intoxicate a wood sprite. The two little ones were slumped over, holding each other up at the shoulder. The tall one, however, was staring at the human mourners with a malevolent look in his bright blue eyes, appearing cold sober. His gaze landed on me, and I pretended to look through him as I dabbed at my damp eyes with a tissue.

Inside, I shuddered. That tall fairy was bad news. I

fingered the necklace at my throat and sent out vibes of love, peace, and exhaustion. I didn't expect love or peace to work on that guy, but sleepiness might. When he yawned, I put my tissue back in my purse and redirected my attention to the service, which was just about to break for volunteers to come up and say a few words.

People began to move around their seats and whisper to one another. I thought it was about the call for people to come up and speak, but then I saw the cops. A man and a woman in uniform strode past me down the aisle, scanning the crowd and then surrounding Jasper and Birdie.

Murmurs and silence, shock and awe—everyone stared as the female cop hooked both hands around her wide utility belt and gestured for Birdie to follow her outside.

Looking shocked, Birdie stood.

And then, like an unhappy wedding procession, the two cops led Birdie down the aisle and out the door.

Chapter Twenty-Five

I spun around to ask my father if he'd overheard the cops say anything to explain why they'd taken Birdie, but he was gone.

Of course he was gone. He'd probably fled long before their squad car had turned in to the driveway, maybe the moment they crossed the unincorporated boundary of Silverpool. I had to admit his talent for appearing and disappearing *tout de suite* was magnificent; more admirable than his knack for nicking things.

While the celebrant attempted to restore order, I bolted out of my seat and ran after the cops and Birdie. They were already putting her—handcuffed—into the back of their car.

I hurried over. "What are you doing? Birdie, what happened?"

The male cop stood hands on hips between me and the car. "Ma'am, please stand back."

"But that's my friend. Birdie! That's Elizabeth Crow."

"We know that, ma'am. You're going to have to stand back," he said.

A tingling between my shoulder blades told me somebody was using a spell on me from the back. As I turned to see who, the cops got in the car and drove off.

Riovaca Police. I'd have to go to the station and see what was going on. Or maybe I could lock the wheels—

"Don't," Jasper said in my ear.

"Was that you?" I drew a triangle in the air, a sign for magic.

"I was afraid you were going to do something stupid." He nodded his head toward Phoebe Day, who had come out of the building, holding a magic wand disguised as a phone. "She'd drag *you* in, too, if you did anything here."

The Protectorate had put itself in charge of punishing witches who used magic recklessly. It wasn't usually enforced, but it would be at a Protectorate's memorial service filled with nonmagicals.

"What did they say?" I asked Jasper. "What was the charge?"

"Just a few questions, they said."

"But they put handcuffs on her." I took out my keys and unlocked my Jeep. "I'm going to Riovaca."

"But what can you do?" he asked. "Maybe they found something. Something to do with Tristan. Something bad."

"I don't believe it," I said. "I saw her the morning after he died. It came as much a shock to her as to anyone. And I know Birdie—" I bit my tongue.

It wasn't right for Birdie to go to jail for something in the magical community. As a witch, I felt responsible for helping all nonmag people from the dangers of our world. Especially my neighbor. My friend.

At least a dozen Silverpool citizens and a handful of witches had come outside, and all were staring at me. Even the fairies were there, weaving between people's legs.

"I'm going to Riovaca," I repeated.

Jasper put his hand on my arm. "There's nothing you can do."

I stared at him. "Watch me."

To GET to Riovaca I would have to take Vago Highway, a narrow, twisting, two-lane road through heavily wooded hills. It was the kind of journey that made children throw up and gave other passengers a headache, especially if they tried reading something in their lap instead of staring straight ahead, praying for it to be over.

If I was behind the wheel, I didn't get carsick. A bouquet of redwood sorrel and peppermint on the dash helped. And although my Jeep handled like a toaster on roller skates, the rough ride kept me from getting smitten by the fairy song in the forest.

The bright sunshine of the winery had disappeared as soon as I took the first sharp turn into the forest. Redwoods grew close together in clusters, a mother tree and her children often merging together at the base into a single trunk before stretching up to the sky like long fingers on a thin hand. Very long. With the cedar and fir, the shade was thick, misty, magical. Even I, a local witch, had to focus hard on the center yellow lines to keep my attention and my wheels pointed at my human destination and not into the appealing shadows. The soft-focus understory sang a siren song to all travelers, tempting even to the most cynical, experienced locals hurrying home after work.

Off to my left, a warm, yellow light flickered about five feet off the ground. Then another. Like fireflies, but there were no fireflies here. The air tasted mossy and sweet in my mouth. Sexy, delicious. When I found myself daydreaming about the feel of a man's warm, strong chest under my cheek and how satisfying it would be to take a nap there right now, I rolled up the windows and drew a circle around my face to protect me from the call of the forest.

It was a wonder anyone ever made it in or out of Silverpool. Though it wasn't usually this bad in the middle of the day. All the witches in town for the memorial service must've stirred up the fae.

The moment I regained my focus on the road, I saw the tall fairy from the winery, standing on the shoulder. He stood with both hands up, pale-green palms out, displaying the same malevolent expression he'd worn in the tasting room.

Out of nowhere, a massive redwood as wide as a double-wide trailer appeared in front of me where the road should've been.

No! Every muscle in my body went rigid as I jerked the wheel sharply to the right to avoid slamming into the tree. But then the road beneath me disappeared, and I realized, stomach twisting, that my wheels weren't touching anything but forest mist.

In that slow-motion vision you get when you're sure you're about to die, I watched the hood of my Jeep arc downward. I clamped harder on the wheel and braced my legs as the vehicle hit the embankment and rolled headfirst into a bed of sword ferns.

I could hear my heart pounding like goblin drums.

After a long moment to remember how to breathe again, I loosened my death grip on the wheel and looked around to see how bad it was.

Other than a sore shoulder from the seat belt, I wasn't hurt. The driver's-side door was blocked by shrubs and saplings, but the passenger side looked free. I crawled over and climbed out to inspect the damage, but my heels slipped out from under me, and I fell into a thicket of blackberry vines.

I'd worn my nicest clothes to the memorial service: a long embroidered skirt and a lacy top with silk sleeves. Both seemed to have been designed to catch as many thorns as possible. By the time I pulled myself free, my limbs were scratched and bleeding and my nicest clothes were no longer my nicest.

From unsteady feet, I regarded my Jeep half-buried in ferns. It wasn't going anywhere without a tow truck—or magic beyond a single witch's powers. Maybe with Jasper's help I could've moved it halfway, but then it would probably just roll down again, this time hitting one of the redwoods near me.

Who the devil was that tall fairy, and why had he run me off the road? Many witches hated fairies. Until now I hadn't understood why. It was no more sensible than hating tigers, oxygen, or geometry; what existed, existed. As Helen had said, our only purpose as witches was to understand. To know as much as possible. And occasionally bend the rules a little to suit our needs.

I staggered up the bank to the road, planning to find the tall fairy and kick his green ass. At a distance, he would look like a small child, about the height of a three-year-old. Although I found the precise spot where he'd run me off the road, he'd left no trace. Now it seemed likely I'd been wrong about thinking he was a wood sprite. The power to move a car like that came from something bigger and colder, perhaps some kind of water fae.

The fireflies caught my attention again. Low to the ground in the shadows, their lights twinkled like glitter. I saw ten, twenty, two dozen lights. More than I'd seen near Jasper's house the week before.

That was an unusually large number of fairies to be gathered so close to civilization without the wellspring in season. Up in the remote areas of the North Coast, countless fae lived in huge communities, hidden from humanity, doing whatever it was they did. But this close to San Francisco, their numbers only grew significant at the solstice.

Why were they here so early?

I cast a protective spell around me and began walking into the woods.

About twenty feet from the road, I passed through a beam of sunlight and began to hear them. Singing, arguing, chanting fairies—hundreds of them. I moved closer, my footsteps hushed by the soft ground beneath the trees. I listened and strained to count how many little beings were scattered among the sorrel and rotting logs, the sticks and shrubs. With each breath I inhaled the flavor of cherries, earth, jasmine, rain. I was reluctant to turn away, tempted by the unique enchantment of the fae.

I was also concerned for their sake. With Tristan gone, the fae here were vulnerable to demons. I'd failed as a demon hunter, but I had a few useful tricks that might protect them in an emergency.

But when I saw how many there were, I no longer worried about their well-being and began to think about my own. Many were delicate and ephemeral, the local wood sprites, but there were also hair-shirted bridge trolls, gnomes in red velvet waistcoats, dryads wearing robes made from buttercup petals, and goblins in human military uniforms.

They were gathered around a bonfire. Nothing most humans could see—it would be shrouded by fog—but because of the wellspring, I knew what to look for. I'd had practice watching similar celebrations at the winter solstice.

But this wasn't a celebration.

"War," chanted the trolls.

"Poison," hissed the dryads.

"Kill," shouted the sprites.

The goblins in their military uniforms held flaming

chunks of wood over their heads, waving them side to side to the beat of hundreds of bare feet pounding the earth.

"Revenge," they said in unison.

Terror washing over me, I forced my legs into reverse. Back the way I'd come. Step by step. Slowly. Carefully. I couldn't risk turning my back on them.

What was happening? Did the Protectorate have any idea that goblins and dryads, immortal enemies, had formed an alliance? And since when did human-hating bridge trolls march in the forest with gnomes, who had cohabited with humanity for millennia?

Horrified but curious, I searched the crowd for Willy's familiar face. I couldn't see him, but there were so many of them.

Another step. Then another. I stole a glance over my shoulder to see how far I had to run, but the road and my Jeep were out of sight. I'd walked farther than I'd realized.

Now I noticed the sun was low in the sky. How long had I been standing here? The memorial service had been in the morning. This mob of fae had captured me.

Yet they still didn't seem to notice I was here. Maybe it had been an accident—

Human.

The fae spoke in one silent but deafening voice, united in metaphysical malice.

And then they joined together, a cloud of lights, and began to come toward me.

My feet felt as if they'd taken root. Using a shot of magic, I was able to lift my heels and finally turn to run, but the bright swarm, flexible with space, surrounded me. I stumbled back against the trunk of a large tree. Heart pounding, I dug my fingers into the thick ridges of bark and drew upon its power. My necklace wouldn't have been enough to transform me so quickly, but a tree as wide as a taco truck would give me everything I needed.

As the lights and shouts of revenge grew closer, I tore off my clothes. I didn't want to get tangled up in my bra after I changed because, without opposable thumbs, there wouldn't be time to free myself.

Human!

Once naked, I dug my fingers into the bark, closed my eyes, and reached into the core of my power.

Since they didn't like humans, I would turn myself into something else.

Chapter Twenty-Six

I'd never been boiled alive, but I always imagined it would feel like shape-shifting into a cat. Walking the earth as a five-seven, one-hundred-sixty-pound (give or take) house cat wouldn't be practical, so years ago I'd mastered the art of transforming into a smaller shape. The shrinking was what hurt. As the skin melted off my flesh to allow the rest of me to morph into a form I hoped was less offensive to the fae, I closed my eyes and tried to focus on my deep, internal flame of magic to stop myself from screaming.

It was agony, but it was quick. Before I could succumb to the pain and let the fairy monsters do their worst, the transformation was complete. With effortless, feline grace, I dug my claws into the soft bark and scrambled up the trunk of the towering redwood, my enemies and my clothing forgotten below me.

I forgot them because I always forgot who I was for the first hours of my transformation. Fortunately (and sometimes unfortunately), I remembered later what happened during that lost time. Usually it involved torturing something small and feathered, which gave me nightmares and the urge to donate to bird sanctuaries and organizations that worked to reduce the feral cat population.

This time when I became aware of myself, I was clinging to the trunk as far from the ground as I'd dared to climb, and because of the fairies, I'd so far been unable to torture anything small or feathered.

Small mercies. I was cold, tired, and afraid, and the branches were too thin to make a comfortable bed for the long night ahead. My necklace, designed to survive a shape shift, was nevertheless heavy and annoying, and only my human spirit kept me from tearing it off.

Darkness was falling, and the fae were still gathered around the tree below me. Their mixed voices—some high and melodious, others little more than a growl—spoke of revenge, retribution, death, and witches.

Witches. Not humans in general, but specifically the magic-wielding variety. What had witches done to them that merited this furious mob? Was the resentment ancient or something new?

Either from stress or instinct, I began licking myself. Holding complex thoughts was impossible in this shape. I was inside a cat's body. My consciousness was intact, but my intelligence was distorted by the absence of a large brain. Later, I told myself. I would figure things out later. Right now I only had to survive, and a cat is a genius at survival.

I dozed up in the tree until dawn, when the fae gathered in one last chorus of whooping and shouting before fading into the morning mist.

I waited another hour before I climbed down. There was no handsome firefighter to help me, and it took three times as long as it should have because of the vertigo that overcame me whenever I looked down the impossibly long trunk.

The moment my paws touched the muffled ground, I shot through the forest to get to the Jeep—and then immediately returned to the tree when I realized I needed my clothes.

The transformation back into my human form would be less painful than turning into a cat, but the discomfort would last much longer. High magic commanded high prices.

I sat, tail curled around the tree, and tapped into my power. After a single second of torturous agony, I was back to myself—a scratched, dirty, tired, thirsty, hungry, worried, and sneezing human being.

I dressed quickly and hiked back to the Jeep. Other than sending it off the road, the fairy hadn't seemed to do my vehicle any harm, but it was too far down the slope to move without help. The wheels and engine were intact. Purse in hand, my outfit torn and wrinkled, I climbed up to the road and took out my phone.

It was dead. Sensing something strange about the way it felt in my hand, I lifted it to my nose and sniffed.

Overly sweet perfume. One of the fae, probably that tall fairy, had messed with it. I took the phone out of its case and discovered it was now only a thin slab of black-and-white glass.

Well, no wonder it didn't work.

Silverpool was several miles behind me. As I began walking, I pulled a tissue out of my purse and held it to my dripping nose. My throat was swollen, and I wanted to rub my eyes but knew it would make the itching worse.

Being able to transform myself into a cat hadn't made me any less allergic. In fact, with each shift I became more sensitive. I had been up in that tree for over twelve hours, and my immune system had been devastated by the infusion of cat proteins. Even if my reaction was psychosomatic—sometimes just the thought of a cat could make me sneeze—I hadn't yet found a way to overcome it.

It was early Sunday morning, and no car passed me

during the hour it took me to reach the Silverpool Bridge. At the spot on the road where Tristan had lain, I paused and sent out thoughts of peace and rest. His spirit was nearby, voiceless and miserable, and I felt the urge to free him. And the urge to sneeze six times in a row.

"I'm working on it," I told him, touching my necklace with one hand while blowing my nose with the other.

With renewed motivation, I walked around the bend to Ruben's Pump and Chew, the town's only gas station and convenience store. It had an old-school pay phone as well as booze, homemade salsa and apple pie, small electronics, and burl wood lawn sculptures, predominantly of dinosaurs. I needed antihistamines and a temporary phone.

Since I didn't usually go inside, I didn't know the young woman behind the counter. She wore more makeup than I'd ever seen before on a living human being, with foundation slathered on in a layer as thick as the fruit leathers for sale next to the register. When I came up to the counter with my pink box of generic diphenhydramine, she was using the mirror over the chewing tobacco display to readjust her false eyelashes.

"Hi," I said, pointing at the pay-as-you-go phones hanging on the rack behind her. "I'll need one of those too, please. That one on the right is fine."

"Sure," she said, smiling as she got it for me. "Anything else?"

Before I could answer, I sneezed violently into the crook of my elbow. "No," I gasped. "That's it."

"Allergies suck."

"Yeah." I reached into my purse and took out my wallet. And then swore.

She bit her well-contoured lip and then asked, "Problem?"

Inside my wallet, instead of credit cards, a driver's license,

179

and cash, were expired gift cards, hair salon business cards, and leaves.

⚜

I swore. That damn fairy.

"Problem?" the clerk asked.

Although she seemed really nice, she was too young and unknown to me to ask for a loan. "Wrong wallet," I muttered.

"Oh I hate that," she said. "I change out my bag and forget to move my stuff over."

"Yeah." I stepped away from the counter and sneezed again. "I'll have to come back."

"I'm really sorry—"

"No problem. I live nearby." I hurried outside, shoving my fortune in leaves back into my purse, and almost went back in when I saw who was at the pumps filling up her car.

Livia. It was too late to run; she'd seen me.

"Alma, what happened to you?" Her slow, horrified gaze took in my appearance from head to toe.

I finger-combed my hair and considered what spell might distract her enough to allow my escape. "Uh…"

She shoved the nozzle back into the pump and strode over to me. I expected her to demand to know why I hadn't bailed out Birdie the night before, but instead she put her arms around me and squeezed. "I know just how you feel. I'm so upset about it I'm staying with friends for a few days. I just can't believe she would— Oh, it's too much."

"Is there news?"

"News? Of course there's news. Horrible news. Where have you been?"

"I had trouble—" I stopped myself. I could hardly explain that after one fairy had run me off the road, another crowd of them had surrounded me in the forest, and then, to escape, I'd had to turn myself into a cat and hide all night, dozens of feet off the ground, in an old-growth redwood. "I've been beside myself."

For once she shook her head with sympathy, not disdain. "You poor thing. I didn't realize you still—but of course you did."

I crossed my arms—crisscrossed with welts and scratches —over my chest. "Are you headed to the station now?"

"Station?"

"The police. In Riovaca. Wherever they're holding Birdie. I'd be there now, but I had car trouble."

Her caring expression vanished. "Whatever for?"

"To post bail, if possible, bring her ho—"

"Not on your life. After what she did to Tristan?"

"We don't know that she did anything. Just because the police—"

Livia's familiar tone of disgust returned. "The police have impounded her car. She ran over Tristan."

I gaped at her, wondering if my cat brains had heard her right. "No, that's impossible."

"It's absolutely possible. Her Toyota was seen driving away. And there's"—her face contorted—"physical evidence. Linking her to the… crime."

"On the car?"

"Yes on the car! What's the matter with you? You saw them arrest her yourself."

"They must've made a mistake," I said.

"Oh please," Livia spat out. "You and Birdie are the same, cruising along, never taking responsibility for your-selves. I wouldn't be surprised to hear *you* were there too and didn't tell anyone because you were afraid of getting in trouble."

Her vile accusation contained enough truth to make me

redden. "I'm going home." I marched past her, my sore toes aching in my shoes. "I'll find a way to help Birdie."

"You don't even know what she did," Livia said.

I spun around. "Neither do you."

"I know enough. She was there, and Tristan is dead."

"She didn't kill him."

"She was *there*," Livia said. "I can't believe you'd even consider defending her."

"I can't believe you wouldn't." I turned and resumed walking.

"Women were always taking advantage of him." Livia got in her car and slammed the door.

"Don't bother offering me a ride," I muttered under my breath as my tired feet pounded the pavement. "I can walk."

By the time I got home ten minutes later, I was using a protective spell on my feet to stop the blisters from popping, and my eyes were swollen half-shut from my cat allergy. Random greeted me frantically at the door—body spasming, tail wagging, tongue licking—and I let him outside before he lost control of his bowels.

I took the hottest shower I could stand, slapped a few nonmagical bandages on my wounds, and got dressed in a hurry. Whatever evidence the cops had on Birdie, I couldn't believe she'd run Tristan over—at least consciously. Somebody else might've tricked her into doing it, then spelled her to forget. Livia wasn't a witch; she didn't know what was possible.

As I was walking around the backyard cleaning up Random's mess in a plastic bag, I noticed Will standing under his tree, looking unusually serious. When I waved, he didn't wave back.

Chapter Twenty-Seven

Is everything all right?" I asked Willy.

"Your animal was very unhappy last night," he said. "From all the way inside my home, I heard him whimpering."

"I know, Willy. I was in trouble. I couldn't get home."

His eyebrows lifted slightly, softening his expression. "I didn't think you would let another creature suffer if you could help it."

"I wouldn't. I promise." I pointed at my bare feet. Even with my protective spell and first aid, my left pinky toe looked like a grilled hot dog with extra ketchup.

"My Jeep rolled off the road a few miles up the highway. I had to spend the night outside and walk home this morning."

Willy ambled over, blue eyes sparkling, all warm and concerned now. "I did think something like that must have happened. Pardon me for doubting you. I couldn't resist liberating your animal around midnight so he could relieve himself. I also gave him a banana. He enjoyed it. I'm afraid his lack of fingers led to a mess with the peel, however. My apologies for your sofa. He did his best to remove all traces with his tongue."

"You can break the spell into my house?" I didn't have to ask about the dead bolt—of course gnomes aren't affected by human locks. But the spells Helen had taught me…

"Your magic, although strong for your kind, is no match for a gnome of my experience."

I paused to digest that. "Thank you," I said slowly, thinking about the mob in the forest. "How many other gnomes of your experience might there be in the area? Or other fairies?"

He took out his pipe, clamped his lips around it, and shook his head.

I squatted down to face him. "Lately I've been wondering if there are more than we thought. More than witches know of, I mean."

"Some witches suspect our true numbers. That is why they hurt us."

"Who hurts you?"

Shrugging, Willy blew a smoke ring. "Not you, that's all I care about, Alma Bellrose. I am of the domestic kind, and I rely on some, although limited, human companionship. Beyond that I attempt to know nothing. It's safest for both of us."

If he cared about my well-being, maybe he'd help me. "A fairy tried to hurt me yesterday while I was driving in my car. Do you know anything about that?"

"That is very bad, Alma Bellrose. Very bad. You should go inside your house and stay there with your nice animal."

"I need to help Birdie. She's in trouble. You know, that woman, my friend, who lives over there?" I pointed at Birdie's house.

"She is also having others interfere with her car. It was taken. Gone now."

"The human police took it," I said. "They took her away her, too. I hear she's still stuck there."

"Would you like me to open the locks of her cage?"

"No, we need to get her out in a different way. Otherwise we'll get in trouble. And she'll be in worse shape." I'd never asked him for help before, but…

I thought about how he hadn't been with the other fae last night and how he was nice to Random. "That fairy who tried to hurt me did something to my wallet. Can you help me get it back to the way it was?"

Willy shrugged and blew another smoke ring. "Perhaps most certainly."

That made me hopeful. I went inside and came out with my purse. I showed him my wallet, took out a leaf. "This should be a twenty-dollar bill."

Willy inhaled from his pipe. "No, that should be a leaf, which it is."

"I know. He…" I held it up and studied it. "Never mind. I thought maybe he'd transformed it."

"That baby has not the skill. He stole your things and replaced them. They're too far away for me to recover. My apologies."

"Baby—you mean the fairy?"

Willy nodded.

"He's a young one then?"

"A baby. Useless or worse."

"Why does he want to hurt me?" I asked.

"Babies are stupid," Willy said, shrugging. "If they live, some grow brains. Fewer still also develop manners."

While I thought about that, Willy turned away, smoking his pipe, and disappeared into his tree.

The tall fairy was young. And Willy didn't respect him. What did that mean?

I was staring into space when Jasper appeared on the side

lawn of my house. "Alma, are you all right? You weren't answering your phone, and with everything going on I thought I—"

"Jasper, thank God," I said, shoving the leaves and the block of glass into my pockets. "I ran into some trouble."

He looked me over. "You're bleeding."

"Some fairy ran me off the road yesterday," I said. "I only got back just now. Have you heard any news about Birdie? Livia says they impounded her car."

"You should see a doctor," he said, scowling at the bandages. "That bruise on your wrist looks bad. You might have broken something."

"I'm fine. Is there any news about Birdie? I didn't make it to Riovaca."

He shook his head and stared at me. "You said the fairies ran you off the road?"

"Just one of them, I think. Although I did see quite a mob of them gathering in the woods. That's what kept me. They were a little hostile."

"At least you survived," Jasper said. "Another guy wasn't so lucky."

My breath caught. "What? What guy?"

"Some contractor. Nick somebody. They found his truck this morning."

Oh no. I put my hand on Jasper's arm to stop myself from falling over. "Are you sure?"

"You know him?"

"Just met him a few days ago." I took a moment to pull myself together. "His car went off the road too? Where?"

"Vago Highway at Black Snake Road. You know that hairpin curve?"

Only two miles beyond where my own car went over, that curve was infamous for car accidents. Somebody went off the road there at least once a year; the guardrail was dented or missing half the time. "Why are the fairies so upset?" I asked. "They can't miss Tristan that badly."

Poor Nick. A harmless nonmag caught up in forces beyond his comprehension. It was possible the witch's chain around his neck had attracted their hostility.

"They have long memories and long lives," Jasper said. "For all we know, they're taking revenge for something Vikings did in Ireland a thousand years ago."

"I'm almost looking forward to the Protectorate installing a new Protector," I said. Tristan had worked hard to befriend as many full-time fae residents as possible.

"I noticed none of them showed up at a funeral for one of their own."

"Phoebe was there."

He shrugged. "She's young, a nobody. If I were at Tristan's level, I'd expect a bigger show of respect."

"The memorial was Livia's idea," I said. "The Protectorate will have their own ritual."

"Did they invite you?"

"No," I said. "I wouldn't expect them to."

"See? They don't care."

"They care. They just don't care about me."

"They don't care about anyone but themselves and their power. One of these days the fae are really going to revolt, and the Protectorate is going to be shocked." He trailed off and bent over to pet Random, who was bouncing around his legs.

A chill crept over me. My long hours in the tree, watching so many of them gather, had given me a new perspective about the fae's numbers and potential threat. And then to hear they *killed* Nick...

"What do you know about the fae wanting to—revolt, as you said?" I asked. "Revolt against what?"

"What do you think?" Jasper gave Random one last pat,

straightened, and regarded me with a frown. "Against witches. They don't distinguish between us and the Protectorate. We're all the same to them, humans with magic who make their lives small and difficult."

"We protect them from demons," I said.

"They can protect themselves. Do you have any idea how powerful the fae really are? How many of them are living in the shadows, watching us, hating us?"

"How many?"

"I don't know," he said, "but it's a lot more than people realize."

"Since when do you know so much about the fae?"

He rubbed his hand over his mouth. "Listen, I haven't been entirely honest with you. I"—he cleared his throat— "study them. Have for years. That's why I bought the house in Silverpool. There are so many here to watch, woodland and river, domestic and wild, all sizes, all types. Especially on the west side where I live."

"I had no idea."

He shrugged and bent over to pet Random some more.

"Why didn't you tell me?" I'd broken a difficult spell to tell him about the wellspring. He could've told me then.

"You were an agent at the Protectorate," he said. "They come down hard on regular witches who have anything to do with the fae. And even if you weren't working for them anymore, you were close to Tristan. Really close, for a while."

"Me and everybody," I muttered.

"Not me."

"Now I know why you gave me so much of that potion of yours," I said. "You felt guilty about me breaking a painful spell to tell you something you already knew."

His eyes widened. "No, Alma. I didn't know about the wellspring until you told me. I thought the fae loved Silverpool for its geography—the river, the ocean, the forest. I never suspected something so powerful could be so close," he said. "I was blind. All the clues are there. You just have to pay attention. But how often do we really give the fae the attention they deserve?"

I glanced at Willy's tree. How much did I really know about him and his kind? If he could get into my house so easily, maybe he was far more dangerous than I'd assumed.

"Let's go inside," I said, walking to my back door. Being within the boundaries of my protection spells was more appealing than ever.

Jasper followed me into the kitchen, Random at his side, and accepted the can of cold coffee I offered him. "I should've told you," he said, popping the can open. "I'm sorry."

"The Protectorate isn't perfect, God knows, but I don't quite understand why you hate it so much," I said. "I'm a little bitter, for obvious reasons, but I'll get over it. Could this maybe be a little… personal on your part?"

Flushing, he set the can on the counter. "I was only joking about wanting to be an agent. I'd never work for them."

His harsh tone surprised me. He sounded like he meant it. "They don't deserve you anyway," I said. And then, to return to the subject at hand, "I need to get my Jeep towed and get Birdie home."

"Didn't you say the police impounded her car?"

"Yes, but—"

"They must have some pretty serious evidence against her. Why are you in such a rush to help her out?"

"He died of a heart attack."

"She ran him over," he said.

"We don't know that."

"But the police seem to." He gave me an incredulous

look. "I'd think you'd want whoever left him on the bridge to suffer."

For a moment I thought of how I, too, had left him on the bridge. "Until I talk to Birdie, I'm not going to believe the worst."

He retrieved the can of coffee and lifted it to his lips. "How well did you really know her? I know she's your neighbor, but do you know anything about her childhood, her family, her life before coming to Silverpool?"

"I know a little," I said. "She had a single mom, grew up in Santa Rosa, went to the junior college."

"That describes a significant percentage of the nonmag people in Sonoma County."

"Trust me. She's not the type to hide things. Even when she should. She can't stop herself from talking too much."

He grimaced. "I hope she has a good lawyer."

"How would she? She's as broke as I am." Reminded of my useless wallet and phone, I added, "And I was mugged by fairies last night."

"Mugged? You said they ran you off the road."

"They also stole all my money, all my cards, and my phone."

"Let me help you." He pulled his wallet out of his back pocket. "Sounds like you need as much help as Birdie."

It was nice of him to offer, but growing up under circumstances that were less than secure had taught me to anticipate emergencies. "Thanks, but I've got—"

"What the hell?" He pulled a wad of leaves out of his wallet and showed them to me.

"Oh, they found you too," I said, trying not to laugh. Maybe the fairies behind the bar at the winery were responsible. "I wonder if they got everyone who came to the service."

He looked through the rest of his wallet with increasing

irritation. "They took everything. My credit cards, my license, everything."

"Me too."

He swore. "Now I'm going to have to take a day off to go to the DMV. Why would they want my credit cards? They can steal anything they want."

"You're the fairy expert," I said. "You tell me."

"Touché." Sighing, he shoved his wallet, leaves and all, into his back pocket. "Looks like I can't help you after all."

"It's fine. I have an emergency stash here at the house."

"Stash of what?"

"The basics—cash and an extra credit card. Copies of everything else, just in case." I even had a duplicate driver's license. Three, actually, and one was even in my own name.

"That's a good idea," he said. "I wish I'd done that."

"It's the only way Malcolm Bellrose is like a Boy Scout. Always prepared. He drilled it into me that some of the best tricks weren't magical at all."

"Glad he did something good for you."

"Comes in handy more often than I'd like. Every once in a while, I'd like more than the worst-case scenario, you know?"

"I don't suppose you have an extra car, too?"

"Sadly no. Couldn't afford that. Could you give me a ride so I can meet the tow truck? It'll probably have to come from Riovaca."

He scratched Random behind the ears and threw his empty can into the recycling bin near the back door. "Of course. Glad to help."

Chapter Twenty-Eight

The tow truck driver was a short, muscled man who seemed to be on the first day of the job. He struggled with the winch more than I'd like and seemed too nervous to make conversation. Only when my Jeep was safely on the shoulder again did he let out the breath he was holding and offer me a weak smile.

"You're lucky," he said. "The other guy rolled down a cliff. They think he died instantly."

But while he'd fallen, he'd probably been wide awake. I shuddered, imagining Nick's terror, how he might've been cursing the day he met a witch. "Were you… called to the scene?"

"My boss. But there was nothing he could do. The cops could barely get down there to see the body." He patted the Jeep, which was scratched but otherwise undamaged. "Yeah, you're real lucky."

I *was* lucky—and grateful for the magic that had kept me alive. From the copy of my AAA card from my emergency files at home, the driver wrote up my paperwork and receipt, again with the deliberation and slowness of a new hire.

While I waited, trying not to show my impatience, I saw a cop car drive past with Birdie in the back seat.

Headed back to Silverpool.

I waved, but it was too late; she hadn't seen me.

Had they let her go? I stared down the road after her, then searched the forest for any sign of fairy activity. Nothing. Not even a leaf of redwood sorrel twitched in the stillness.

Finally the tow truck driver handed me a copy of my paperwork. "I hate this road," he said. "Everyone does."

I thanked him and returned home, eager to talk to Birdie. But when I walked over, she didn't answer the door.

"Birdie? It's Alma," I called out, then waited. "I brought Random with me." I smiled down at the dog, hoping he would bark a hello, but he only panted.

Jasper and Livia had both been quick to condemn her, and I had to wonder if I was being gullible again. I was the trained Protectorate agent who hadn't been willing to believe *demons* could really be all that bad. Who was to say Birdie, a young woman without money, property, or powerful friends, would risk calling the police after striking a body on a bridge in the middle of the night? Somebody else had killed Tristan —and I'd felt the magic residue of that—but maybe she had been the one to run him over and then run away.

She *had* been acting strange the past day or two.

"Birdie, please answer if you're awake." I knocked again. A night in jail would be exhausting. Maybe she was in bed. Had she been released on bail or because she was innocent?

Had Willy sprung her from her cage, as he'd offered? But no—the police drove her home.

Just as I was turning to leave, she opened the door. "You brought Random? Isn't he so sweet? I promised him a walk, but then I let both of you down." She wiped her nose with a tissue.

She looked terrible. Sunken eye sockets, limp hair clinging to the sides of her head.

"I had car trouble on the way to the police station," I said. "I was trying to find out what happened and see if I could help. I'm sorry I didn't make it."

She stepped aside and held out her hand to invite me in. "I saw an accident on the road on my way back home," she said. "The cop said some man from Silverpool went off at Black Snake Road. They found his body crushed under his truck."

"His name was Nick Takata. Did you know him?"

"Oh no! I used to ring him up all the time at Cypress. He did hardwood floors or drywall or something." She petted Random, scrambling in to greet her, then closed the door behind us.

"Custom woodworking," I said.

Birdie shook her head. "I thought Silverpool would be a safe place to live."

"How are you doing? It's got to be rough, spending the night in jail."

"Thank God, Madge could give me an alibi," she said. "They never would've believed me without Madge backing me up."

Margaret and Chuck Sauter were the eightysomething couple who lived in the neighboring house with the chickens. "You were with Madge when…"

"When somebody I guess stole my RAV4 and ran over Tristan. After he was already dead? I don't know because I wasn't there, which they didn't believe until they talked to Madge. Thank God, they finally talked to Madge. We were playing Yahtzee."

"There's physical evidence on your car," I said.

I didn't mean to sound like I was doubting her, because I believed her completely, but she got defensive.

"Ask Madge if you don't believe me. She got Yahtzee twice. Not like she's going to forget that in a hurry. She was so proud of herself she kept the scorecard and stuck it on the fridge with little red Sharpie stars all over it. Usually we use a pencil and write lightly so we can erase and reuse them. Neither one of us wants to use good money on new Yahtzee scorecards."

"I believe you. I was just trying to figure out who could've stolen your car."

"I didn't know it was stolen! The cops say it was, but I never saw it missing. That morning you gave me a ride to Livia's, I tried to drive it and the battery was dead. I can't afford fixing it until I get paid on Friday, so I just used my bike for a few days. I didn't look at it again. But…" She trailed off.

"What?"

"There was blood all over the bumper and the wheels. They wanted to know why I hadn't noticed."

The thought of Tristan's body under the wheels of her SUV made me recoil. It took me a few long moments to recover. "Your garage is dark."

"That's what I told them. I don't usually bother to turn on the light because when the garage door opens I can see, but by then I'm inside the car, backing out. Except I wasn't because the car had a dead battery."

"You're right," I said.

"About the dead battery?"

"No, you're right about being lucky Madge had two Yahtzees that night," I said. Nonmag police never would've believed her story without corroboration.

"I didn't feel lucky at the time," Birdie said. "I kept rolling fives."

"Five can be lucky," I said softly, thinking how I could look for another kind of evidence. I'd spelled my house to repel ill will, but Birdie had been vulnerable. Most fae weren't as powerful as Willy—at least I hoped not. "Do you mind if I look around your garage?"

"There's still police tape around it. You can't go inside. And the car is still impounded."

"I'll just walk around the outside, if that's OK."

Birdie looked at me, head tilted to one side, oddly quiet. "Sure," she said finally. "Thanks."

"It's probably hopeless," I said. "It's not like I'm a cop."

"I'm glad. After last night, I don't even think the Riovaca cop is so cute anymore."

"Maybe I can see if there are footsteps coming from the road or another neighbor," I said lamely. What could Birdie expect for me, a supposedly normal person, to find that the police hadn't?

"Hey, maybe Random will smell something important," Birdie said. "Bring him with you, see how he reacts."

"That's exactly what I was thinking," I lied, picking up his leash. It would've been a great excuse if I'd thought of it myself.

Random and I went out her front door and around to the detached garage to the side of the house. Bright yellow tape, stretched around the old, gray-green structure, fluttered in the breeze.

When I was still ten steps away from the driveway, I felt the residue of magic lingering in the cracked asphalt.

I knelt down and set my palm on the ground. "How about you, Random? Smell anything?"

Random was sniffing everything the way he always did but didn't give anything away.

I put my hand on my necklace and cast out my senses to detect more of the magical residue. It was faint, already tram-pled by humans and dogs, birds and sunlight, but there was no doubt it was magic. Like an odor, it spread from the trees into the driveway, fading at the edges and hard to detect after inhaling it for a while.

I made a show of looking at the ground for footprints, but I'd found what I feared. Something or someone of magical means had been near her house, probably in her garage, but I couldn't be sure of that. As her neighbor, I could've attracted the fae, witch, or demon myself, and I was only detecting the fact that they'd been nearby.

But knowing her RAV4 had struck Tristan made me think magic was used to steal it. Or somebody wanted me to think it was.

"Well?" Birdie asked from the front yard.

"I don't know. I just… I just don't understand." Unable to pinpoint the magic further, I walked over to her.

She looked away, sighing. "Thanks anyway. You're nice to try to help."

"I'm sorry—"

"Don't be sorry. I should've locked the garage. We're not far from the main road. Obviously somebody came up here looking for an easy ride to steal and brought it back after they ran over a guy and freaked out."

Her analysis didn't seem entirely plausible to me, but I nodded. "Let me know if there's anything I can do." I guided Random to the road, knowing if I hurried, I would be able to drive to Riovaca in time to buy myself a new phone before they closed. If I saw the tall fairy again, I'd run him over.

"The only other possibility is Livia got really upset with Tristan and took it."

I turned. "Took what?"

"My car. She had a set of keys."

Chapter Twenty-Nine

Staring at Birdie, the thought hit me that the last time I'd seen Livia, she'd been in a hurry to leave town.

The expression on Birdie's face was unusually hard. "It would be like her, don't you think? To get so angry with a person she'd run him over? Even if she was—no, especially if she was in huge love with him. She might've found something out, and that was the final straw. Bam. She's smart enough not to use her own car, so—"

"I don't believe it," I said.

"I do. I don't think she could kill somebody close up, but I've seen her drive around town in that SUV as if it was a tank, gliding through stop signs and speeding over crosswalks if she sees a pedestrian and doesn't want to slow down because she's too important and has things to do."

I was shocked by Birdie's uncharacteristic venom. Having had my own rough night, I empathized with Birdie's short temper, but it was obvious she was too tired to think clearly.

"First of all," I said, trying to reason with her, "he had a heart attack. It wasn't a car that killed him. Secondly—"

"Maybe she scared him first, threatening to run him

down, watched until he keeled over, and then waited a few minutes before finally driving, so to speak, the message home." Angry tears shone in Birdie's eyes.

"Secondly," I said quickly, "what you're describing sounds like a crime of passion. She wouldn't drive up here, get your car, run him over, drive back, put the RAV4 in the garage, and then return home."

"All right, so she planned it. Way in advance. You know what she's like. Really organized. And she did it not because she was actually in love with him, because who could put up with watching him sleep with everyone else all the time and never with you? But because she thought he was going to leave her something in his will." Birdie's eyes narrowed. "You don't know how bad she needs the money. She lost every-thing trying to save her family winery in Napa. She acts rich, but she's as broke as we are. Broker."

"Forget it, Birdie. How could she have done it without being seen? One of us would've seen her huge white SUV. We both went out at some point. And why use your car? It makes no sense," I said. "Besides, why would he leave her much of anything in his will? He's been rejecting her since they met."

Birdie turned away, nodding, and began to walk unsteadily to her front door. "You're right. Forget it. I'm hysterical. You should slap me like they do in old movies."

I wanted to tell her she wasn't crazy, that there were beings and forces she couldn't see or comprehend but did indeed exist.

But smart witches didn't do that. We'd learned the hard way.

"How about I bring over something for you to eat?" I asked. "I don't know how to make a casserole, but I make an excellent quesadilla."

"No, please don't. I'm getting in bed. I'm going to put in

my earplugs and cover my eyes and pretend none of this is happening. I'll go back to dealing with life tomorrow."

"If you need any—"

She waved before she hurried inside and shut the door in my face.

Deciding Birdie had a sensible plan for the rest of the day, I returned to my house, planning to do the same. I could get a new phone when I went to Santa Rosa for a replacement (authentic) driver's license. And my antihistamines had kicked in, making me feel as if my limbs weren't quite attached to my body. My episode as a cat also led to a bone-deep exhaustion that demanded hours, sometimes days, of sleep.

I stretched out in bed, thinking that whatever was going to happen next, I would need my strength to deal with it.

Eyes closed, blankets pulled up to my chin, feeling Random curled up against my thigh, I began to drift off into a soft, pleasant dreamland.

Until I remembered what had happened to Nick. If I hadn't tracked him down because of the cabinet, would he have died last night? Like Birdie, he was a powerless nonmag, a bystander.

I rolled to one side, telling myself magic was everywhere, Shadow was in every corner, I didn't have the power to protect everyone. If I wanted the strength to find out what had happened, I needed to sleep. The cat shifting had drained me. Sleep, just sleep.

But when I closed my eyes, I imagined Nick's panicked face. I could almost hear him screaming.

It was useless. Helen was right—I couldn't rest with so many questions. My ignorance was an itch I had to scratch. I sat up, turned on the light, and let myself think.

Somebody or something had driven him off the road.

What if it hadn't been the tall fairy or the other aggressive fae I'd seen in the forest? And why kill Nick?

Anyone walking by could have seen him talking to me at the taqueria. And those close enough could have heard us talking about a key and a cabinet.

Although my mind was restless, my body was weak and unsteady, so I indulged in a drop of wellspring water in a can of coffee. Just a drop. A dangerous habit to develop, but it was an emergency.

Refreshed, I told Random I'd be back as soon as I could and drove to Tristan's house. Since I'd been able to search the cabinet even without Nick's help, I'd forgotten about it. But nobody knew I'd searched it but me. They, whoever they were, might assume I needed Nick's key.

As I drove up the driveway, I braked for Donna, who was walking from the direction of the tasting room, carrying two wine bottles. She signaled for me to stop and came over to my window.

"It's one thing to go through his things," she told me, shooting a sour glance at the house, "but something else to bark orders at me. I don't work for them."

"Who's barking orders at you?"

"Some girl. She waved some papers at me and said she had permission to go inside."

I looked up the driveway and glimpsed the rear bumper of a familiar BMW. "You said 'them.' Who's with her?"

"They just drove away. Movers, they said, but I'd never hire them." She made a face. "They broke the cabinet into pieces. I'm glad it's gone, but they dragged it through the house without even picking it up right. Scratched the floors like you wouldn't believe. Terrible. Really, unbelievable. Tristan must be rolling in his grave."

So the cabinet was gone, with Phoebe directing the show.

I gestured at the bottles in her hands. "Who asked for the wine?"

"That girl. She's probably not even old enough to drink." Donna straightened. "Not my business. I'm out of here at the end of the week."

"For what it's worth, she and Tristan worked for the same people. She's probably following orders."

"'People,'" Donna said, raising an eyebrow. "I know what you mean. At least they got that thing out of here. Are they the new owners then? That girl and… you know, the same 'people' Tristan worked for?"

"I don't know."

Shaking her head, she resumed walking toward the house. I thought about following her and asking Phoebe about the cabinet or Nick but thought better of it. I'd only end up having to answer questions of my own.

The Protectorate had the cabinet with all its nasty hexes and Shadows. The men with Phoebe had to have been witches with enough power to overcome the spells Tristan had left behind. One of them had probably been the Emerald witch who had put me under the secrecy spell years ago. Phoebe didn't have the power on her own.

Would any of them kill Nick to stop me from seeing what was inside? From learning Tristan wasn't as law-abiding as his reputation?

Or did Nick mean nothing to them, and they continued to search for the torc?

I returned home and fell into bed, finally overcome by exhaustion and allergy medicine. Nick and Tristan haunted my dreams.

FOR THE SECOND time in a week, Livia woke me up in the morning by appearing in person on my doorstep.

"Why didn't you tell me?" she demanded. The shrubs hadn't gotten any smaller since her last visit, and she kicked away the rosemary branches that sprawled over the welcome mat.

I'd slept on the sofa again so I could watch the door. "Tell you what?" I asked wearily.

"Is that why you were so friendly with her? I'd always wondered why you buttered her up when nobody else did. You must've known."

I was tempted to slam the door in her face, but I was too curious. "You'd better come in."

I walked to the kitchen without waiting to see if she'd follow. After opening the back door for Random, I decided to use my actual coffee maker and the good beans Jasper had given me recently. Some mornings a refrigerated can just wouldn't cut it.

"I thought you'd left town." I flipped on the grinder just as she opened her mouth.

"She—" When the machine whine ceased, she snapped, "She called me."

"Who?"

"Birdie! She accused me of stealing her car and— It's insane!"

"I told her the same thing."

"Why would— You did?"

"You wouldn't have used a car that could be traced back to you so easily."

Livia turned a dark shade of red and said, very tightly, "I wouldn't have used *any* car."

I measured the coffee grounds and tapped them into the filter. "But if you did. Just saying."

"You think this is funny? She humiliated both of us," Livia said. "Of course she won't even come to the door."

"It's not her fault they arrested her at the memorial," I said. "Thank God she has an alibi."

"How can you—" She let out a frustrated sound and sat at the table. "All right. He slept around. I know that. Everyone knows that. But to leave her the winery? I've been —I was—a true friend to him. I really cared." Tears welled in her eyes, but she scowled and wiped them away.

I had been slow to realize what she'd been trying to tell me. "Birdie? And Tristan?"

She nodded, still scowling.

"I don't believe it," I said.

"He left her the winery."

Chapter Thirty

I fell back a step. "No. He couldn't. She didn't even know him. Who told you that?"

"She did," Livia said. "When she was accusing me of stealing her car and running him over. She called me late last night and asked me outright why I'd done it. She wanted to know how I'd found out about the will, that he'd left her the estate. She figured that was why I'd flown into a rage and —" She made the noise again, halfway between a scream and a growl.

"What did you say?"

"What do you think? I told her she was nuts. On both counts."

I sat across from her at the table. "And?"

"She said never mind and hung up." Livia snorted, eyes wild. "Never mind!"

"She realized you hadn't known about the will."

"Of course not! He wouldn't have told me he'd left the winery to his latest... toy... and not to his dear friend and experienced winemaker who—" She slammed her hand on the table, rattling the vase of dried lavender. "But you hadn't known either, so there you go. He hid it from both of us. He humiliated both of us."

"I can't believe there was anything romantic between them." Not only did I believe it, I knew it. I'd never seen them together, but I realized there was a connection, something I should've noticed earlier…

Livia gave me a contemptuous eye-roll. "The man was obviously not particular."

I cleared my throat. "Ahem."

She looked down at her hands, twisting her fingers together and playing with her rings. "On top of everything else, I just found out he slept with my best friend." It wasn't quite an apology, but close enough.

"Carolyn," I said.

"No. Meredith." She stared at me a moment and then swore. "Seriously?"

I sent a silent apology to Carolyn for spilling her secret. "No, I was just guessing. She's the only friend of yours I know."

"Nice try." She got to her feet, her mouth turned down and quivering the way it did right before throwing up. "I should've guessed. I can't believe I—" She made the noise a third time and flung open the back door. Random ran in; she stepped out.

I got up to follow. "Look, I'm sorry—"

"Save your breath. This is embarrassing enough without *you* feeling sorry for *me*. You should thank me for exposing Birdie's lies."

"Thanks," I said.

She marched to the side yard and out of my sight, and a moment later I heard her SUV peel out of the driveway, sputtering gravel.

Letting Random follow me, I walked over to talk to Birdie. Why hadn't Tristan told me? Our relationship was brief, and he never hid his many relationships. Perhaps there was something awkward he wanted to keep to himself. He'd left her his fortune. Something unique about Birdie—

Of course.

As I rang the bell, I cast a spell at the threshold to make Birdie forget why she didn't want to answer the door. It took a few minutes for the magic to trickle through the cracks and reach her where she waited inside, probably peering through the curtains.

Her face was a little dazed when she appeared in the open doorway. "Alma?"

I gave her a huge smile. "Thanks for inviting me over. I was thinking about you."

"I invited you over," she said.

Not wasting a second, I followed Random inside before she shook it off. "Livia just came to see me. She told me about Tristan's will."

Birdie ran a hand over her face. "Everything is so screwed up."

"She thinks you were sleeping with Tristan. She's upset, but I don't—"

"Oh my God. No." Birdie stuck out her tongue. "Why would— Oh. I guess that makes sense. Yuck."

"You can't hide this for much longer."

"What's crazy is I didn't know about it until the police accused me of killing him for his money. I was like, what money? And they told me Elizabeth Mary Crow was named as the beneficiary of the house and buildings and everything, and I was like, no way, but they'd seen a copy of the will."

"You didn't know."

"I barely knew the guy. I wasn't sure I wanted to."

My feelings about Tristan were getting more and more complicated. He'd hidden a big secret from me. I wondered if he ever would've told me himself, if I'd known him at all.

I took off my shoes and set them by the door. "When did he find out he was your father?"

Her eyes widened. "You know?"

"I only guessed a few minutes ago. Now that I look at you, I can see the resemblance. You smile the same way he did." I felt a wave of grief. "It's a great smile. Very— Very charming."

She smiled weakly. "My mother had me send a letter to him after she died. That was two and a half years ago."

I rubbed my temples. He could've told me.

"To be fair to him," she continued, "I never introduced myself. I figured if he was really curious about me, he'd track me down."

"You didn't use a fake name," I said.

"But I didn't make an announcement or anything. I got the job at Cypress, but everyone calls me Birdie. My name tag says Birdie. My coworkers probably don't even know my last name, which is my mother's anyway." She sat on the floor of her kitchen and put her arms around Random. "I'm so sorry, Alma. I was so worried you were going to hate me for not telling you. It just got so awkward, and the longer I waited, the more impossible it was. Besides, until recently I wasn't totally sure. My mom wasn't always honest."

As Birdie got more upset, Random became frantic, licking her cheeks and jumping into and out of her lap.

"How about I make us coffee?" I began opening cabinets.

"I don't have any. I can't handle caffeine. I'm already high-strung, lately even more. I start shaking." She held up an unsteady hand. "I can't sleep. I never got to know him, and I lived just down the street for so long. I saw him come into the store and never had the guts to introduce myself. I was afraid he'd take one look at me and be like, yeah so? And after I'd lost my mother and I don't have anyone else, that would've been too much. Except now I wish I had, because he's gone and I'm alone."

She began to cry, and Random's tongue went berserk. I hoped she hadn't put on much makeup that morning because so many chemicals couldn't be good for a dog's stomach.

"You're not alone," I said. "Can't you see the dog having seizures in your lap?"

Smiling through her tears, Birdie nuzzled Random's neck. "Good dog."

I found two glasses, filled them with tap water, and offered her one. The trace of wellspring water might make it easier for me to read her. "So you don't get dehydrated," I said.

She accepted the glass, smiling under the dog tongue onslaught. After taking one sip, she offered it to Random. "Thirsty, puppers?"

He licked the glass and, seeing she was calming down, began to settle as well. With a loud sigh, he flopped on the floor and went to sleep with his chin propped on Birdie's bare foot.

They looked sweet together, but I wasn't feeling it. Ever since Livia had told me about Tristan's will, my mind had been churning with the implications of Birdie being a Protector's biological daughter.

Was Birdie a witch? Did she inherit power as well as property? Did she know anything about magic, what Tristan had been?

I walked into her living room and made myself comfortable on her couch. "Let's talk," I said, patting the cushion next to me.

Chapter Thirty-One

Every move Birdie made now seemed suspicious as I considered the possibility that all this time she'd been using spells to confuse me, and only now was I awake enough to see the illusion. If she'd hidden her story so well earlier, why not now?

What secrets and lies had she hidden in the goofy blathering? If she was a witch, she could've met Tristan, given him a heart attack, driven over his body, and then visited the neighbor—manipulating that neighbor's memory of time to give her an alibi.

It all hinged on how powerful Birdie might be—or how evil.

Random jumped up on the cushions between us as we sipped our tap water.

"I don't really know anything other than what my mom told me at the end," Birdie said, stroking Random's fur. He arched back into her lap, paws quivering in the air. Friends for life. "A long time ago, she said she had a fling with a weird blond guy and I was the result. When she got sick, she worried about how young I was to be alone in the world and so finally told me his name. I'd been bugging her all my life, but she finally caved. Although at the time I was suspicious that she'd made something up just to change the subject."

"She said he was weird? Anything else?"

Birdie glanced at me and then quickly looked down again before shaking her head.

So. She knew something.

"What kind of weird?" I asked.

With her head lowered, her hair shielded her face, hiding her eyes.

If she wouldn't tell me, I'd find out indirectly. "Did you quit your job because you knew you were inheriting the—"

"No!" She pushed the hair out of her face. "I just couldn't bear to lie about who I was anymore. I realized it was true; he really was my dad. The day before he died, that envelope appeared at the store with the pictures of him and my mom together."

"Anonymously?"

She shrugged. "I knew it was him. He's the only one who would've had the pictures, and then later he... he sent a letter. I think it was his way of telling me he knew who I was and would wait for me to make the next move."

I wondered if that's exactly what she'd done. But... Birdie? Could she really be hiding so much power? If she was Tristan's daughter, she could've inherited quite a bit.

But I was skeptical she could hide her real personality, which seemed so genuine. Why pretend to be so awkward and silly for so long—over the years, with everyone—if you weren't? There were easier ways to deflect suspicion from yourself.

Like pretending to be in love...

"Livia was furious about your getting the winery," I said. "She was mad at me too until she saw I wasn't in on the secret."

Birdie grimaced. "I feel bad about losing my temper with her. I'm tempted to give her the house so we can be friends again."

Once again I studied her with all my powers, trying to tell if she was putting on an act.

But I felt nothing false. Not the tiniest hint of a deflection spell. I couldn't see any jewelry or herbs on her body, no tattoos. I couldn't smell anything burning, or the acrid odor of a nasty but protective floor wash—nothing suspicious in the least.

"I'm not sure her friendship would be worth the price," I said.

She smiled. "I know, I know. She's totally a mean girl, but she was usually nice to me in her own way." She ruffled Random's neck fur. "But you're right, she probably won't forgive me. That's why I quit. I'm going to move to Windsor, or maybe Sonoma. Somewhere pretty, and start over."

"What about the winery? You don't want to move in and take over?"

She made a face. "Me? I don't know anything about wine."

"You could learn."

"Why are you being so nice to me? I lied to you."

I wasn't really being nice. Part of me was testing her, trying to figure out her motives. "I know what it's like to have a complicated relationship with your parents."

She laughed a little. "You got that right. I used to fight with my mom a lot—I mean, all the time—and then she was gone and all I had to turn to was this rich weirdo who didn't know I existed."

"There's that word again," I said. "Weird how?"

"You know."

I paused. "I do. But do you?"

Dislodging Random, she got to her feet and walked over

to the TV, an old thing that wasn't much bigger than a computer monitor. "You mentioned your parents," she said.

"Yes?"

"I thought you were raised by your dad." She spun around and said quickly, "I only ask because I used to think we had that in common, being raised by one parent. But then you just mentioned your parents, plural, and I wondered... Do you have two?"

"Kind of like you do," I said.

"You don't know your mom?"

I needed to know what she knew about my world. "I don't like to talk about that."

"That's so funny."

"Not usually," I said.

"I only meant that's what I used to say. When people asked about my dad. People don't ask very much about a missing father, though, do they? Because they might never know you exist. But it's kind of hard for the mom not to know you exist."

"I'll tell you about it if you answer my earlier question," I said.

"About weird?"

"Yeah."

She buried her face in her hands. "I'm afraid to say it. He kind of swore me to secrecy."

"Tristan? I thought you never spoke."

"We didn't. He... he wrote me a letter. At least I think it was him. He mentioned the photograph and then said we could meet if... if I accepted something about him. He said what it was and asked me to burn the letter while I thought about it, so I did."

I got to my feet and looked at her steadily, without magic but intently. "You burned it because you thought he was crazy."

GRETCHEN GALWAY

"I burned it because he told me to." Her voice fell. "And I was afraid."

"But you didn't actually swear anything? You just burned the letter?"

"What's the difference?"

I let out my breath. If she'd truly sworn to Tristan and then had broken the promise, she could've been in some danger, like how I'd felt after telling Jasper about the well-spring or how the gargoyle on the cabinet had knocked me out. Not all spells expired at death.

"You did as he asked, so you're fine," I said.

"You're like him," she said. "Aren't you?"

I nodded.

"Holy moly," she said.

"You never...," I began. "Did your mother—"

"She only said he was weird."

"Did she ever think she could do magic?" I asked. "You know, play around with herbs?"

"She chopped cilantro for guacamole, rosemary for chicken, maybe basil if the snails didn't get it first."

I tried not to laugh. "Right. More than that. Burning plants, sprinkling leaves around, that sort of thing. Weird things."

"No, Mom wasn't into weird. She worked for a medical billing service."

Tristan had played a dangerous game, mixing with so many women who weren't aware of the magical world. It was interesting to think he'd kept the photo booth snapshots of himself with Birdie's mother, as if she'd been important to him.

"Your turn," Birdie said. "You said you'd tell me about your mother."

"No, I said I'd tell you if I had two parents." I went back to the couch and sat next to Random for fur therapy while I

214

talked about my least favorite subject. "I assume I do, because as powerful as my father is, he can't create life from thin air. Distort it, sure. But create it? No."

She sat across from me again. "So you don't know why your mother left?"

"I don't know if she did. He may have stolen me in the middle of the night, the same way he gets everything else he wants." I crossed my legs and leaned back in the sofa, determined not to get upset about ancient history.

Birdie's eyes widened. "You don't know?" she whispered.

"I don't know anything." I smiled. "Maybe she owns a winery somewhere."

"Maybe she— Maybe she's looking for you."

"If so, she's not looking very hard," I said. "My father is kind of famous. In a bad way."

"To magic people, maybe—"

"Witches. Might as well call us what we are."

She frowned, not from anger but from concentration. "Right. Witches. Maybe she's not a witch, just somebody norm... Uh, not a witch."

"Nonmag, we say. Nonmagical," I said. "But she has to be a witch. I know she is."

"How can you know? Did he tell you? Or is it..." Her eyes widened. "It's a genetic thing, is that it? And because you have powers, she must have powers. But then why don't I — Ah. Is it only on the maternal line?"

I reminded myself not to underestimate Birdie. "A daughter inherits her mother's powers. And also, sometimes, her father's. But not always."

"How about sons?"

"Same story in reverse. Sons get the father's powers and possibly the mother's. Mixed marriages have unpredictable results."

"But how do you know you don't just have your father's powers, and your mother is nonmagical?"

"It's the kind of powers that I have." We were getting into the gray area that had shadowed my entire life. "I don't want to get into specifics, but I have too many for them only to have come from my father." And different ones he didn't have.

Birdie stared at me without blinking. "Wow. What— I mean, what—"

"You're Tristan's daughter," I said. She might not tell the truth, but I had to try. "He was a powerful witch. Do you have any power of your own?" I prepared my magic to gauge the truth of her answer.

She laughed, clapping her hands together. "I can't believe we're talking about this so seriously."

"I know, right?" I tried to smile.

"I would love to be a witch with amazing powers," she said.

So far she'd said nothing I could determine to be false. Her statements were either sincere or carefully evasive.

"Have you ever done something you thought was impossible?" I asked.

"Well, sure, but…" She leaned closer, hugging a pillow to her chest. "Can you teach me? Is it like learning spells and waving things the right way?"

"Sometimes. But it won't work if you don't have any power."

"Can you tell if I have any power?"

I'd been trying to figure that out for the past hour. Innate ability couldn't be determined, only the act itself. Should I admit I couldn't tell? If she was playing me, that might give her too much ammunition.

"I'll leave you to figure that out for yourself," I said, adding a smile in case she was as innocent as I hoped.

I could be evasive too.

She buried her face in the pillow, shaking her head. "So cool, so cool," she said, her voice muffled.

Although she had a motive and possibly the ability to give herself that alibi, I just couldn't believe she would hurt anyone. Either I was a good friend and neighbor or the biggest fool in the witch world.

Chapter Thirty-Two

I left Birdie's house before she could ask me more pointed questions about magic. Until I knew for sure who and what she was, I couldn't risk teaching her anything.

Across the street, a surprise visitor was waiting for me at the edge of my driveway, pacing and muttering to herself, obviously unable to get any closer and annoyed about it. Phoebe Day, alone this time, wearing a black dress, long black cardigan, pointy lace-up boots, and a purple scarf. Her BMW was parked at an odd angle, its front wheels in the drainage ditch to the left of the driveway—as if she'd been driving onto my property before something unexpected had shoved her car to one side.

I indulged in a quick smile before approaching.

"Phoebe," I said.

She held up a thick silver chain between us and began muttering under her breath. The spell was protective, surrounding her in a cocoon of white, fuzzy light. "I'm here to talk." She sounded nervous.

If she hadn't intended me any harm, I doubted my house

spells would have driven her car into the ditch. Whatever she wanted to talk about, her intentions weren't good for me personally.

While Random skittered out of sight, giving our visitor the widest berth possible, I approached Phoebe, only stopping when I was immediately outside the cocoon. Not hiding a yawn, I zipped up my sweatshirt. Autumn was just around the corner, and the fog was cold that morning.

"Nice outfit," I said. "Did you get that at the Junior Witch department at Macy's?"

Her lips tightened. "I apologize for Mage Lorne's behavior. I didn't realize he had a history with you and your father that made him incapable of objectivity or..." She swallowed. "Compromise."

"There's nothing to compromise about," I said. "I don't know anything about—"

"Of course not. But maybe you and I could come to a private arrangement that would trigger your memory." She turned, waving the chain in a circle around her like a rotating sprinkler head. The white mist grew thicker, sealing her back inside her safety blanket. "Just between you and me. Lorne doesn't have to know."

"I don't have the torc," I said, "and I don't know who does. At this point, I probably wouldn't tell you if I did."

"It doesn't matter what you do or don't know. Lorne and the Protectorate believes you're guilty, which will mean an end to the way you've been accepted in the ways your father is not."

"Just how am I accepted? I was fired."

"Honorably discharged with an Incurable Inability is quite different from being shunned," she said, "or hunted as a common demon."

"I've done nothing wrong."

Her beautiful eyes narrowed. "But your father has. Listen

carefully. If you give me the torc, I'll make Lorne believe it came from another thief. Your father, and therefore you, won't be implicated. Lorne isn't willing to negotiate with Malcolm because of bad blood, but I'm more flexible." She waved the chain again, rustling her purple scarf. "I won't make this offer again and will deny it if asked. This is your only chance to clear your family's name."

That chance had already faded before I was born, when Malcolm Bellrose had famously stolen the dragon-shaped door knocker from the main entrance of the Protectorate office in London. Its eyes had been rubies, which he'd told me—when I wasn't yet tall enough to reach the knocker, had it still been on the door—had practically been an invitation to rescue it from its precarious location.

"Anybody could've stolen it," he'd said. "I've sold it to somebody who knows how to take better care of nice things."

I wondered if, with more time to search Tristan's house, I'd find it among his other treasures.

"When is Tristan's funeral?" I asked Phoebe.

"That was held the night after his death," she said.

I'd told Jasper how I hadn't expected to be invited, but hearing that it had already happened, without a word to me, still hurt. As Phoebe had guessed, I didn't enjoy living under the same infamy as my father.

"And the new Protector?" I asked. "When should we expect one?"

"That's another reason you should accept my offer now. It's not safe here until a new Protector is assigned, even with all this crude soft magic piled up around you." She lifted her chin as if daring me to deny my methods. "Hearth witch," she sneered.

"Crude but effective," I said, walking past her, making a point of staring at her car that was beautifully not in my driveway.

"There are malevolent forces stirring up the fae," she blurted. "Tristan told Lorne there was intentional harm occurring here in Silverpool."

"Other than murder, you mean?"

"Harm to the fae. Even I'm not supposed to know." She lowered her voice. "My telling you is a show of my good faith."

"What kind of harm?"

A wave of verity spells broke out of her cocoon and surrounded my head. "Tristan reported poisoning near the winery. A potion of some kind. But since his death, we have discovered the deliberate contamination"—she paused, watching me carefully—"of the forest near the wellspring itself."

I thought of the mob of fairies in the forest that had kept me in a tree all night. "That makes no sense. Who would want to do that? Why harm fairies?"

"If it weren't for Tristan's presence here, naturally we would blame demons. But his power fighting demons"—she gave me a contemptuous glance—"was unwavering and unmatched. None would approach while he was here. It must be a human."

"The nonmag are always careless with chemicals. Maybe somebody dumped—"

"Only magic could touch fairies." She brought out a second chain and drew a circle with it between us. "It had to be a witch." Then she lowered her hands enough to stare at me over her trembling fingers.

I realized she was accusing Malcolm of a worse crime than stealing a necklace from the Protectorate.

"Do you know where the wellspring is?" she continued.

"Yes." I felt Phoebe's verity spell tickle my cheeks.

"Have you visited recently?"

"I tried, but it's dry this time of year." I told a partial

truth because it was possible she already knew I'd been in the area after the bramble spell was triggered and because her implication was too crazy to be insulting.

"Of course it is," she said, sighing as she lowered her arms completely. "And even if it was at its fullest, you obviously couldn't be the one harming any fairies. After all, you ruined your life because you didn't have the steel to hurt *demons*. Those monsters deserve whatever they get. Unlike the poor little spirits who share this earth with us."

That comment alone told me how sheltered she must've been in her short life. Nobody had ever let *her* wander alone in the woods all night or dance naked under a full moon on midsummer's eve.

"And after all, I'm harmless," I said. The irony of her trembling behind her steam bath cocoon of protective magic wasn't lost on me.

"Because of the suspicions on your character and that of your father, it would be beneficial to both of you if someone understanding and forgiving was appointed here," she said. "You might find it increasingly difficult to mingle in mainstream magic society now that Tristan is dead and the torc is missing and your father... well. We know about him."

Was she threatening or bargaining with me? "What do you care about the Protector appointment in Silverpool?"

She frowned and looked away.

Could she possibly believe she had a chance of being appointed Protector? That was impossible. No matter why he favored her, Lorne would never get away with giving such a coveted position to his niece, a low-level underling, still basically a Flint. Dozens of more experienced, more powerful witches, wanting the post for themselves, would destroy him if he tried.

The magic cocoon around her had taken a tremendous

amount of effort to create and was already beginning to fade around her feet.

It was so easy to forget about the feet. Our instincts were to protect the vital organs and the face, and those poor toes, heels, arches, and ankles became vulnerable.

Although she was an agent at the Protectorate, her training must've rushed some of the basics. I didn't need to knock her off her feet to get what I wanted; my spell could slip under the boundary of her protection and measure her motives through any exposed body part. Before she could wave her silver chain again, I broke through the gap, coasted up both high-heeled boots, through the laces, the leather tongue, the delicate stocking, and encircled the bare skin of her ankles with a tendril of power.

And listened to the weather of her thoughts.

"Do you expect to be Protector of Silverpool?" I asked quietly, enhancing the question through the bond I'd tied around her feet.

I saw the torc, a shining, open hoop of gold. I smelled Lorne's cologne, the distinctive scent I remembered from my time at the Diamond Street office. I tasted a woman's lust for power—a dark, sticky, hot craving that made my stomach clench.

Tightening the bond, I had a stunning glimpse of how cold, Shadowed, and grasping Phoebe was beneath her lovely face. Yes, she did think she would be Protector. Why did she—

"Stop that!" Phoebe shouted, rushing me with the chain in her fist.

More afraid of the fist than the chain—the idea of any part of her touching me was suddenly repulsive—I stumbled backward. Then she bent over, and as she began slapping the chain against her ankles (hitting hard enough to bruise), the spell I'd snaked under her feet broke away.

"You need to be more careful," she said, her voice high and loud. "Who do you think you are? You're— You're— You're nothing! You— Is it your father? How do you—" Swinging the chain at me like a whip, she began moving away, slow then fast, toward her car.

I didn't try to follow. I'd seen more than I'd wanted to see, learned more than I wanted to know. The woman was ambitious and cruel with a lust for power I associated with nonmag tycoons and politicians.

As I watched, she pulled off her scarf and threw it in the air between us, staring at it with the concentration of spellcasting. The thin fabric burst into lavender smoke, fluffy but opaque, completely shrouding her body and her car. A few moments later a car engine roared, its wheels spun in the ditch, the shoulder, and finally the asphalt. Her BMW burst out of the cloud and sped away down the street, trailing purple tendrils.

"Holy smokes," I muttered.

A man coughed politely behind me. "Not very holy, actually," he said. "But I suppose you already knew that."

Chapter Thirty-Three

I didn't need to turn around to identify Seth Dumont. I would always remember that voice, and I was familiar with his habit of sneaking up on people. Came with the demon job, I supposed.

"Her name is Phoebe Day," I said. "Or have you already met?"

"I avoid witches as much as possible."

"If only," I said.

He grinned. "You're different."

"Sometimes I wish I weren't."

"Never say that." He pointed down the road, still hazy with purple smoke. It was midday but still foggy, exaggerating the effect of Phoebe's spell. "Given the alternative, I'd say the world got lucky with you getting so much power."

"Power? Me?"

"She's not here anymore, is she?"

I scowled at the tire marks from the ditch into the road, knowing they'd be there until the first heavy rains came, in October at the soonest. "For now. But she keeps coming back."

"You have a magnetic personality," Seth said.

Random, who had run away when he'd seen Phoebe, now reappeared, wagging tail a blur, and greeted my unwanted visitor with embarrassing delight.

"You're the magnet," I said. "Do you have salami in your pocket?"

He stopped patting Random to shoot me another grin.

"Cut that out," I said. "Your charms don't work on me."

"Because you're a very powerful witch." He began rubbing Random's belly. My fearsome and fearless guard dog had rolled over for him in spite of my cold tone and aggressive body language.

"Because I'm tired and annoyed and you shouldn't be here." Seeing how comfortable Random was with Seth made me suspicious of both of them. Demons weren't supposed to get along with dogs, but Seth had always been different.

Or maybe I was just fooling myself.

"I came by to tell you to be careful," he said. "Stay home if you can."

Tempting, but I was in too deep. "My neighbor's car was the one that ran over Tristan," I said. "Do you know anything about that?"

He stood up and faced me. The flat white light of the sky made his eyes look more gray than blue. "I know she wasn't the one driving."

I hesitated to tell him anything, but if I gave him information, he might give me some. "She's his biological daughter. I'm not sure if I can believe she didn't have anything to do with his death. She acts like magic is all new to her."

"I don't know anything about your neighbor. But I do know who took her car."

"And this person ran over Tristan?"

"Not a person," he said.

The hair rose on the back of my neck. I glanced at

Birdie's house, hoping he was telling me the truth. More than one magical creature was playing games around Silverpool lately. "Come inside before you tell me more. It's safer."

He rubbed his chin. "I'd rather not. You've made a few additions to your fortress since I was here last."

"Surely they're not effective on a creature as powerful as yourself?"

"Surely you don't expect me to test it and find out?" he asked.

I crossed my arms over my chest, trying to decide if he was humoring me as usual for motives of his own or if Helen's magic really might be stronger than he was.

"Only those who mean me harm should be prevented entry," I said.

"I'd like to steal your heart. For that alone, your ancient magic might interpret me as a threat." His voice was as smooth as his smile.

Rolling my eyes, I sent out a probing spell to confirm we were alone. "A demon was on the bridge that night?"

He paused and took a deep breath as if he expected an argument. "No. A fairy drove the car that night."

"That's im—" I stopped myself. Fairies could move things, hide things, break things. But drive? And why use a human machine when magic was so much simpler?

"His name is Launt," he continued. "He's... lake fae."

"But why? Why would any fairy hurt people? Why run over a witch?" My voice rose involuntarily. "Did he kill Tristan before he ran over him? Is he capable of that?"

"I don't know."

"Is he a nasty green one, excessively large for his species?"

He drew back in surprise. "You've met?"

"He ran me off the road. Me in my Jeep and then later, I think, a man named Nick Takata. They found him dead this morning."

Seth turned aside and put his hand over his face. After a long moment, he turned back to me. "Where's your car now?"

I pointed toward my house.

He approached the driveway. After first stepping gingerly into the cracked asphalt, he walked slowly, flinching. "Blueberry leaves?" he asked me over his shoulder.

"And a few other things."

Eventually he reached the front bumper, held out a hand over it, and paused. Never touching it, he shivered, glanced at me, and then inhaled deeply.

"Launt," he said tightly. "We've got to find him. Today. Now. He's gone too far. He could've killed you."

I tried not to be flattered by his show of concern. "It's typical around here for fae to steal things, but a car? I wouldn't think they could even if they wanted to. Hide the keys, lock the doors, loosen the parking brake, deflate a tire —sure. All the time. But drive a car? It's so big and mechanical."

"So human," he said.

"You're sure?"

"I'm sure. Launt can drive. He's big enough, you see, and he's got a vengeful heart." He splayed his fingers over the bumper and added, his voice low, "Like so many of his kind."

"I've never seen lake fae around here," I said.

He turned suddenly, frowning at me. "How did you see Launt? He wouldn't show himself to you."

Regretting what I'd revealed, I kept my face expressionless. "I can't tell you that."

We stared at each other.

"Can all hunters see the fae?" he asked.

"I can't tell you that either."

"I don't think they can," he said. "I think you've got an interesting secret."

"Why is this fairy on a rampage?" I asked. "And why haven't you stopped him? You obviously have no trouble seeing him."

He threw up his hands. "I'm working on it. It's not as easy as you might think."

"There's no Protector here to stop you." I pointed toward the bridge, where I still felt Tristan's unhappy spirit lingering. "I thought demons could do what they wanted with fairies when nobody stopped them."

"Perhaps they can," he said. "But I can't."

He spoke casually, but his words struck me. The Protectorate had been unable to tell me of any crime he'd committed, any evidence he was more than a man. I'd felt his magic, yes—more than I'd ever felt on any human being. But nothing evil or ancient.

I'd always wondered… I'd always doubted…

Was he really a demon?

"You're a witch, aren't you?" I whispered. "Some kind of Shadow practitioner maybe, or—"

"You know I'm not a witch." He frowned. "Come on, you can do better than that."

"If you're not a demon, and you're not human, then… fae?"

"You're getting close." He took my hand in his and looked down at it. "You have a name for my kind. You just don't want to believe it."

ONLY MY HUNGER TO acquire knowledge kept me from pulling my hand away. I couldn't resist a witch's most valuable treasure—a secret.

"Tell me," I said.

He brought my hand to his face. "I wasn't born in this

body. I wasn't born in any body of this earth but a body of the spirit people."

My pulse quickened. Even witches didn't believe in all the fairy tales. "Spirit people?"

"I was born fae. Lake fae. Wanting a glorious future for her son, my mother switched my soul with that of a human baby." He pressed my hand against his cheek. "I was a baby myself, in fairy terms, and I didn't know what I was until I was older. I loved my human parents, my friends, other people."

"A changeling," I said wonderingly. "I didn't know you—things like you—existed." The warmth of his face, the roughness of his stubble, told me he was very real.

He patted the back of my hand on his cheek. "Here I am."

Because he'd started smiling again, I finally pulled my hand back. "Why did the Protectorate say you were a demon?"

"Because they wanted you to kill me." He sighed. "I didn't realize that Protectorate guy was going to overreact so badly to a few questions."

"What guy?"

"The big cheese in San Francisco. Not as powerful as I'd expected from a boss at the Protectorate. I made him talk to me for a few minutes, and he really didn't like it."

"Lorne," I said. "I worked for him."

"Should've been the other way around. He was much too easy to capture. I'd tracked Laurit to Las Vegas but then lost him," he said. "I was asking Protectorate witches around all the cities on the West Coast if they'd recorded any odd fairy behavior in their regions."

"Asking?"

"Well, first I had to trick and capture them before I could

ask questions. Usually I was only able to catch young agents. But in San Francisco I nabbed the director."

Even now I was embarrassed for the San Francisco office that Lorne was in charge. "Why didn't you make him forget what you'd done?"

"Some other guy came and freed him before I could get to that," he said. "A better witch. He was too strong for me, and I fled."

"And then they sent me and my partner after you."

"To be fair to your Protectorate friends, most witches can't tell changelings and demons apart," he said. "After all, we are possessing spirits. We don't belong in your bodies."

I took a step back, agreeing with him. "Why were you tracking Launt in the first place? Was he— You said he's lake fae. Like you. Is he a... relative? A—?"

"My twin, spiritually speaking." He put his hand on his chest. "This is his rightful body."

Unable to control the feeling of revulsion that washed over me, I took another step back. "Why are you following him? Are you trying to kill him?"

"No. No, never. His death would be— No." He shoved his hands in his pockets. "I want to talk to him. I— I feel responsible."

"Responsible for what he's done?"

"Responsible for his existence."

I wasn't sure I could believe Seth—demon or changeling —could experience human morality. Only human beings felt guilt.

But I did know one thing. I wanted to see Launt for myself. "I'll help you find him. And then I'll..."

"You'll what?"

"I don't know. Something." My training had centered around protecting fae, not hurting them. But I was motivated.

He stared at me a moment. "I don't want him to suffer."

I paused, thinking of Nick's horrible death. "Why not?"

"He's my brother."

If he didn't have genuine human feeling, he was putting on an excellent imitation. "Why did he come out here?" I asked. "Was he drawn to the wellspring like everyone else?"

He opened the passenger side of the Jeep and, to my shock, climbed in. "I'm not sure. I'll ask him."

Random ran around to the driver's-side door and looked at me, clearly expecting to join Seth.

I let him into the back and told Seth, "I need to get my stuff." Although I didn't have my driver's license or a phone, I never left home without cash and a credit card, just in case. And a jacket. And a few extra beads and a can of coffee. And my staff, which wasn't powerful away from home but might have other uses.

After I'd gotten my things, I put it all in the back seat with Random and got behind the wheel.

"I've noticed human females can never just leave the house," he said.

"And I've noticed changeling males are really annoying," I replied, starting the engine. "So. Where are we going?"

He rolled down the window and inhaled deeply. Handsome nostrils flaring, he took another breath, held his hand out the window, waved it around a moment, then brought it to his mouth. Licking the tips of his fingers, he shook his head.

"The coast. At a boundary of sea and freshwater," he said. "We have to catch him before he hurts himself."

"Before he hurts somebody else," I said, backing out of the driveway. I turned around in the remaining purple mist, rolling over the marks Phoebe had left in the road.

He tapped his fingers on the dash. "That's what I said."

I glanced at the police tape around Birdie's garage as we

drove past. What did Launt want? When I'd been in the winery for the memorial, he hadn't seemed interested in me. It was only later, after Birdie had been arrested.

My thoughts churned through the possibilities. I had been going to Riovaca to help Birdie when Launt stopped me, suggesting it was Birdie who was really the object of his animosity.

But why Birdie? Because she was Tristan's daughter?

We drove west into the forest between Silverpool and the ocean. The road was narrow and twisting, dappled with shadows, and I gave my attention to it for the next fifteen minutes while I tried to remember if anyone at the Protectorate had ever mentioned changelings. Not that I could think of.

"The Protectorate believes a witch is intentionally poisoning the water in Silverpool," I said, watching Seth out of the corner of my eye to see his reaction. "Using some kind of potion to harm magic species. It's upsetting the fae enough to make them dangerous. Could Launt be, I don't know, fighting for revenge? For the injured fae?"

"Launt doesn't care about anyone but himself." He rolled down the window and held out his hand, fingers forward, feeling the wind. His voice grew serious. "He's slightly inland, on a creek bank. Turn off at the next road. Left."

"There is no next road before we get to Highway 1."

"Brake now," he said.

There was a gap in the trees. I braked, turned left onto a narrow dirt road. A small campsite with pit toilets sat at the entrance of a small redwood grove.

"Now where?" I asked.

"Keep going. He's following the tide up the creek."

"The road stops. Should I park, or—"

The dead end before us opened up, revealing a dirt track that snaked through the forest. Emerald green moss, curtains of lichen, and wet fog created the impression of a tunnel's entrance.

"Never mind," I said. "I see it now."

"I hoped you would. That's a useful trick."

At the end of the track, I turned around and parked the Jeep facing out for a quick escape, if necessary. Random's doggy breath over my shoulder smelled foul, but the air of the forest was sweetly delicious and cool.

"What do you think he wants?" I asked.

"He's grown up hating both human and fae. As far as I know, his only aim is malice, destruction, pain, suffering. War."

"You know this because…"

"I can feel him. We're bonded. My happy life with human parents was a constant torture for him." He cleared his throat. "The lake fae in that area aren't always nice to their own children, let alone the ones they foster."

"Abduct, you mean."

"I was raised as a human," Seth said. "I share your horror with the tradition."

I unfastened my seat belt. "What are you going to do when we find him?"

Seth let out a long breath. "Talk to him. I think I can get him to stop hurting people," he said. "If I could just talk to him."

I heard the longing in his voice, the hope. I didn't share it.

Chapter Thirty-Four

"**D**o you feel him?" I asked.

Seth closed his eyes a moment. "He's close."

I stared out the car window and heard a weird, angry singing from the direction of the river. Like a cross between heavy metal and a baby's cry. "I think he's in the water," I said.

Seth stared at me. "You can *hear* him, too?"

I didn't want to tell him everything, so I looked away. "We should walk. Sneak up on him. Unless he can feel you coming?"

"I learned long ago to turn off his sight through my eyes," he said. "His own control is more unpredictable. I can feel him now but not always."

"Why not?"

"He's drunk," Seth said. "Or maybe just distracted. He's watching the moon and the sun, searching for the boundary of sea and freshwater in the creek as the tide comes in."

Such transitional points in nature were particularly powerful, especially to fairies. They preferred to live in between the two states as much as possible, never committing to one pure condition or another. The dawn, the dusk. The moment water froze or ice melted. A day with both moon and sun in the sky or a night without either.

"What do you think he's doing?" I asked.

"Swimming, I imagine. Enjoying a day at the beach."

"You mean, for fun?"

"He's lake fae. He craves the water. This time of year, the river is too shallow for him. He needs the tidewater flowing upstream to give him room to splash and dive."

I heard the longing in Seth's voice, more sincere emotion I'd ever sensed in him.

"You want your body back," I said softly. "You miss your old life."

"This is the only life I remember. But yes, I am prepared to make an offer to Launt. This body belongs to him. I can't live a full life in it, knowing the bones were stolen."

"You would give up that—" I stopped myself from complimenting his human body's appearance. I didn't want to encourage more of the aggressive flirting he liked to inflict on me. "You said prepared to but not wanting to. Do you mean you'd rather stay in that body?"

"It's complicated." He opened the car door. "Let's go." He looked back at Random, nodded his head, and the dog flopped down on the back seat, sighed, and closed his eyes.

I grabbed my staff and got out of the Jeep, dwelling over the obvious bond between Seth and Random.

"Tell me the truth—is he your dog?"

Seth held his hand up into the air like he'd done earlier, searching for Launt. "Nope. But his ancestors liked the water almost as much as mine." He lowered his voice to a whisper. "Very close."

I adjusted my necklace, checking in with my power, and held the staff, point in the earth, on my right side. "What's your plan?" I asked quietly.

Seth turned to me, his face serious. "If he accepts my offer, you'll know the danger is past and can go, your mind at ease."

"How will I know?"

"In a few minutes, if the short, ugly one tells you you're hot, you'll know it's me." He winked.

"What if he doesn't?"

"Then I'll have to disarm him the only way I know how," Seth said.

I looked at his bare hands, his high-top sneakers, his faded jeans and navy-blue sweatshirt. No fae of any kind could be taken by physical force, but he didn't have any objects on him a witch would consider powerful enough to command an unwilling spirit—no silver, no gemstones. Not even an earring.

"How?" I asked.

"The Protectorate mistook me for a demon, right? There must be something dangerous I can do."

Squeezing my staff, I tried to pull on its power. Only a faint glimmer ran up my arm. "I just want to know why he ran over Tristan."

"And that little thing about almost killing you, not to mention the carpenter," Seth added. "Come to think of it, you should stay here. His power won't be as strong out of the water."

I focused on the path ahead, using my necklace now to concentrate on a thousand possible steps I could take, a blur of still images, almost all of them false, but I didn't know which. I saw Seth and Launt embrace, I saw them jump into the water together and disappear, I saw a flash of light, I saw Launt scream in pain, I saw Seth scream in pain. I felt pain of my own. Most of the images were violent, but some were sweet, with Launt and Seth laughing together like long-lost brothers.

"I'm coming," I said. "You might need my help." And I needed to see whatever happened for myself. A changeling and the human spirit he'd evicted, reuniting under a sliver of moon and afternoon sun—I needed to see such a sight for myself.

The staff under my palm became warm, which was either a sign of impending danger or simply evidence my nervous hands were sweaty. I glanced at Seth, hoping he'd pull something out of his pocket like a shining sword inlayed with rubies, emeralds, and obsidian, but he only rubbed his hands together as if the cold wind off the coast was affecting his circulation.

After only a few minutes' walk, we turned a bend and saw the creek ahead of us, quiet and slow, its surface white in the sunlight and dull black under the trees. On our side of the creek was a narrow, sandy bank with a small figure sitting on it, his side to us and his bare feet in the water.

He wore only a pair of children's running shorts in lemon yellow with white stripes down the legs. His hair was a greenish brown, long and lank, shiny, slimy. His face and shoulders were green, but his belly was as white as a marshmallow.

Now that I knew Launt's fae body had once contained Seth's spirit, I decided it was unusually hideous by any standard, human or fae. It smelled bad. It smelled wrong. Rotten, sour, dangerous. And while a fairy's song should be lovely to hear, if a human was capable or invited to hear it, this fae's voice was cruel and vicious. I had to hold the staff with both hands to stop myself from covering my ears as he sang a song about making babies bleed.

"Regret not waiting at the car?" Seth asked me, sounding cheerful.

"Do something, or I will," I said.

Seth looked over at me, glanced at the staff, and nodded. "You see him?"

I paused. "Yes."

"He won't expect that," Seth said. "Use it to your advantage."

Launt was on his feet now, facing us. Still singing, which was terrifying.

"Anytime now, SD." I bent my knees slightly, preparing for battle. When they'd fired me, the Protectorate had mentioned my clumsiness in hand-to-hand combat, but neither of these supernatural brothers needed to know that.

Seth held out his empty hands in the universal gesture of harmless greeting. His lips moved, but he made no sound I could hear.

For the next minute, Seth continued to speak in the voice I couldn't hear, and Launt continued to sing—unfortunately in a voice I heard only too well, and it was getting louder and louder.

Eventually Seth shook his head and stopped talking. His face twisted with grief. The fairy, still murdering infants with his song, stepped backward into the creek until the water reached his knobby knees. His arms and legs were covered with red spots, and I could see green veins like a network of spiderwebs shining underneath his pale skin from head to toe. He shook his hair, sending water droplets flying, and took another step backward.

I felt power growing between the two but didn't know which one of them was sparking it. Seth stretched out his arms, and for an instant he looked like the vision I'd had of him embracing the estranged fairy-human—but then he brought his hands together in a single loud clap.

The explosion knocked me to my knees. When I recovered enough to lift my head, bracing my weight on the staff to regain my feet, I saw Launt sinking below the surface of the water, his mouth and eyes wide with shock. When he went under, several large bubbles came to the surface and burst foul, yellow gas.

And then Seth fell facedown in the sandy mud, his arms beneath him.

"Seth!" As I stumbled over to him, I sent out my power to feel for his heartbeat, the pumping of his lungs, the magic in every cell of his stolen body.

I crouched down and looked for a safe place to touch him. If the magic was still active, I could be hurt by the contact, but...

Oh hell, I would take the risk. I put both hands on his shoulders and rolled him over to his back. His complexion was ashen and his eyes were closed, but I found a pulse at his throat.

I looked behind me at the creek, searching for Launt. If he was lake fae, I had no chance of finding him here. He could live under the surface indefinitely or float the short distance to the ocean.

"Seth," I said again. "I don't know if I can carry you. I need to get you to a friend of mine. He's better at healing than I am."

Seth's eyelids fluttered open, but his gaze was unfocused. "What happened?"

"You clapped and then everyone fell down," I said.

"Launt?"

"Gone. Under the water."

He closed his eyes. "Whoops."

"Changelings say 'whoops'?"

He started to speak but had to cough first. Then said, "From... Minnesota."

"So you keep saying. You're very proud of that, aren't you?"

He managed a weak grin. "Are my fingers missing? Because it feels like they're missing."

I checked. "They're where they should be." I worked my arm under his back to help him up. "Come on. I can't carry you to the car by myself."

"You can do a lot more than you know," he said.

"You're only saying that because you're too lazy to walk."

"Don't you want to hold my defenseless body? You could do whatever you wanted to me right now, and I'd have to let you."

"Save your energy for walking," I said.

He chuckled, but his eyes were closed, and I had to support most of his weight to get him to his feet.

"I'd tell you to leave me here, but then Launt might hurt you," he mumbled.

"He looked in pretty bad shape himself when he went under."

Seth coughed, turned his head to the side, and spat a mouthful of blood. "That explains a little," he whispered.

"What?"

He shook his head. "Need to focus. Walking."

It took us ten minutes to reach the car. Every few steps he had to stop, cough, spit, and offer to be my boyfriend again. Random was sticking his head out the window, watching for us, and jumped out and ran over in spite of Seth's feeble commands to stay in the car. I already half believed Random was his dog and didn't try to interfere in their reunion.

"Easy, buddy," Seth said, too weak to stop Random from jumping up on him.

"Sit," I said.

Seth leaned against the Jeep. "I'll wait until I get in the car. I'm not sure I can"—he coughed, spat—"get up again."

I opened the passenger door, dragged a frantic Random

into the back seat, and helped Seth climb in. When I was finally behind the wheel, I asked, "What happened to you?"

Seth leaned back in the seat and closed his eyes. "Not good."

"I can see that. But was Launt able to do this to you? How could a lake fairy—"

"What I'm feeling, he's feeling," Seth said. "I think."

I pulled out of our narrow parking spot in the dirt and headed for the road home. Heavier fog had rolled in, reducing the daylight, erasing shadows. The drive through the trees was a flat, dim gray. I turned on the heater and headlights.

"Did your spell reflect back on you because you're bonded?" I asked.

"I don't use spells," he said. "I'm not a witch."

"I don't understand what you are."

"The first step on the path to truth is to learn what you do not know," he said.

The Protectorate had taught me demons were liars who could convince people of anything. His claim to being a changeling could be a clever trick that preyed upon my desire to uncover secrets. As Helen had said, I coveted knowledge.

"What I don't know is why I'm helping you," I said. "I should've driven that spike into your heart that night. Right now I'd be sitting in a nice, cozy condo in Pacific Heights, watching sailboats floating on the bay, telling my app to get me takeout dim sum."

When he didn't reply, I looked at him. His head had slumped to one side, tilted back too far, and his mouth was open.

"Seth," I said loudly, grabbing his knee. "I don't mean it. Stay with me."

Without moving his head, he mumbled, "Aren't you clingy."

Random was trying to climb into the front seat to lick Seth to death, and I was tempted to help him do it. The death part, not the licking. I wished I'd never met him.

But who else was going to help me understand what was going on? Jasper had asked me to leave him out of it.

Well, too bad for Jasper, because he was going to have to help me now, like it or not. He had that potion in his kitchen that had helped me so much; maybe it could help a demon. Or a changeling. Whatever he was.

Chapter Thirty-Five

Before hitting Silverpool's shopping district, I turned left on the road to Jasper's house. If the wellspring had been in season, I might've risked running down the ravine for a drop of the water to help Seth. But with it dry and the spells triggered the last time I'd visited, it wasn't worth the risk. Thinking Seth was a demon, the Protectorate spells would be much worse the second time around.

And Seth didn't look like he was up for much of a fight. His skin was ashen and shiny, and his breath rattled. The coughing came more frequently now, and he'd bloodied the rag I kept in the car for wiping the morning condensation off the mirrors and windows.

It was worth the risk of telling Jasper about him. As an independent witch, he was under no magical obligation to kill dangerous supernatural creatures. Moral and social, possibly, as were all normal people. But Jasper was an independent thinker.

"Where—" Seth began, cracking open an eye.

"Witch friend," I said.

"No, no, no," Seth said. He bent over, coughing.

"We'll just—" I drove up the hill, turned, and saw Jasper's cottage under the trees.

And Phoebe's car in his driveway.

I braked so suddenly Random stumbled over the center console and head-butted my elbow. Throwing the Jeep in reverse, I drew upon my power for a quick hiding spell. It would only work if they weren't watching for visitors.

What was she doing at Jasper's?

"What's going on?" Seth asked.

I turned the Jeep around as quickly but silently as possible, focusing on hiding the roar of the engine and the bumping of its knobby wheels in the potholes. When I was headed downhill, I put one hand on my necklace to strengthen the spell.

Seth waited a few minutes before speaking again. "Fae? A lot of them around that place."

"Witch," I said. "A young agent from the Protectorate who is not my friend."

"With someone who is?"

"Yes. But it looks like she's with him at the moment. He doesn't know anything about the torc or Protectorate politics, but… she's got it in for me."

"The torc?"

Under stress, I'd forgotten I wasn't going to tell him about that. "Something they think my father stole."

"Ah—" His words were interrupted by another coughing fit.

Jasper talked bitterly about the Protectorate, but hadn't he wished he'd been an agent? Was it all just sour grapes?

My instincts told me that if Phoebe offered him a way in, Jasper would jump at the chance to fulfill an old dream he was too ashamed to admit he still had.

Had she already made him an offer?

It was only another few minutes to my house. When I parked in the driveway, I kept an eye on Seth to see if the fortress of protective spells were hurting him, but because he was already in such bad shape, I couldn't tell. If I kept my hand on him, guiding him through my property myself, the magic should welcome him inside.

Should.

Luckily Willy wasn't near his tree when I helped Seth into the backyard and up the steps to my kitchen door. Instinct told me they wouldn't like each other at all. Loyal domestic gnome and changeling... No, that felt like ancient animosity brew to me.

Seth staggered over the threshold, throwing the bloody rag at the new gargoyle I'd set behind the recycling bin, whether by intention or accident I wasn't sure, and then into the living room.

"Let me rest here," he said, sprawling on the sofa. "I'll be fine. I just need—"

I ran to the bathroom to get him an old towel to bleed on. My furniture wasn't fancy, but it was all I had.

While he coughed his guts out, my worry intensified.

"I have some herbal tea," I began.

He swore, rolling his eyes.

"It's from a witch in San Francisco who really knows her stuff," I said.

"Useless," he gasped. "On me. For... this."

"For what? What happened to you?"

He smiled blearily. "I stole a human body and then harmed my true one."

"So it's what, bad karma?"

He turned serious. "Exactly. That's exactly what it is. You understand."

I didn't understand anything, but I could see he didn't have much time. The signs of demon death, so eagerly sought by the avenging Protectorate agent, were all present: waxy complexion, perspiration, bloody cough, muscle weakness.

"For a changeling, you sure look like a sick demon," I said.

"Possession," he gasped. "Same costs."

I hurried to my file cabinet and opened the bottom drawer. Breaking through my own guardian spells took a minute I might not have had; I heard Seth's coughs growing weaker.

But as soon as I pulled out the vial of wellspring water, he sat up and began to protest with renewed energy.

"No," he said. "I can't."

"Why not?"

He closed his eyes. "Addictive personality," he said weakly. "Dangerous."

"It's that or die," I said. "What's it going to be?"

He let out a long sigh. After a moment, he lifted his head. "Fine."

"I'll just give you a little," I said, tipping the vial onto my fingertip and then pressing my finger to his lips.

With a shudder, he licked the drop off my skin. There was nothing pleasurable about it for either of us. Wellspring water captured the fae's attention like nothing else on earth. The Protectorate believed demons were drawn to wellsprings because it made the fae vulnerable, easy to catch, consume, destroy.

He sat up and wiped the sweat off his brow. "Please put the rest of that poison away."

I corked the vial and held it behind my back. "Are you all right now?"

The color had returned to his cheeks, and his lips were no

longer thin and cracked. "If you don't put the springwater someplace secure, I'll rip you apart to get it."

I'd heard Seth make a lot of jokes, and that didn't sound like one of them.

I put the vial away. And locked the cabinet with every spell I could remember off the top of my head and a few I made up on the spot.

"I swore never to touch the stuff," he said.

"To yourself?"

"To my fae mother." He was looking better every second. The sparkle was back in his eyes, which wasn't a good thing. "She had other plans for me, like mating with a nice human girl such as yourself."

Against my will, I shuddered. Something about the thought of a water fae thousands of miles away stealing human bodies for breeding made me want to reopen the cabinet, take out the iron spike I'd kept as a memento, and drive it through his skull.

"I was just kidding," he said. "Don't look so disgusted."

"Don't be so disgusting." I sat on the floor and took a moment to catch my breath. Seth wasn't going to die anytime soon, but Launt was free or dead. "Could Launt have killed Tristan?"

Seth paused. "No. He's working for somebody else."

"What? The fae are organized like that?"

"No, they are not. Not yet, anyway."

"Demons?" I asked.

"Please. Demons rather liked Tristan. He made deals with them sometimes. Not a bad witch, really."

"I thought you hated him."

He grinned. "Personal reasons. Not professional."

"Did *you* kill him?"

"It's interesting you asked me that question *after* you saved my life."

"I asked you before, too. You didn't answer. I kept you alive so I can get the truth out of you."

"The truth," Seth said. He opened his mouth and froze, eyes widening. "You've got some good magic in here. I just tried to lie to you, and I couldn't."

"Why should I believe that?" I asked. "You could just be saying that so I swallow the lie you feed me next."

He chuckled and got to his feet, smiling at me with blood-spattered lips. "You're cute when you're smart."

"Go home and wash up," I said. "Where is home, anyway?"

"The only home I deserve is inside that ugly body you saw earlier today. When I get out of this witchy house, I'll track him down again." He walked to the front door, rubbing his mouth with my bath towel.

"Could he be dead?"

Seth closed his eyes. "Not now," he said. "You gave me the wellspring water. That saved both of us."

"Great," I said flatly.

"I suppose I'm grateful."

"I suppose I'm not," I said.

He laughed. "Alma, I'm going to miss you."

Before I could stop him, he'd thrown the second towel against another gargoyle and walked out the front door.

I hurried after him to see where he went, but he'd already disappeared.

At 11:59 p.m., I received a summons from the Protectorate. A male witch in his late teens roared up my driveway in a motorcycle, banged on my back door, and greeted me in a black leather jacket heavily decorated with silver zippers, gold buttons, steel snaps, buckles, and chains. Even the thread had strands of silver woven into it.

Barefoot and groggy, I wore only an old T-shirt and running shorts. I'd intentionally left my staff out of sight inside the doorway and locked Random in the bedroom, where he now barked furiously. As soon as I'd woken and seen the time, I'd known what kind of summons this was.

To put up any resistance would be to invite violence upon my person.

"Alma Bellrose, you are hereby instructed to deliver your-self to the San Francisco Diamond Street office," the boy said. He had very short hair and warm brown skin and looked about fifteen, although I hoped he was older. The Protectorate wasn't supposed to give a silver jacket to anyone under sixteen. And he wouldn't be alone; another pair of witches, more powerful and important than he was, would be waiting outside the periphery of my protected property. I hadn't heard their vehicle, but they were there.

"Now?" I asked.

"You are expected at first light," he said.

First light. Seriously? The ancient operating procedure had made more sense before everyone was forced to drive motorized vehicles on crowded six-lane highways to get around. The witches in the *olde dayes* had been imagining a stroll across the village green, not a two-and-a-half-hour slog in bumper-to-bumper California traffic.

I glanced at the night sky. "When is that on a real clock, exactly? I don't live by the old ways anymore."

Without moving his head, he glanced to either side, obviously unsure. He'd been given a message and nothing more.

I raised my voice. "When is that on a real clock, please? Hello? You guys probably know."

A man's voice, unsure and annoyed, called out from the darkness. "Can't you Google it?"

"I lost my phone. I need you to look it up for me." I watched the boy in the jacket, considering how much power it would take to drive him off my property. It was tempting. I was angry. But it was probably wiser to be difficult in less obvious ways. "You don't want me to be late for some stupid reason like that, do you?"

"Just show up early," a third voice shouted. It sounded as if she was halfway down the street. They must've heard scary stories about me from Phoebe, which made me happier than I wanted to admit. When I'd left the Protectorate, everyone had been laughing at me for being weak.

Pushing aside the rosemary branches, I stepped out next to the messenger in the silver coat. He jumped back about three feet.

"And wake up Lorne before he's ready?" I called out again. "You want to be the one to knock on his bedroom door?"

"I'll look it up," the kid said, holding up his phone. "Just… stay in your house."

"But I thought I was supposed to go to San Francisco."

He took another step backward, glancing nervously between me and the phone. "At first light, which is…" He tripped over an overgrown agapanthus.

"Just be there at six a.m.," the other man called out. "We'll tell him we said six."

"You're sure?"

"Raynor will tell him. Don't worry," the kid said.

"Hey," the man said. "I told you not to share my name."

I knew Raynor by reputation. An Emerald-level agent based out of New York, he was considered the best demon hunter in the United States.

Lorne had sent *Raynor* to bring me in? I had to admit I was flattered. Amazing what a little pee floor wash would do.

"I'll be there," I said. "By the way, what's the charge?"

The kid in silver, moving away without ever showing me his back, paused and looked at somebody over his shoulder, then back to me.

"You're a person of interest in the murder of Protector Tristan Price," he said.

Chapter Thirty-Six

S o, they were going to try blaming me for everything. Surely they knew I hadn't done anything, but simply wanted to punish me to get to my father—right?

I wished I knew for sure.

Raynor and the woman left first, leaving me with the kid and his Ducati. Teens could be dangerous driving a family minivan; an Italian sport bike would be suicidal. And I wanted a few hours to prepare.

The moment he roared away, I ran to my bedroom to soothe Random and prepare him for a trip to Birdie's house. I had no idea how long it would take them to be convinced I hadn't killed Tristan—several well-equipped mages at the Protectorate office could get the truth out of most people in a few days—but they might keep me longer if they'd discovered I'd found the body and hadn't reported it. An agent would've called Diamond Street office immediately. A fired agent, in my opinion, had no such obligation.

It was almost one in the morning when I brought Random and his food over to Birdie's house. He was happy to trot over to her place and jumped up on her enthusiastically when she opened the door.

"I'm so sorry if I woke you, but—" I began.

"I wasn't asleep. I got all turned around, being in jail and then napping all day." Birdie squatted down and laughed as Random licked her face. "His breath isn't very good. Do people ever give dogs mouthwash? I've never had a dog. I'd be tempted to get out the mouthwash, but maybe that would kill them. That would be horrible, to kill a dog just because their breath smelled nasty. That wouldn't be right. Cruel and unusual—"

"Listen, I need to ask a favor. I need to go away for a little while, hopefully back by tomorrow night, but—"

"No hurry. I can keep him forever." She smiled behind Random's busy tongue.

"It won't be forever." I hoped. "I plan on being back as soon as possible."

"Right, right." She scratched Random's skull, gazing down at him, and they gave each other melting, open-mouthed smiles.

"I brought his food." I set a tote bag just inside the doorway. "And his bowls. He likes to go on walks, not that I've been able to—"

"We will so go on walk, yes we will, yes we will," she exclaimed, using a high-pitched voice that made Random lose control of himself, running and jumping and panting.

"Thanks so much," I said.

"Is there anything else?"

I stared at her, then at Random, who had trotted into her house and was sniffing the floor, making himself at home. "No," I said. "Thanks again."

Birdie closed the door, and her cheerful voice continued. A pang struck my heart, and I considered knocking and asking for him back—he could come with me to San Francisco, stay at Helen's again—but that would be selfish of me. I needed to face this challenge by myself.

Knowing I would need to be sharp, I tried to grab an hour or two of sleep before I left, but it was hopeless. Around two in the morning, shooting a final, longing glance at Birdie's dark house, I hit the road. I could get to San Francisco more quickly leaving early, and it might give me time to talk to Helen. If she was willing to answer the door, she might tell me if she'd overheard anything through the window.

If she was willing. I couldn't risk bringing the remaining wellspring water with me to pay for her information; the Protectorate agents might find it on me and have a real crime to charge me with. Witches passed around tiny amounts all the time, but if they wanted to charge me with something, it would be a convenient excuse.

Even though I was anxious, I almost nodded off a few times as I drove south in the dark, quiet night. A can of coffee helped a little. So did chewing on a bouquet of peppermint leaves that made my lips numb.

When I was in the city, several blocks away from Diamond Street, I parked at the top of a steep hill overlooking the Castro. Cars lined up perpendicular to a sidewalk that was so steep it had stairs. Lorne wouldn't be expecting me for at least two more hours.

I took a roundabout path to Diamond, finally walking down a hidden pedestrian stairway through an urban forest in the middle of the block to reach Helen's house. If she could tell me what Lorne thought he knew—

"Alma Bellrose," Raynor said, stepping out of the shadows on the stairs. A colossal man, he could look down at me even from several steps below.

I hadn't felt the slightest hint of him waiting in the shadows. Apparently the demon killer deserved his impressive reputation.

"It's hours before first light," I said, brushing past him. Like me, he reeked of coffee.

"Lorne will appreciate your consideration in coming early. He's eager to talk to you." He followed less than a step behind me, as if I'd try to run away.

I didn't look at Helen's house as we walked past it to the Protectorate building, but I sent a silent alarm in the form of a rattling window, exaggerating the noise from an approaching garbage truck.

The Protectorate house windows were lit, even the room upstairs I used to inhabit when I worked there. That, more than anything, made me nervous. Midnight was a popular time for witches, but at four in the morning, even the youngest, most energetic witches should've been asleep.

I walked up the steps to the portico and waited. Knocking would be redundant. They knew we were there.

"Touch the plate," Raynor said. Next to the door was a shiny metallic square about the same size as the button for an automatic door but freshly polished. "Like this." He held up his hand, palm out, fingers splayed, but didn't touch the plate himself.

That was new, and I didn't like it. Formal submission to metal at the doorway put me in the power of the witch who had cast it until I left the building.

I looked up at Raynor. He was at least six five, with every muscle that magic, DNA, and nonmag science could get him.

He gave me a pitying smile. "You have no choice. And we both know you're no match for me. You may have had power over Lorne and a Flint in your own kitchen, but here, with me—" He raised an eyebrow. "Don't bother trying."

I put my face in my hands and sighed, trying to look as if

my Incurable Inability was the great tragedy of my life. Meanwhile, I brought up a generous mouthful of spit and licked the skin of my palms. If I was lucky, it would form a protective barrier. The bushel of peppermint I'd consumed should help strengthen the potency.

The first birds had begun to sing, and I was exhausted. I didn't have to fake my yawn as I tapped my palm on the plate. I hope he didn't notice the wet smear on the metal.

"Good girl," Raynor said. "Now give me your silver."

"I don't have any."

"The chain of your necklace."

The door opened to a young male app in a gray suit. He said nothing but bowed to Raynor.

I didn't want to give up my power so easily. "The chain is too thin to matter," I said. "Surely."

"Don't waste Mage Raynor's time," the app said.

Nodding, I reached up to my wood bead necklace with its silver chain, stepped into the doorway, and gave the young witch a painful butt pimple right before I unclasped the necklace and handed it to Raynor.

"So sorry," I muttered.

The app in gray was tugging at his trousers as we walked by.

"Lorne's office is—" Raynor began.

"I know where it is." I strode past him, took two short steps to my right, opened a glass door, and then climbed up a steep, narrow staircase to the top floor. From there I walked left, through another small door, down a hallway, and then to another door. Helen's house with its rooftop garden was on the other side of the wall to my right.

I put my hand on the plaster and sent out a thought—

The door opened.

"Alma, child." Lorne stood before me. Like his app downstairs, he wore a gray suit, although his clothes matched his gray hair and gray eyes. Even his teeth were gray. Seriously, the witch was a black-and-white photograph.

"You must be terrified," he said.

"Of you?"

His phony smile froze on his face. "Of the fae. If you help us, you have nothing to fear."

"The fae?"

He jerked his head for me to enter. "Let's talk. I really hope you'll be cooperative."

Knowing he would have other mages working to determine the truth of anything I said, I chose my words carefully as I stepped over the threshold. "I'll help if I can."

What I was capable of doing was a gray area, which gave me wiggle room to tell half-truths. Since gray was his favorite color, he should've liked it.

"You were smart to come right away," Lorne said. "Silverpool has gone wild, and much of the North Bay is simmering with fairy mobs. Sporadic fae violence has been reported over the Bay Area."

"But—"

"Since Tristan's death, nonmag police departments we monitor have reported an increase in minor acts of vandalism. Theft. Inexplicable alterations in the landscape."

He couldn't seriously be blaming me for weird fae activity like that. "Landscape?"

"Seemed to erase Mount Tamalpais. Obviously they couldn't keep up the illusion for more than a few seconds, but that was long enough to alarm the nonmag populace."

I looked around his office. He'd replaced all the ornate Victorian décor and woodwork with hard modern angles. Lots of glass and steel, everything in gray and white, as colorless as he was. I chose a chair near the wall, just in case Helen was there listening. "What could any of that have to do with Tristan's death? Or me?"

"The torc was stolen the same night," he said.

"Look, I don't know anything about the torc." I said it loudly and clearly. Let them sift through every syllable with the best magic they had. It was true.

He paused, as if expecting an agent to rush into the room and tell him I was lying.

But he finally said, "We know your father took it."

"Why not blame the fae? We don't know how powerful they—"

"We know it was your father, Alma. We know it."

I clamped my mouth shut. If I tried to argue with him, the verity spells would catch my insincerity.

"Why all this activity now that it's stolen?" I asked finally.

He cleared his throat. "Tristan reported the poisoning of some kind of fairy in Silverpool two weeks ago. We have evidence of additional fae deaths in the past week."

"Deaths," I whispered, thinking of the mob in the forest. Only magic could kill the fae. "And now they want revenge."

"Yes," he said.

"OK. They're upset. What does that have to do with me?"

"Alma, please," he said. "Surely after all this time you aren't loyal to your father. When he wasn't dragging you into his life of Shadow, he abandoned you with strangers."

"I'm not loyal to him," I said. "That's why you should believe me. I don't know anything about him, the torc, the poison—"

"But Tristan did. And now Tristan is dead," Lorne said.

"Yes. I know."

He steepled his fingers. "What do you know about a witch named Sheila Zalek?"

The abrupt change of topic unnerved me. "Who?"

"You claim not to know her name?"

"I don't know the name," I said. "Never heard of her. Who was she?"

"You were seen sharing a meal with her nonmagical boyfriend. He wore a witch's chain that was visible to all who saw him." He gave me a gloating look. "I'll be generous and allow you to change your statement now. How long have you known Sheila Zalek? Where did you meet?"

Nick's ex-girlfriend was mixed up with the Protectorate? And now he was dead. What did that mean? "I only met Nick Takata that once to ask about a carpentry project. I noticed the witch's chain, and he said it was his ex-girl-friend's. That's it. I didn't know her name, and I certainly never met her. He wouldn't talk about her."

"She was Freewitch, as I'm sure you know. We found her body yesterday after tracking the chain on Nick Takata's body to her house in Belvedere." He held out his hands. "So you see, we know nearly everything. We just need you to fill in the gaps. For your own sake. Your confession is the only thing that will save you."

Hadn't Nick said he was working on a job in Belvedere? Maybe he saw his ex-girlfriend more often than he'd implied. And she'd killed him, or somebody had killed them both…

"Well?"

"I've never met her," I said. "I've never heard that name before."

Lorne glanced expectantly at the empty couch. Then he frowned at the empty air and snapped his head to face me again. "How well did you know Tristan?"

I shrugged. "I slept with him." That wasn't admitting anything important. After all, who hadn't?

"Tristan hired Malcolm to steal the torc."

I tried to look shocked, although it was what I'd suspected when I'd found the cabinet. "Hm." Where had he put it? Who had it now?

"Your father stole the torc for Tristan but then killed him to keep the money and the torc for himself," Lorne said.

"My father would never kill anyone," I said. I still believed that. "Not even for— What exactly does the torc do?"

Lorne frowned. "Don't you know?"

I raised my voice. "I don't know what power the torc holds. I don't know who took it. I don't know where it is." My words bounced over the modern Scandinavian design like marbles on concrete. Surely somebody was sitting there, under magical cover, listening to me and weighing my honesty.

Lorne's expression, which until now had been conciliatory, even bargaining, became contemptuous. "You don't know," he said sarcastically.

"I don't."

There was a long silence. No reply from the invisible truth-screeners.

He scowled at something behind me, his face reddening. "Get her out of here. She's lying to us." There was a pause. "I don't know how, but she is. Put her upstairs until you figure out how."

I glanced at the black, armless leather sofa. "Who are you talking to?"

"You went too far, Alma," Lorne said. "I might have believed you if you hadn't gotten carried away."

I felt my arms and legs grabbed by invisible clamps—like fingers but icy cold and hard—and jerked upward. My butt came out of the chair and bumped a silver orb off Lorne's coffee table as I floated past.

"Careful," he snapped.

I hung my head back and met his gaze. "I'm more graceful when I'm allowed to walk myself."

"Enough. Shut her up." Lorne pointed at the sofa again, and in a moment I felt my lips glue together.

The invisible hands hauled me out of the room and into the hallway and up another flight of stairs to the attic. Oh, not good. Maybe I should've made something up, something they wanted to hear.

How could I convince them? Would they ever believe me? Nobody would come fight for me, certainly not my father.

Adding insult to injury, a dozen agents, some I recognized, stared at me with narrow-eyed suspicion from three rows of desks. Most of them, I knew, had invisible blankets and pillows hidden under their chairs. Lorne only pretended to mind. The dormer windows and their lovely view were heavily curtained to encourage work and prevent daydreaming.

Their beds were more comfortable than mine was likely to be.

Wrists and ankles stinging from supporting my own weight, I floated away from my old pals toward a door at the other end of the attic. It flew open, I flew in, and then everything went dark.

Chapter Thirty-Seven

I don't know how long the sedation spell kept me dazed and stupid on the floor, but when I came to, I felt as if I'd been in a drunken bar brawl. After taking a moment to remember where I was, I turned my attention to my surroundings.

I felt rough wooden planks under my hands, heavily grooved and pitted with the years, but no dust or grit. I could smell flowers, a burnt potion. A dove was cooing nearby.

Opening my eyes, I saw I was alone in a tiny room, perhaps a converted closet. It wasn't completely sealed away; a window was closed and shuttered, but not magically. The old building had shifted more than enough over the decades to leave a gap around the frame.

I got to my feet and crept over to investigate. Very carefully I held my hand over the latch of the shutter. A small buzz shot out and bounced against my palm.

It didn't hold. I smiled and cracked open the shutter. The sky was bright with midday sun shining through a heavy layer of fog.

The spell set into the metal plate at the front entrance had been designed to prevent me from touching any boundary object inside the house—door or window. But my bare skin hadn't touched the plate the night before. The spit had worked.

Don't get cocky, I told myself, wiping the smile off my face. I was still trapped in the attic, and my head was pounding.

But it had been so sweet to fool Raynor, the famous demon hunter.

I lifted my wrist to my face and sniffed the residue of magic clinging to my skin. The shackles he'd carried me with had been a powerfully unpleasant touch. No furry padding for Raynor's bondage gear; it had been horribly plain. A man who was comfortable with his role as a judge, jury, and executioner, with the power to act like a god.

But not this time. I unlatched the window and pushed it open as high as it would go. There was no screen, no security bars.

I indulged in another smile. There were advantages to being underestimated. But now the hard part would begin.

As a security precaution, the Protectorate didn't allow shape-shifting within the walls of its offices and had global spells woven into each structure. Too distracting for daily business to wonder if that mouse skittering by your desk was a rodent, a Shadow witch, or your boss.

I would have to find another way to get down to the ground.

Above me in the hills, the thick fog covered Sutro Tower and Diamond Heights, limiting my view to the neighboring houses, the elementary schoolyard up the hill, the Protectorate backyard, Helen's rooftop garden next door, Helen…

Helen.

A floor below, she was sitting on the glass roof of her

conservatory, feeding parts of her bagel to a dove perched on her knee. Once again I was impressed with the irritable woman.

She caught me watching and waved. After shoving the rest of her bagel in her bra, she made the old-fashioned hand gesture for telephone, thumb and pinkie extended at the side of her face.

For a second I thought she was actually suggesting I pick up the phone. Then I remembered that I was, like her, a witch, and although the Protectorate had cast countless spells over the house, communication might not be one of them. They'd taken my beads, but those were primarily for amplifying my power. I didn't depend on them. Helen was strong, and she was close—I could try to use her the same way.

I propped my elbows in the open window and focused on her eyes.

"Hello," I said softly. At the very least, we could try to read lips.

Frowning, she wiggled her hand, still splayed out next to her cheek.

She was old and eccentric and seemed to want me to do what she was doing. I brought my hand to the side of my head in the same gesture. "Hello," I said into my pinkie finger, feeling ridiculous.

She grinned. "That's better." Her voice was muffled, as if we were children in a swimming pool, playing games with each other under the water.

"They're convinced I know something," I said. "I need to get out of here."

"Yeah," she said. "No kidding."

"I'm going to land on your roof."

She flapped her hands and shook her head. "No, no. Not mine."

"I have to," I said.

Helen pointed at the neighboring property on the other side. Even if I could've reached it, landing there would be pointless; when I'd worked at the Protectorate, the Emerald-level witch in charge of security had lived there.

"You don't have to do anything, just let me—" I began.

Helen flung down the imaginary phone and turned her face away, reclining on her chair as if she were on the beach in Maui, not a care in the world.

For Shadow's sake. I turned away myself and paced around the little room. Who else could rescue me from the Protectorate? My own father would sell me out if it would help him. Jasper was nice, but he had his own life, and we weren't close enough for him to risk his neck for mine. Birdie was sweet but knew nothing of magic. Even if she had inherited power from Tristan, she didn't know about the Protectorate and certainly not how to get me out of it.

I'd let myself become too isolated in the world. In limited ways I'd leaned on Tristan, but Tristan was dead. I had to look out for myself.

The window had been charmed to keep me from opening it, but I'd opened it. If I'd been able to turn into a cat, I'd take my chances with the gutters and drainpipe and wall trellis, and climb out.

But I couldn't shift. I stuck my head out the window and looked down, left, right, and up. The only witch I saw was Helen, still on her roof. She'd retrieved the bagel from her bra and was eating it.

I stuck out a hand, then an arm. No resistance, no magic. The only security was the spell they thought they'd put on me at the front door.

To my surprise, I felt insulted. They never expected me to be daring. To them I was just a coward with an Incurable Inability.

And if they couldn't get anything out of me to solve the

mystery, they would keep me in custody anyway, even if they didn't think I had anything to do with it. Lorne could assure New York that they'd apprehended an accomplice, possibly the culprit herself. A disgruntled former employee. A born criminal. Nobody from New York would have to come and poke around San Francisco Protectorate business. Lorne's magical ineptitude could go unchallenged another day.

Something furious and powerful rose up from deep inside me. I retreated to the room, audibly buzzing with rage magic. This was the feeling you were supposed to tap into before you killed a demon. Zap. Boom. Dead. Until now, I'd never felt it.

Until now.

Chapter Thirty-Eight

I stopped pacing and sat cross-legged on the floor. Holding my breath, I pulled nine long hairs from the crown of my head and spread them carefully on my thigh.

I split the nine into three piles of three and then slowly knotted all hairs together at the top, having to stop several times to lick my fingers to keep them from floating away. When they were all tied together, I brought the knot to my lips with a spell of intention, imagining its length and strength, and then lowered my hands.

A loud banging drew my attention to the door. It wasn't on my door but in the hallway outside, where the apps would be walking during their daily grind. There was an explosion, a long pause, then laughter. The distinct odor of pizza wafted through the cracks in the doorway.

Lunchtime. Pizzas at the Protectorate weren't usually acquired legally. Somebody would wait in the windows of the top floor until a car delivering takeout for one of Noe Valley's restaurants approached. Everyone would gather, link hands to enhance their talents, and practice teleportation. The results could be messy—thus the explosion—but something edible usually made it through.

If the agents were busy fishing from Uber Eats cars for lunch, they might be too distracted to notice anything odd happening in the backyard. Now was the time to move.

I braided my hair into a focus string, careful not to fumble in my haste. Each turn of the plait was stronger than the one before, and as I worked I sent a Rapunzel vision into my hands, filling each hair with ambitions of grandeur. When I ran out of hair, I pinched the ends together and brought them to my lips. Holding them in my mouth, I walked over to the window and slung a leg out without looking down. If I thought about what I was doing and how I'd never done it before, I might lose my nerve.

As the wind blew the featherweight braid against my cheek, I pulled my other leg through and sat on the sill, bent over to fit in the window, remembering what it was like to be a cat. A graceful, fearless cat. I couldn't be one, but I could evoke the attitude.

I flipped onto my belly, butt in the air, and dangled my legs out the window. Then I pinched the braid, removing it from my lips, and reached it into the room as I cast a small gravity spell to pull the window down.

Just as the window shut, I brought Rapunzel to life. My delicate braid became a monstrous rope with a life of its own, rippling and grasping, swinging outward. I didn't want it to fall down into the Protectorate backyard, which was surrounded by high fencing on all sides—I needed to get about twenty yards to the right. To Helen's roof. She might not help me, but she wouldn't actually act against me, right?

I told myself to think cat, kitty, feline. Nine lives. Meow.

Helen frowned at the end of the rope as it landed beside her. Shaking her head, she picked it up, turned away, and climbed off the roof of her conservatory, dropping out of sight.

For a few terrified breaths, I waited to see if she would anchor her end of the rope. If not, my journey would be brief and much more vertical than I preferred.

And then: a sharp tension in the rope told me she'd done as I hoped. I nearly fell out the window in relief.

Now I had to try another trick: invisibility. Raynor—I assumed he was the other witch in Lorne's office—had given me the idea. If he could do it, why not me? My father had never succeeded at invisibility, much to his shame because he'd attempted it many times, so I'd never really tried myself.

Nothing like the threat of imminent, painful death to clarify the mind. As I turned my focus to camouflage, I discovered the rope of my own hair was like an antenna for my powers, providing more amplification than my confiscated redwood beads. Had I known that, I would've extended the enchantment to the rope itself before I'd jumped out the window. Too late now. I drew the bubble of invisibility around myself and hooked a leg over the rope to begin my journey. When it seemed to hold, I grabbed it with both hands, swung my other leg over, and began wiggling my way beneath it down the line.

My first thought was that I needed to go to the salon for an intensive conditioning treatment. On my head, my hair seemed silky enough, but under my bare hands—damn. Tree bark would've been softer.

Kitty, kitty, I'm a kitty, I told myself.

But the amplification of the rope had changed the balance of power, and now as I clung to the rope, more than twenty feet of open air beneath me, I felt my fingers tingle with the beginning of emerging claws.

Not now! I wrapped my hands with its opposable thumbs around the rope and told myself I was a human being. I only needed to slide upside down a few seconds longer. A minute at the most. I was wriggling as fast as I could go.

It took all my strength to avoid hitting the lattice top of the fence between the Protectorate and Helen's house as I glided past, and then I was accelerating through potted lemon trees and vertical trellises heavy with bougainvillea to the deck.

The rope came to an end near a yellow lawn chair. To function as an anchor, she'd placed the remains of her bagel, little more than a mouthful, on the loose end, and now stretched out in full recline as she waited for me to arrive.

I landed on my butt, let go of the rope, and collapsed spread-eagled, breathing hard and maybe whimpering a little.

"Alma?" Helen was staring at my general direction but not into my eyes.

I sat up, proud of myself. "Can you really not see me? Or are you just humoring me?"

She blinked hard a few times. "There you are. Good one." She scowled. "Where'd you learn that trick?"

"Oh, it's just a little something I picked up."

"You forgot to hide the rope," she said.

"I needed you to see it, didn't I?"

She removed the bagel from the rope, which went flying into the air. "Now would be a good time to make it invisible. I don't want the Protectorate agents climbing over to bother me."

"I don't think I can. It's too big now."

"Do something. It's your hair."

The rope was swaying over our heads like a water snake. "If I could touch it, I could shrink it back into its original size."

"Put your hand on your head, you fool. That's the only hair you need."

I did as she said, felt the hum of the power in the massive hair extension, and reluctantly sent the enchantment into itself. On my next breath, it was gone. All that remained were the original nine strands of my hair, in its natural size, wedged into the attic window next door.

It took me a moment to recover from the loss of so much power. In fact, I had the sudden need to sit down and found myself collapsed in a ball under the lemon tree planter.

A heavy jacket fell over my head and shoulders. "Take this," Helen said. "And then get the hell out of here."

"I don't feel very good. I think I need to stay"—I yawned —"a few minutes. Just a few minutes." My vision was going dark.

"You have to pay the price for that pretty spell, but not yet. Tell your body to wait until you're safe to let yourself rest," she said. "This is the first place they'll come looking."

Knowing she was right, I staggered to my feet and took deep, invigorating breaths. I'd been up all night, knocked out, magically drained… I was running on fumes.

I pushed my arms into the jacket, a fleece anorak that reeked of sage. Some kind of burr, clinging to the cuff, scraped my wrist. Turning my face away from the Protectorate house, I walked inside to Helen's kitchen.

Helen closed the door to the deck and waved her hand over the latch. It made a sizzling sound like eggs on a hot griddle. Then she walked over to the table and sat down, brushing imaginary crumbs off the surface, still not answering my question. Knowing Helen, she was probably thinking about demanding payment for my trespassing.

"I don't have any wellspring water with me this time," I said. "You'll have to help me out of the goodness of your heart."

"Do you have the torc?"

"Of course I don't have the stupid torc."

"Don't get snippy. It was a simple question," she said.

"If I had it, I wouldn't be here. I'd hand it over to Lorne and be cleared."

"Oh, don't do that," Helen said. "You'd be much better off keeping it for yourself."

"I would?"

"You would." She raised an eyebrow.

I slapped my hands on the kitchen counter. "You know what it does!" I declared. "Tell me."

"One condition."

I thought of the Protectorate building next door. Any minute now they would notice I was gone and send up the alarm. "Name it," I said.

"One vial of springwater, drawn at midsummer under a full moon."

"There is no springwater at midsummer," I said. "That's—"

"There is with the torc," she said.

I paused to absorb the implications of that. "The torc makes a wellspring in summer?"

"Not just anywhere. It has to be a natural site already, like the one in Silverpool. The torc can draw it from deep underground. Not just a little trickle, but deep, unlimited quantities. Water drawn that way at midsummer should have special qualities. I'd like to learn what." She nodded, scratched her armpit. "So that's what you'll get for me. Please don't get caught before you can make it happen."

If the torc could make springwater, that made it valuable to demons and fae as well as humans. Anyone might have taken it or kill to acquire it.

I stared in frustration at the assorted canisters of herbs, dried fruit, bark, and disgusting mysteries on Helen's countertop. "But where is it?" I asked. "Everyone seems to want it, but nobody knows where it is. My father's looking for something. I didn't find it at Tristan's house. The fae are forming angry mobs, which isn't something they would do if they had a wellspring on tap. I haven't seen any sign of them having a party the way they do at the solstice. Launt—"

"Who's Launt?"

I regretted sharing his name. My instincts told me to keep Seth's secrets to myself. "A fairy with a bad attitude," I said. "He's been causing trouble in Silverpool. And I don't know why. Again, this isn't a creature pleased with his situation because he's got a rare object that could make him rich and powerful among his own kind." Whichever kind he was, fae or human.

"Sounds like an unpleasant spirit," Helen said.

"Very."

"I recommend staying away from him. Even quiet and lovely fairies can lose control of themselves when there's springwater at stake. A malevolent one—"

"Yes, I know. Thanks to you, my house is quite secure now. It's not like he could just climb through a win—" I cut myself off as a terrifying thought struck me.

Oh no.

"What?" Helen demanded.

I stared at her. "If there had been something about Random, would you have noticed?"

"Who's Random?"

"My dog." I flinched. How quickly I'd accepted him into my life. "The dog I brought here. He just showed up the morning after Tristan's murder."

"What are you thinking?"

"Could… Is there any way…"

Helen pushed to her feet impatiently. "What?"

"Could Random *be* the torc? Tristan had been experimenting with shifting when I knew him, and he collected a lot of nasty Shadow magic at his house that I only learned about after he'd died. What if—"

"No. That black dog you brought? He was a real dog. No witch could create spirit out of a hunk of metal."

"But what if…" My thoughts raced. What if the torc was *inside* him? A shrinking spell, a wad of peanut butter… No. It would've gone right through him. But other spells could've embedded it among his organs.

"I have to go." I felt sick. For that kind of treasure, even a human being might kill a dog. Fae and demon were even less likely to worry about hurting him.

"How many people know he showed up the morning after Tristan was killed?" Helen asked.

"I don't know." A jumble of memories danced in my head. I had to get to Silverpool. "I can't remember."

If only I'd left him at my house. He would've been safe in there. But he was at Birdie's, as vulnerable as a rotisserie chicken in a swamp full of hungry alligators.

"You'd better run," Helen said.

"I prefer driving." I raced through the house to the front door.

Chapter Thirty-Nine

U nder a fresh bubble of invisibility, I jogged up the hill to my Jeep. The Protectorate could track me in whatever I drove, so I didn't see the point in delaying my escape by looking for something else, like Helen's old Volvo. There was a spare beaded necklace under the Jeep's front seat, and my own wheels would make me more flexible to take a sudden detour if necessary.

Breathing heavily, I approached the corner where I'd parked, searching for any sign of defensive spells. A calico cat sat in a patch of sun on a balcony, licking its paws, and I waited a moment to see if it reacted to my presence before I unlocked my Jeep and got behind the wheel.

I reached under my seat for the spare necklace. It was worth the five-second delay to get it fastened around my neck before I hit the road, even though it had lost power during the months it had sat unused in my car. After I'd traded my demon-hunting job for quiet Silverpool, I hadn't expected to need emergency power again. Lesson learned.

Anything could happen from here on out. Hands sweating, I slanted the wheel and hit the gas to get out of the heavily sloped parking spot, alert for any sign of a magical alarm going off.

Nothing. I roared up the hill and turned at the corner to double back and head north. In the middle of the day it would take me at least fifteen minutes, maybe thirty, to get out of San Francisco. If I could reach the Golden Gate Bridge, I might be able to block any witches from following me. Boundaries like the Golden Gate had power I could draw upon. And it was always busy, with enough nonmagicals around to prevent the Protectorate from taking dramatic action that might be witnessed, recorded, and uploaded to the internet.

I didn't have the same hang-ups about publicity. With every moment that passed, I was less interested in saving the reputation of the Protectorate from anyone, magical or non.

Perhaps Tristan had put the torc inside Random and sent him to me. His secret had gone with him to his grave.

And I'd been too stupid to see it.

Maybe.

Where did Phoebe fit in? She was probably behind my recent incarceration, and from her presence at Jasper's house, I feared she'd convinced him to work with her. At the very least, I had to assume he was sympathetic to helping her.

As I drove, my mind ruminated over everything I'd learned. The fae were gathering in Silverpool and increasingly causing trouble for miles around. They were doing this because somebody had poisoned them. Somebody had also killed Tristan. With Tristan's death and the revolutionary fae, Lorne would need to install a new Protector in Silverpool as soon as possible, perhaps without vetting the witch too closely. Especially if she was his niece. The authorities might not have time to prevent the assignment or would give her the benefit of the doubt in the short term.

It was the only way Phoebe, at her age, with so little experience, could achieve so much power and status.

My thoughts churned and churned.

With me locked up in San Francisco, Phoebe would be free to cause even more trouble in Silverpool—stir up the fae with another poisoning, perhaps. Then she could whip out the torc—which had never been stolen?—pump out a few gallons of fresh, irresistible wellspring water, distribute it to the fae, and take credit for the peace and happiness that settled across the land.

The young heroine would be appointed Protector. She would probably claim to have found the torc on my property, guaranteeing my confinement in San Francisco until after a new Protector was appointed.

But would Jasper really help her do that? He might not know what she'd done to me—at least I certainly hoped not. He was one of the few friends I had.

With each mile, my suspicions of Phoebe Day seemed increasingly plausible. When she had showed up the morning after Tristan's death, crying about the theft of the torc, it could've been a plot to trick Jasper into helping her. Because of the location of his house near so many fairies, Jasper had developed the skills to bribe and manage them, at least to a degree. He didn't believe in the honorable history of the Protectorate—in fact, he'd been critical. Jealous. Bitter. He knew I wouldn't get the job, so why not help a beautiful woman who asked for help? She'd probably offered money and magic. Maybe more.

When I passed the last exit before the Golden Gate Bridge, I felt the snapping of the last thin strand of magical tension binding me to the house on Diamond Street. My car lurched forward, freed from the magical leash, and I almost rammed a pickup in front of me.

I hit the brakes. I'd never get to Silverpool if I killed myself on the road.

By the time I was driving through Riovaca an hour and a half later, I'd mastered a spell that kept the traffic moving. The nightmare image of Random's disemboweled body kept flashing before my eyes. As soon as I'd passed out of Riovaca, I hit the gas and used my magic to keep me from losing control of the Jeep.

The road narrowed, and the redwood, cedar, and pine rose up on either side, throwing me into shadow. I had the first tingling sensation of danger since I'd left San Francisco.

I was being followed.

Chapter Forty

As I sped through the forest, I isolated the sensation to be a human threat about thirty miles behind me on the road. Witches. Powerful enough for me to feel them at a distance. I'd set a boundary spell in Marin, knowing it wouldn't hold but hoping I'd sense its breaking.

I did. The Protectorate was coming.

Thirty miles was better than none. I might have time to get Random safely locked up inside my house. There wasn't anyone I could trust with him. If his body hid the torc somehow, even Jasper might be tempted to extract...

I wouldn't let myself think about it. I took a sharp turn and for once didn't feel the pull of the fae in the enchanted forest to either side of the road. Their sweet song couldn't tempt me today.

Of all the names I'd given the dog, why hadn't I chosen something luckier than *Random*? I was practically begging for him to be a victim of fate.

Before I reached the Silverpool Bridge, I began to smell smoke. Just outside the drive to Tristan's house, I saw the first flames. The Silverpool Vineyards sign was on fire.

Surrounded by gravel and drought-friendly plantings, it hadn't yet spread to the grass and shrubs along the road—and therefore to the house and winery. But it was only a matter of time.

A dozen fairies surrounded the blaze, chanting and dancing. I didn't see Launt, but the snarling little creatures in their human children's clothes reminded me of him, although they weren't as tall as him—each was about the size of a human baby. I recognized an apple-green face.

Without braking, I sent out a hurried blast of cold, wet power, hoping it was enough to dampen the flammable plants and structures near the fire. This time of year, the dry hills could ignite in seconds, and the resulting firestorm might take out not only Silverpool—and her house—but Riovaca to the east as well.

I turned the bend and saw another fire, this one on the bridge itself. Right in the middle, where I'd found Tristan's body, a mass of something was burning. A twisted pile of machinery. I recognized a lawn mower, a toaster oven, a rusted-out water heater. The smell was acrid and nasty. Since it was the only road into town, I had to pull over to the shoulder and climb out. The rest of my journey would be on foot.

Two dozen rainbow-clad wood sprites, the tallest no bigger than a Big Gulp, stood with their backs to me in a semicircle, facing the bridge as they sang for it to burn.

There weren't any police or fire vehicles, which suggested the calls for help weren't reaching Riovaca.

Three cars were stuck on my side of the bridge, and the passengers were standing outside their vehicles, talking to each other and shaking their heads, blind to the fairies. One guy got back into his car and began turning it around.

Good idea. It was a good time to avoid Silverpool. The fae were trying to burn it down.

I walked to the bridge and kept going. The fairies turned, saw me, and danced over with garish smiles on their small green and blue faces. A line of fire ignited at my feet where they pointed.

I paused. It spread around me in a ring, but the flames were short and flimsy, only as tall as the fairies themselves. A normal human being would respond to the sudden appearance of a wall of fire by running away, but I stepped over it and gave the fairies a little wave of my hand. I knew it wasn't real. The fae had a talent for deception, but I had a strange ability to see through it.

Their almond-shaped eyes widened, realizing that I could see them. Their smiles, and the ring of fire, slowly died down.

"Go home," I said.

Startled, they looked at each other. One of them, a small fairy with yellow teeth, flung a burning chunk of metal at me. I recognized him as one of Launt's companions at the memorial service. I hopped out of the way just in time but was annoyed enough to put my hands together and use a spell to push him away from me. He flew over the railing, farther than I'd intended. When emotions ran high, power could rise to match it, surprising even the most experienced witches.

The other fairies ran over and peered through the railing at him down below. As river people, they weren't natural fliers, although they weren't constrained by the laws of physics as mortals were.

After a long moment, they turned and gaped at me in horror. A greenish glow formed around each of their quivering bodies, as if their fear had been made visible. Suddenly they ran away, their delicate feet barely touching the ground as they fled to the forest side of the bridge.

I paused, surprised by their terror. They were acting as if I'd done something worse to the yellow-toothed one than throw him—a spirit creature—into the air. In spite of the bonfire sputtering nearby, I strode to the spot where he'd fallen and looked over the railing.

Below in the shallow current, the fairy was sprawled face-up, wide-eyed and motionless. The rocks and the shallow current were keeping him from floating downstream. His skin was shrunken and gray, and the distinctive long nose had collapsed upon itself like an empty tube of toothpaste. The yellow teeth were exposed in a grimace, as if his last moment had been torture.

A wave of nausea overcame me. I'd killed him? But how? He was fae. He had no skin to bruise, no bones to break. Only magic could hurt—

I stared at his diseased, shrinking body.

Tristan reported poisoning near the winery, Phoebe had said, but I hadn't believed her.

It was true. The river itself must've been hexed.

I ran across the bridge toward town, ignoring several nonmag humans who were standing around, gaping at the bonfire, taking pictures and complaining with one another. I had to get to Random, but I'd just killed a creature in the same spot Tristan had died. The worst kind of karma.

But I hadn't meant to kill him. I hope that mattered, karma-wise. And more importantly, fae-wise—they wouldn't forget, and their natural lives were long.

I pushed through the summer grass and branches to a dirt path that led down the slope to the river. The fairy who I'd seen the night Tristan died usually slept under the bridge on the Silverpool side, unseen by most, but today he'd been one of the fae I'd seen near Tristan's winery, setting the sign on fire. That had been strange in itself; he should've been bonded to the spot. Something powerful must've broken to let him roam.

As soon as I reached the riverbank, I realized what that had to have been.

And who was truly responsible for the death of not only the little yellow-toothed fairy. Which meant—

I had to be sure. If I was right, Birdie might need my help. And Random could be in more danger than ever.

Chapter Forty-One

I ran past the nonmag people still watching the bonfire and headed for my house. I wasn't much of a runner, and the journey up the hill at full speed made me winded. To reach Birdie's more quickly, and hopefully unseen, I cut across the Sauters' backyard. The house where Birdie played Yahtzee was the first one on our street, backing onto, as mine did, the bluff overlooking the river.

Just as I was dodging Madge's raised bed of stubbornly green tomatoes, a pair of gnomes in black leather jumped out of a towering incense cedar and flung a ball of fire at my head.

Screaming briefly, I slapped my hands over my sizzling ponytail and extinguished it before I went up like a tiki torch. The two gnomes—a male and a female—began to send another blast at my head, but I released my hair, pointed the water spell at them, and sent them into the air like bowling pins.

Gnomes hated to be knocked over because it reminded them of the manufactured statuary nonmag humans kept in their gardens. Unfortunately for them, gnomes, like turtles, had difficulty rising from their backs, especially when they were angry and had just used up their energy on sending bolts of fire at a witch.

I hoped they would be stuck for at least five minutes and then would be too embarrassed to attack me again. Having already killed one of the fae, I refused to hurt another two. What I'd seen at the river justified their anger.

I maneuvered through several more raised beds of late-summer vegetables to reach the narrow strip of land behind Birdie's detached garage. I put my hand on the stucco and felt a residue of magic. Now that I'd had the pleasure of spending more time with Launt, I recognized the feel of him in the lingering magic, like burnt rubber on asphalt. An unpleasant member of the fairy population for sure.

I hurried past the garage toward the driveway, keeping myself out of sight from the house. More than common sense kept me from just walking to Birdie's front door and ringing the bell. The magic in my veins warned me to stay away—or better yet, run. In cat form, if necessary, and then climb a very tall tree.

If Random was in trouble, would he bark? Did he know I was outside right now?

When I turned the corner of the garage and saw the white BMW parked in the driveway, I sucked in a breath. Phoebe was there. Phoebe with the heart as foul and grasping as any demon.

Speaking of demon-like individuals…

I retreated behind the garage and put my hand on the new necklace I'd strung around my neck. It wasn't strong—the Protectorate had taken that one—but I'd worn it when I'd been an agent, and it was still attuned to my one and only prey. Since I'd let him go, we'd interacted—well, I hated to say *intimately*, but there was a social element to our conversations—and the magic in the beads jumped at the fresh connection it felt inside me.

It took me less than a minute to find him. I couldn't see him, but I sensed he was standing near the huge sycamore next to the driveway, less than twenty feet from where I stood. Distinctive power came off him in slow waves, like ripples in a lake. The Protectorate had trained me for over two years to find ripples like that so that I could sneak up behind whatever it was and kill it. "Before it killed you or anyone else," had been the lesson, but I believed it less now than I'd ever had.

With the lessons on detection had come other lessons. Reluctantly I used one now.

Against his will, Seth left the safety of the sycamore and walked stiffly over to me. His face bore a tight smile, but I knew he was angry.

"Sorry," I whispered when he reached me beside the garage. "It's an emergency. I need to know—is Random inside the house?"

"Who?"

"The dog. My dog. Have you seen him?"

"You put me under a Compulsion to ask about an animal?"

"Yes," I said.

He glared. "I suppose you just walked through the fairy rebellion on the way into town?"

"I couldn't drive. The bridge was on fire."

"But that didn't stop you," Seth said.

"I'm worried about my dog."

Seth rubbed his face. "I saw him set the fire on the bridge."

"My dog?"

Seth pointed at the house. "Launt."

"Where is he now?" All the forces were coming together. I was beginning to understand why.

"On the doorstep. Waiting for his master." He turned to me. "I've got to talk to him again."

His master. Confirming my suspicion. What witch wouldn't care about sparking a fae war? Who might even find it interesting?

"I don't want Launt. I'm here for what's inside the house." Not only Random but Birdie was stuck inside with Phoebe, who wouldn't hesitate to use power, however hurtful, to get what she wanted. "You take care of your brother, and I'll deal with my kind."

The sound of a dog's frantic barking came from the house. I began to rush forward, but Seth stopped me with a hand on my arm.

"Not yet," he said.

Shaking him off, I reached for my necklace as I moved toward the front door.

"Alma, please," he said, getting in front of me. "I need to talk to him first. You might hurt him."

That didn't sound too bad.

Seeming to read my thoughts, he added, "And therefore me."

I liked him more than I wanted to admit, but I couldn't leave Birdie and Random in danger. "You have teleportation powers of some kind?"

He frowned, then nodded warily.

"Get them out of there," I said. "Birdie and the dog. Then we can deal with the others."

"It's not that easy."

I pushed past him to move to the door.

"All right! All right! Give me a minute!" He took a deep breath. And vanished.

Five loud thumps of my heartbeat later, he appeared with

a jet-black dog in his arms. Random appeared unharmed, cheerful as ever. He wriggled to the ground and began sniffing. After circling in place for a moment, he squatted to relieve himself.

"I can't get Birdie," Seth said. "There's too much power in there directed at her. And humans are more complicated."

When Random was done with his business, I knelt down and felt him for any bumps, lumps, possible incisions, finding nothing. My magic had been unable to detect anything sinister about him before, but I tried again, this time looking for foreign objects, silver, iron, concentrations of power, anything painful. To my relief and frustration, I found nothing.

"Is there anything inside this dog?" I demanded of Seth. "Metal of any kind, hidden with magic?"

Seth frowned, looked at Random for a long moment, and shook his head. "No. Nothing."

I let out my breath. If the torc wasn't inside him, then it had to be...

"Help! Somebody help!" Birdie cried, rushing out the front door.

Chapter Forty-Two

✿

Not seeing Launt, Birdie ran right past him, down the steps to the sidewalk, waving her arms and continuing to yell for help.

She reached the driveway, perhaps headed for the Sauters' house, when she saw me and Seth standing there in the shadows. Her mouth formed a grateful *O* and then—

A rain barrel flew through the air and struck her from behind.

It hit her left shoulder, knocking her to the ground. With a pained cry, she rolled over to see who had thrown it at her. But she wouldn't be able to see Launt the way I could. She must've felt as if her life had become an incomprehensible nightmare.

I rushed forward, hands raised, already drawing from the well of angry power I'd refused to use on Seth those pivotal years ago. The monster had hurt Birdie, who deserved better than she'd gotten from life, from her father, from me.

But Seth was ahead of me, moving with supernatural speed, and the next thing I saw was Launt flying into the air, spinning like a maple seedpod, the human slippers he'd been wearing knocked off his fairy feet.

"Hear me, Launt," Seth declared, standing over the tall fairy's prone figure. And then he said something in a language I didn't understand, something both cheerful and horrible, like carnival music in a horror movie.

Any moment, Phoebe could appear and make things worse. Why was she staying inside?

I continued running to Birdie, who hadn't yet risen from the ground. Before I could reach Birdie, a fountain of blue, smoky liquid sprayed from the barrel. No! Another potion, another poisoned liquid.

Always the liquids.

It scorched the grass around it, setting one of Launt's fallen shoes on fire, and then—

Birdie screamed. I grabbed her under the arms, cringing at the heat, and dragged her away from the center of power.

No fairy could have power like that. Not without help.

I huddled with her on the driveway near Phoebe's car. Her eyes were wide with terror, no awareness behind them. Her hair was singed on one side, her skin dusty. I could feel the Shadow snaking through her pores into her blood, racing for her heart. I tore off my necklace, pushed it under her T-shirt, and held the beads in a fist over her chest. A spell a teacher had taught me years ago came to my lips, ancient magic that needed to be spoken, and I repeated it over and over as I begged fate not to punish my neighbor for my slowness.

Aya, baya, ayu, bayu, I whispered.

I should've anticipated the threat to Birdie's life. As soon as the will had become public, her life had been in danger. I'd thought her nonmag ignorance would protect her, but Tristan's daughter would always be a threat to the witch who'd murdered him. A witch's blood would seek justice.

Her rain barrel. She'd been proud of collecting last winter's rain in it for her small container garden where, inspired by Margaret next door, she'd grown a few vegetables. One way or another, sooner or later, she would have ingested whatever was inside. When had it been contaminated with potion? If it had been days ago, it might be too late for her.

A glimmer of light grew stronger around Birdie's heart and then spread to her lungs, her stomach, her abdomen. The latent power inside her was joining mine, fighting the threat. I spoke the words again, pressing harder on the beads, but the progress was slow; if I moved my hand, she wouldn't be strong enough to fight it.

"Birdie, you're doing great," I said. "You're stronger than you know. Keep fighting. Hold on."

Random appeared from the shadows and began licking the soot and singed hair off Birdie's face.

Meanwhile, Seth was standing between us and Launt, offering a hand to the prone fairy. "I have a deal for you. But you've got to stop hurting people."

A bicycle appeared out of nowhere and came hurtling at me and Birdie. In the split second before I flung up a spell to push it aside, I noticed the front tire's rim was inverted, its spokes jutting out to pierce flesh.

Seth shouted and knocked Launt across the yard.

I turned my attention back to Birdie, now trembling violently. During my momentary distraction, the poison inside her had regained its hold and was growing again. It would take more than me to free her from it. The beads were helping, but her own efforts were getting weaker, not stronger, with each moment. She had to find her own latent abilities, wherever they were, however weak they might be, to fight off the infection.

"You've got power, Birdie," I said. "You can feel it. Find that weird little thing inside you and grab on to it. Grab it!"

Her eyes came into focus for a moment. "Weird."

I grabbed her hand and set it over the beads on her chest. "Do you feel that? It amplifies your power. Pull on it. Wrap it into a ball. Pretend you're making bread. You want it to grow. You're the boss."

"I'm cold," Birdie said.

I put my arms around her and cast a warming spell. "How's that?"

She closed her eyes, but after a moment she said, "Nice trick."

My own body began to shake. The warming spell drained all the heat from my own body. If I kept it up for too long, I would get hypothermic. Poor Random seemed to sense the danger, because he turned his head to me and began licking my face instead of Birdie's.

"Thanks." Birdie's voice was stronger. The poison inside her was wavering, drawing back.

"You're doing it," I said. "You're claiming your power."

"Cool," she whispered, smiling.

Across the yard, Seth was trying again with Launt. "Come back with me to Minnesota. Your human parents have left us a house. Land. There's a lake. You can regain what you lost."

Launt spat at him. "I go nowhere with you."

"I can show you how to live as you were meant to live. You can have my life."

This time Launt laughed. "I take it now!"

"Kill me now, and you'll die as you are," Seth said.

"Kill you, and *you* die."

"There's a wellspring there too," Seth said. "You can see the ones who raised you—"

A propane canister flew at Seth's head, and he disappeared for a moment. He reappeared several feet to the left, holding something round and shiny in his hands. A crown?

"With this, both human and fae will respect you. You'll be welcomed. Powerful."

The object in Seth's hand was a large, open ring of gold. It looked like a headband or a tiara and glowed with its own warm light.

The torc.

That lying, Shadow bastard, I thought.

"You can find a wife, human or fae, and enjoy a long life," Seth said. "Longer than most humans. I'll give you the land of your ancestors and never return."

"Lies," Launt said.

"No," Seth said. "I owe you. The debt is too great for me to bear." He held out the torc, showing how the light caught it, hovered near it, called more light to it.

All right, this time I *was* going to kill him.

Chapter Forty-Three

❦

"No land, no lakes," Launt said. "No humans."

A leaf blower spun through the air and struck Seth in the back of the head. He cried out and dropped the torc.

Birdie was too weak for me to leave her, even for a moment. I had to hold her and watch as Seth stumbled forward, picked up the torc, and tucked it into a pocket.

"You're already dying," Seth said. "The fairy form can't hold the human spirit forever. Your lease is about up."

"Lies, lies, lies." Launt inhaled as if drawing in power.

This time Seth stopped him by blowing a kiss that knocked Launt onto his back. "Let me help you, brother."

But I could tell Seth was losing hope. He spoke quietly, almost to himself.

Launt rolled onto one side and pointed at Phoebe's BMW. As the hood ripped free, I grabbed Birdie's arms and dragged her away, drawing on the beads in her hand to give me more strength, but not so much that it left her vulnerable again to the poison in her blood.

The hood shaved past Birdie's head, barely missing it, and

clattered to the driveway. Eyes widening, she looked at me in terror, losing her hold on the beads. The grip she had over her own magic broke.

"Hold on, Birdie, hold on." I fumbled around her body and the ground for the beads, needing them as much for myself as for her, but I couldn't find them.

I reached down into my default self, the core I was born with, the small well that held magic like a cup held water. My Witchwell. It was weak, weaker than usual because I was injured and without my beads to focus.

What was the fairy doing to me?

No, not the fairy. It was the poison inside Birdie. Whatever it was had contaminated me as well, seeping into my own flesh, searching for another victim.

Panic rose in my gut. If I fell, who would help Birdie? I had to fight. The sensation was similar to the pain I'd felt when I'd broken the Protectorate silence spell, the pain Jasper's recovery potion had been so quick to dissipate.

The car began to shake and give off heat. I thought of the fire on the bridge, the burning machinery, and staggered to my feet. I had to get Birdie away from her house, but she began to shake as well, arms and legs going stiff as she had some kind of seizure.

"Seth! Dammit! Do something!" I cried. "Help her or I *will* put a silver stake through your eyes!"

Flames flicked out from under the hood. Birdie and I were too close. I couldn't leave her; I couldn't move her. Random began to whine and nip at my elbows to pull me away from danger.

Just as I heard the beginning of the explosion, I gave up on Seth and wrapped Birdie and Random in a protective sphere of bright, soft energy, heavier than air, hotter than fire, stronger than metal. It drew from my heart like a straw sips the last dregs of liquid from the bottom of a glass. I gave it the last drops of power from my personal well. I lost my sight, then my hearing. I forgot my name.

And then I snapped awake. I was slumped on the ground, Birdie and Random in my arms, with the burning wreck of Phoebe's car just outside the protective globe of my spell.

Something was feeding me energy I didn't have, enough for me to get to my feet and drag Birdie to safety, never releasing the shimmering sphere that protected us. I set her in the soft green grass of the Sauters' yard and told Random to sit there with her. Both were awake, watching me with clear eyes. Whatever I'd created had cast out the poison as well.

Movement in the shadows of Madge Sauter's tomato planter caught my eye. A familiar red coat. A pale hand holding a pipe.

And then he was gone.

The strength of my magic seemed effortless now, but I didn't trust it. I'd been far too trusting for far too long. I dissolved the sphere and turned to face Launt and Seth with renewed vigor.

I found them both on the ground, arms wrapped around each other like lovers. Seth's eyes were open, and his gaze turned wearily to mine. Coughing, he pulled away from Launt and sat up, not quite upright. His skin was ashen, hollow, a sheen of sweat on him.

"I'm sorry," he said, coughing again. "About the torc. Trying to protect you."

Apparently he was going to continue lying to me. "You were going to give it to your—" I looked at Launt, saw the stillness, the impossible angle of his neck, the glow on his skin. "He's dead."

Seth jerked his head once in a rough nod.

"But—what happens to you now?"

He reached into his pocket and took out the torc. It glowed faintly. "Doesn't matter," he said. "Put it in a safe place, witch, or somebody might try to hurt you again." With shaking hands, he held it out to me.

"Ethan, fetch!"

I spun around at the sound of my father's voice. Malcolm was in the driveway, pointing at Random, my dog—*his* dog—who shifted into a small but glorious dragon and took flight. The black fur was now a rainbow of scales, shining and iridescent, and his canine jaws stretched open not with a long, pink tongue but with a cloud of fire.

As his master had commanded him, the dragon flew directly at Seth.

Chapter Forty-Four

❧

"**N**o!" I lifted my hands to strike, but I was unwilling to hurt my dog, even now.

Seth released the torc and clapped his hands together like he had at the river. Ethan—Random—hit the ground before the torc even reached Seth's lap.

Seth fell to one side, motionless, perhaps dead. He'd killed his twin, the body that was his true form—did that mean he was dead too? I felt for a pulse, but he was cold, so cold.

I spun around and ran toward the dragon's quivering figure, but Malcolm got there first, lifted the shiny body in his arms, and disappeared in a blast of white light.

My talented father had teleported away with Random, who was Ethan, who deserved a more caring guardian—just as I had.

Shaken, I returned to Seth and knelt down to search for his pulse again. This time I felt it, slow but steady. His skin seemed a little warmer. Maybe Launt's death wouldn't guarantee his own. Unbidden relief washed over me.

But then I was reminded of Random in my father's arms

and of Seth hiding the torc, and I was furious again. So many selfish people, human and fae, taking and killing and lying and hurting.

Seth's eyes opened. "You let me live."

"Of course I did," I said. "Kicked out of the Protectorate for being weak, remember?"

He took a deep breath, nodded. "Thank you." He rolled to one side and pushed himself up onto his feet. "I'm getting tired of saying that."

"I'm tired of hearing it."

He brushed the dirt off his pants with unsteady hands. "Don't be mad at the dog. It's not his fault."

"I know that. More than anyone, I know that." My father must've been thrilled to find a minion who couldn't talk or complain. I'd always annoyed him, saying no, being miserable, asking for friends, school, a permanent home.

"I'm sorry I hurt him," Seth said. "It was reflex. Self-defense."

"Was that why you took the torc out of my house where my father hid it?"

He nodded, which seemed to make him dizzy. When he recovered, he took another deep breath and said, "I was trying to protect you."

If only Malcolm had felt the same, Protectorate agents wouldn't be approaching with orders to take me into custody. Even without my beads, I could feel them getting closer.

"You should've told me," I said.

"Your ignorance saved you," he said.

"You couldn't resist its power. You're just like the rest of them," I said.

He pinched the bridge of his nose, avoiding my gaze.

The front door of Birdie's house banged open, revealing Phoebe with a wand in her hand. Her posture sagged to one side, as if she'd been drinking. When Jasper appeared behind her, I realized she *had* been drinking something, something he'd given her to keep her inside when her car had exploded.

"Demon!" Phoebe shouted suddenly, pointing her wand at Seth. She marched down the steps and came full speed toward us. "Step aside, Alma. I recognize his picture. I'll take care of him this time."

"No, he's not—"

Without waiting, Phoebe sent a blast of exorcising magic at Seth's heart. Taken by surprise and already weakened, he caught the full force of it in the chest. He glanced at me with an expression that looked an awful lot like regret before crumpling to the ground again.

With a triumphant grin, Phoebe took out a small pocket knife—silver, folding, regulation Protectorate—and flicked it open as she moved in to finish the job.

I stepped in front of her.

Phoebe recoiled. "What are you doing?"

"You have no right to kill him," I said.

"I have every right. I have a *duty*."

"He's not a demon."

The look of contempt on her face was mixed with pity, which made it worse. "Sure he isn't."

"He's done nothing to you, nothing to anybody." I looked over her shoulder. "Unlike Jasper."

Jasper was slowing taking in the disaster in the front yard: the dead body on the grass was Launt, not Birdie.

I'd saved her life, but I still felt terribly guilty for leaving her so vulnerable to Jasper and his fairy henchman.

Jasper, my friend, who was a killer. He'd always had a knack for liquids.

"Jasper poisoned the river," I told Phoebe. "Tristan caught him in the act, so Jasper killed him."

Phoebe scoffed. "You're just angry he won't help you hide your father's crimes."

"For a while I thought you'd helped him," I said. "You thought if Tristan was out of the way, you could be Protector."

"You're pathetic," Phoebe said. "Jasper told me how you cry on his shoulder about losing everything, about being such a loser."

I looked over at the charred BMW. "You really should wash your car more often. You know, to make a good impression."

The car fire had gone out with Launt's death, so only now did Phoebe notice what had happened.

"My car!"

"Jasper is responsible for that too," I said. "He told his fae accomplice to kill Birdie. The car was collateral damage."

Jasper spoke for the first time. "Where is the poor girl now, by the way?"

The residue of so much magic from the battle with Launt and Seth must've blinded him to her presence. She'd moved into the Sauters' backyard, near the spot where I'd glimpsed Willy in the vegetable garden, and was hiding behind the raised beds.

"She's harmless," I said, suddenly unable to hide my rage. "She's untrained and ignorant and harmless. Only a monster would want to kill her."

"Demons like him are the monsters," Jasper said. "Don't you think, Phoebe?"

"Yes, yes, of course." Phoebe raised her knife and tried to push past me.

"Don't be stupid," I said. "Don't you see what he's doing? He's trying to get you to fight Seth so he can blame your death on him and get away with everything."

"You're the stupid one," Phoebe said. "That demon is a threat. They are *always* a threat. That's why we exist."

"He's not a demon," I said. "He's a changeling. His spirit is fae."

"I always knew you were crazy," Phoebe said, "but I didn't believe anyone and certainly not a witch screened by the Protectorate could ever have perverted thoughts about the enemy."

I knew how severely injured Seth must've been when he didn't raise his head and wink at me. Which meant anything Phoebe did could finish him off for good.

"I won't let you murder him," I said, raising both my hands. I still didn't have my beads, but my rage gave me focus. Hopefully it would be enough to deal bare-handed with Phoebe and Jasper until the Protectorate guys arrived.

Hopefully very soon.

"We don't have time for this," Jasper said, reaching into his jacket.

I grabbed Phoebe's sleeve. "Listen to me. Jasper's the one you want." I tried to turn her around and face Jasper, who was now holding a thick silver chain in his fist, but she jerked away and tried to get to Seth with her little knife.

"Demon filth," she said.

"She makes this so easy," Jasper said to me as he aimed his fist at Phoebe. Silver fire the same thickness as the chain spiraled through the air and hit the young, ambitious witch in the shoulder. It knocked her to one side so that she fell facing him.

Chapter Forty-Five

"They'll blame the demon and the rebelling fae," Jasper told Phoebe. "I'm really so lucky you're here tonight. A Protectorate agent, greedy and stupid, pretty face, well connected. They'll go crazy when they find your body."

Phoebe's mouth was locked open in a silent scream, her body frozen in a sideways crouch. Her eyes fixed on Jasper, wide with dawning comprehension.

Yeah, I thought. He's the one.

She'd dropped the knife as she'd fallen, and I hurried forward and snatched it up. I could see from her softening expression that Jasper's spell was already wearing off, and I didn't want her making a last-ditch attempt to kill her favorite enemy.

"When the war begins," Jasper said, "humanity will finally be forced to attack the ancient fae threat. Witches have lived in bondage"—he pulled the silver chain between both hands—"long enough."

"You're… crazy," Phoebe said, crawling to her knees. She had her wand out again, this time aimed at Jasper.

I glimpsed movement on the road. It was almost time.

While Phoebe and Jasper began to enact fighting spells in the air between them, I turned to Seth. He was awake, staring at the sky, making no effort to escape.

"Go," I said. Evening had become night. Soon the stars would be out.

"Go where?"

"Anywhere, just go!"

Seth rolled his head toward me. "I thought I would be dead by now."

"You will if you stay here."

He sighed as if that wasn't such a bad thing. But when a tendril of Jasper's magic shot past Phoebe and narrowly missed his nose, survival instinct kicked in and he held out a hand. I took it, impatient to be rid of him, and pulled him to his feet.

"Take the torc before I leave," he whispered, patting his pockets.

"I already did."

He gave me one last grin before disappearing.

At the same moment, one of Jasper's spells hit Phoebe in the throat. She spun through the air and landed on her back with a sickening thud. From the way her hands jutted upward, it looked like she wouldn't be getting up anytime soon. Trainee agents called it the "dead bug" pose.

"That's it?" Jasper demanded, sounding genuinely put out. "That's the best she can do? I'm only using folk magic with a fae signature."

"You always were too impressed with Protectorate agents," I said, preparing a defensive spell in the back of my mind, readying for battle.

"You won't mind if I finish the job," he said, taking a step toward Phoebe. "You hated her too."

I got in front of him with my hands fisted, telling myself

the beads and silver were only crutches that directed power, not power itself. "I won't let you."

He frowned at me in surprise. "I don't want to kill you," he said. "I never did."

"It's over, Jasper."

"No, it's just beginning." He flicked the chain at me, just to test the waters.

I absorbed the energy without a word, not letting the pain show on my face. "You're a killer. No more than that."

"I'm much stronger than anyone suspected. More than Tristan, more than that stupid fae, more than Phoebe, more than you."

"Being a killer doesn't make you strong," I said.

He laughed. "That's how you make yourself feel better, isn't it? So young and already such a failure." He sent another flick of magic at me, as small and deadly as a laser point.

I swallowed it like the last one but was unable to hide my flinch as it nicked a vertebra. "If you sit quietly, the Protectorate might take you in without killing you."

"The Protectorate thinks you're the criminal. Didn't they take you in last night? Phoebe assured me they would get the truth out of you." He snorted. "Those idiots couldn't even hold on to a sweet little hearth witch like you for more than a few hours. But they'll get you. They're probably on their way."

I drew a circle in the air between us to stop his laser-like attacks. "They are. Give up now."

He gave me a pitying look. "I will kill you, don't you realize? I love you, but I'll do what I have to do."

"Time's running out," I said.

He punched the air with his fist, and a meteor shower of red light spattered my shield. Most fell apart, but two—no, three—broke through and struck me in the stomach, ear, and shoulder.

"Give it up, Alma," he said, angry now.

I shook my head, tasting blood. "You killed the fae. You killed Tristan. You tried to kill Birdie and a Protectorate agent."

"But I didn't kill you, and I could have." He began frantically searching his pockets. "This is your last warning. Please, Alma."

"This is *your* last warning, you idiot. Sit down and—"

"You can tell the Protectorate that you fought the demon as I tried to save Phoebe's life."

"He's a changeling," I said.

Jasper didn't care what Seth was or wasn't. "We can both come out of this better than we went in. The Protectorate will know you tried to save Phoebe, but... sadly, as they know, you are unable to *kill*, so she's dead." He pulled a vial hanging from a chain out of his pocket. "And she will be, Alma. Why should you be blamed for it?"

"Time's up." I dropped the shield and waited.

He frowned at me, fiddling with the vial in his hands. "We both know you can't kill me. Why do you want me to kill you?"

"Just try."

"I meant what I said. I love you. Doesn't that mean anything?"

I turned my attention inward to the well I always had with me.

"Your love is crap," I said.

His head snapped back as if I'd blasted him with a silver-driven punching hex. It took a moment for the rage to hit the boiling point, but when it did, I was ready.

He flung the open vial at me. True to form, he did it underhanded.

It spun through the air, spraying white raindrops of death for anyone it touched. I was too close to jump out of the way, and my clothing would be useless against the Shadow magic embedded in the liquid. My shield would stop most of it, but the single drop or two that got through would be enough to destroy me. Willy had helped me earlier, but I didn't feel him now. Maybe he'd only gotten involved to protect Random, the animal I'd neglected too many times.

But I still had my Witchwell, the magic that was unique to me. It was magic that had failed me with my father, who would've loved me more if only I'd been the right kind of daughter. It had failed me with the Protectorate, who would've given me power and prestige if only I'd been the right kind of witch. And now I was asking it to save me from Jasper, who would kill me for not being the right kind of friend.

Like so many powerful feelings, it rose up from my stomach. Then it spread to my chest, my heart and lungs, and then down to my toes and up to my eyes. Finally it was strong enough, like a song getting loud enough to hear the words, and it pumped down my arms and pooled in my bare hands.

Power like nothing I'd ever experienced before vibrated through me. Time slowed, allowing me to see each droplet, each molecule, each atom of magic shimmering and burning through the air.

Yet I discovered that even now, I couldn't kill him. My hands wouldn't move; my well of magic wouldn't serve as a weapon. All that power wasn't enough.

For my weakness, this damn weakness, I was going to die.

But then I thought of Random, damaged and abused, in my father's arms.

I thought of Birdie in the neighbor's vegetable garden, injured, motherless, fatherless, alone.

I even thought of Phoebe, who I disliked intensely, powerless to stop her own murder.

Angry and desperate, I pulled up my shield and fueled it with every trace of power inside me. I fed it as if it were a lost child, a starving dog, a dying grandmother. I gave it everything.

And this time, luckily for me, it was enough. The shield held firm, forming a solid wall of impenetrable energy. The vial struck the center and ricocheted, its glass walls shattering as it spun in the opposite direction, spewing its poison at its sender.

But more than that: the shield followed the vial, shaping itself into a funnel, directing the spray toward Jasper's face. When it reached him, it formed a globe around his head, trapping him inside with the mist so that even when he tried to pull out another vial to save himself or use the silver chain in his fist, he was unable to reach his mouth, his nose, his eyes. The poison was inside him.

Which, really, since that's where it had come from, was where it belonged.

Chapter Forty-Six

J asper collapsed not downward in a heap but like a tree falling, stiffly and with a lot of noise.

Shaking, I stared down at his body and tried to be glad he was dead. Instead, I turned aside and doubled over to vomit.

I'd killed a man. A witch. A friend. A person with thoughts and feelings, a mom and a dad. He'd told me once about a sister in San Diego. Now they would hear he was dead and grieve, cursing life, cursing me.

A man came out from the shadows and patted me on the back. "Excellent work, Bellrose."

I froze, feeling the urge to be sick again. After a long moment, I turned to Raynor. "Took you long enough to get here."

"I was watching to see how things played out."

"You would've let him kill me," I said.

"Oh no," he said.

I didn't believe him.

"Agent Day is still alive," I said, gesturing at Phoebe. I

didn't want him to bother Birdie. The last thing she needed tonight was more questioning by the Protectorate.

Raynor shot Phoebe a distasteful look. "Indeed." He turned to the road. "Lorne should be here shortly."

"Why isn't he with you?"

"The disturbance on the bridge was too much for him." Raynor's contempt was obvious. "He waited for his agents to clear it so his car could get through."

"You walked." I'd glimpsed him on the road. Quite a long time ago, relatively speaking. He should've seen enough to know the whole story, but I didn't trust him to share it with the Protectorate. Maybe with Jasper's dead body, the evidence of his potion, and both Phoebe and Birdie as witnesses, they would believe me.

But I wasn't counting on it.

"I don't think she's seriously hurt," I said. "But she needs some help."

"She'll probably be all right. Lorne can take her somewhere."

"Jasper hit her with a Shadow hex," I said. "Intending to kill."

He gave me a funny look. "You're worried about her comfort?"

"I need her as a witness. Just last night you and Lorne had me locked up for conspiracy, theft, and accessory to murder."

"His decision, not mine," Raynor said. "But you'll have come to San Francisco to make a statement."

"Not tonight." I needed to get both Birdie and the torc safely into my house.

"Now the Protectorate has the opportunity to right the wrongs you've experienced." Raynor nodded at Jasper's rigid body. "Your skills have matured. Perhaps your status within the Protectorate could be reevaluated."

"Now that I can kill people?"

He made a face. "Don't be childish."

I resisted the urge to stick out my tongue. "I'm going home." They could make me return to Diamond Street now, but not without a fight. I would go willingly after I had some sleep.

Raynor looked me over, perhaps coming to the same conclusion. "Tomorrow," he said. "When the sun sets. I'll see to it you're treated well."

"You? Not Lorne?"

Raynor's lips curled in a cold smile. "After the events of recent weeks, combined with the behavior of local management and"—he glanced at Phoebe, who had rolled onto her back and was groaning softly—"his regrettable protégé, I've been given full authority, in a provisional capacity, over the San Francisco office."

I was too tired to care. "Congratulations."

"Thank you." He took a little packet of herbs out of his pocket and sniffed it. "You can also thank me for allowing the changeling to get away."

"So, the Protectorate always knew he wasn't a demon, but they—"

"I'm only repeating what you said," Raynor said. "He seemed like a demon to me."

"He killed his... brother. The human in his fairy body." I hated to ask Raynor anything, but I couldn't resist. "Is he going to die?"

"If he's really a changeling, yes. That's the lore." He put the herbs back into his pocket and shrugged. "But who knows?"

Who knows. Not very comforting.

Raynor turned to face the road where a row of headlights was snaking up the hill. "If you want to avoid making a statement tonight, you might want to get out of here before

Lorne arrives. I'll go inside and pretend I don't know where you are."

"Me? Got away from the great Raynor?"

He shot me a warning look as he walked up the steps to Birdie's house.

I waited until he was inside before striding over to find Birdie slumped against Madge's tomato planter. She held a tomato in one hand, regarding it as if it were a crystal ball that held the secrets of the universe.

"Come on," I said softly. "I'm bringing you home to my place."

She let me help her to her feet but didn't put down the tomato. "I'm so confused."

I spun the weak threads of my power into a hiding spell around us and guided her into her own backyard just as a car roared up to the house in front.

"I know," I whispered, supporting her weight as we walked toward my house. "I know."

Chapter Forty-Seven

It was the next day, just after sunset, and I'd driven down again in my Jeep. Raynor sat behind Lorne's old desk, and a female app in gray robes I didn't know sat beside me, taking notes. I hadn't seen Lorne since I'd arrived, and nobody had mentioned him.

"When she's strong enough to travel, Phoebe will be moved to Los Angeles," Raynor said.

"For treatment?" I asked, knowing the most prestigious witch clinic on the West Coast was down there.

"For reassignment," Raynor said. "Given her family connection to the ex-director, it was thought best to give her a fresh start in a new location."

As much as I disliked Phoebe, she hadn't been responsible for any of the actual crimes in Silverpool. "She didn't know Jasper had done anything wrong," I said.

"She should have."

"I didn't figure it out until last night."

"Understandable. He was a friend of yours," Raynor said. "And you weren't on duty. She was."

I nodded and looked at my hands. The fight with Jasper

had left a black tattoo on my left wrist—an arc like the ones he'd had on his arm to mark the passing years. Would I have another one appear next year? Already I was dreading my birthday.

"Speaking of duty," Raynor continued.

"I don't want a job," I said.

He smiled. "It's been a stressful few days. We'll talk about that later."

"Only if you happen to be in Silverpool," I said. "Otherwise, I doubt we'll be talking about anything again."

He flattened his lips, but I could tell he was humoring me. "Of course. Now, since you're so eager to leave, you can begin giving your formal statement and return to your lovely, fae-infested backwater."

"Don't knock it. It would be on the cover of *Sunset Magazine* if they could find it."

The app next to me snorted, and Raynor pointed at her pen and notebook. "You don't need to write that down. Only the statement." He turned his gaze to me. "Begin. Please."

"Did Jasper kill Nick Takata? And if so, why?"

"After you tell us what you know, then—"

"No, you have to tell me now. It's the final piece of the puzzle. Then I'll tell you everything." Mostly.

After a long pause, he took out his herb case and snorted a pinch up his nose. "Nick Takata once dated a witch named Sheila Zalek."

"Lorne asked me about her. He said she was a Freewitch."

"As a hobby more than a vocation," Raynor said. "She seemed to have gotten bored easily. She'd inherited the Zalek fortune but worked as an interior designer, staging big, fancy houses for sale, which is how she met Nick Takata. Like Tristan and her father, she had a love of beautiful, unusual things. That turned into a preference for Shadow artifacts, which led her to a Freewitch meeting in Berkeley. That was years ago, but recently she got more involved. She'd been on our radar on and off for years, but last June she began going to meetings every week. Right around the time she began taking advanced potion lessons from a tutor in Silverpool. She paid for the lessons by decorating his house for him."

"Jasper," I said.

He nodded. "I was assigned to track her last June, which is how I know so much about her. I followed her to Silverpool but unfortunately was too stupid to notice anything suspicious about Jasper Holland. He never attended a Freewitch meeting himself, never left a trail online."

"He was good with computers," I said.

And he'd had a rotten soul I'd never suspected. When he'd seen me talking to Nick at the memorial service, he must've panicked, afraid I might connect him to his secret life and therefore the murder.

"So Jasper had a fairy run Nick off the road," I said softly. "But why leave the necklace on the body, which led you to a known Freewitch?"

"It told us nothing new. They were inciting war between humans and fae. But it didn't explain who had killed Tristan. Sheila Zalek was dead."

"How—" I began. But I knew.

"Poison," he said. "In her coffee."

I gripped my knees. If only I'd seen what was right in front of me. If only I'd paid better attention to other people instead of moping around in a self-centered funk after the Protectorate had canned me.

"I had no idea he was so… *hateful*," I said.

"He applied to the Protectorate every year for a decade," Raynor said. "Many who join the Freewitches are merely nursing a sore ego after being rejected by us."

"Maybe you should've let him in," I said. "He's got the bloodthirsty instinct you guys seem to go for."

Raynor stood up and went over to the small wet bar under the window, where he lifted a water pitcher and filled two glasses. As he brought one over to me, I could feel the buzz of sweet, delicious wellspring water.

"It's just a drop," he said, taking a sip, perhaps to show me it was safe.

I'd never been affected by the springwater like everyone else, but I didn't want him to know that. I pretended to be eager as I took a mouthful and smiled as I swallowed.

Within seconds I could feel Raynor's truth spell hit my bloodstream. Expecting the famous demon hunter to have done something like it, I'd lined my bra with oak leaves. Itchy but effective. I didn't plan on lying, but I liked the option. "Thank you."

"Oh, by the way," Raynor said, shifting in his seat. Turning to the app, he made a spiral gesture in the air. "You and I share a secret in common."

"You and me?"

Raynor leaned back in his chair and stared at me. "Yes."

I looked at the app, who now had a slack expression on her face. A string of drool hung over her lower lip, which kind of ruined the effect of her carefully applied makeup.

"You blanked her," I said.

"The first time you give your statement, you will include all details." He nodded at the notebook that had fallen into the app's lap. "The second time, you'll exclude the details that expose your gift of fairy sight and sound. Neither you nor I want others to be aware such an ability exists."

I stared at him as the app snored softly. *Interesting.* Maybe he'd heard how I walked through the fairy mob on the bridge or had seen me watching Launt.

Did he know why we had this ability? I was tempted to lie, to hide my precious secret, but I was too curious.

And so was a certain witch who lived next door.

Without speaking, I glanced at the painted-over window next to Raynor's desk. He saw the direction of my gaze and smiled.

"Dr. Helen Mendoza can't hear what we're saying." He took out his herbs again and pinched a small amount between his fingers.

"You can't be sure of that."

A grin flashed and was gone. "She hears *something*. She just doesn't know it isn't everything. Eventually, maybe, she'll figure it out. But not yet. So please, before my app falls on the floor, tell your tale."

"What does it mean that we can hear and see the fae?" I asked.

"If you come work for me, I'll tell you."

To hide my annoyance, I squeezed the glass in my hand and kept my face bland. Shadow's balls. I wouldn't pay that price.

I took another swallow of the springwater to enjoy its healing properties, even with the truth spell embedded in it. "I don't know how much you already know."

"Don't worry about that. I won't be bored."

I looked down at the black ring tattoo on my wrist and rubbed my thumb across it. "It was the fairies who woke me up. I'm usually aware of them in the back of my mind, their singing and arguing, but this was…"

Raynor leaned forward and clasped his hands together on his desk. "Yes?"

"It was unlike anything I'd ever heard before. They were…"

"Angry?"

"Afraid," I said. "And one of them was calling for help."

"Help from whom?"

"I don't know. Me, another witch, anybody. I followed the voice and found Tristan on the bridge."

"We found no trace of you on his skin." He arched an eyebrow. "No *recent* trace."

"I didn't touch him. I knew— I knew he was dead." I paused to swallow over the lump in my throat. And then I told him everything.

Chapter Forty-Eight

J asper had studied fairies for a long time and apparently hated them. He also hated the Protectorate for having rejected him year after year and for having all the power and prestige he lacked as a witch without family, power, wealth, or connections. Sparking a war between them would be a personal triumph. Having a reason for it—the Freewitch movement—wasn't necessary. He would've done it anyway. But it gave him an excuse that what he was doing was for a greater good, and Jasper, even at the very end, was still arguing that he was a good guy.

The night of the murder, Jasper poisoned the river, probably by pouring his potion off the bridge into the shallow water below. He wouldn't risk climbing down to the riverbank, not with the green-faced river sprite there all the time and other fairies who already hated him for the experimentation he'd been doing near his house.

The potion he used that night didn't work right away. If it had, I would've felt it sooner. Instead, he must've developed a spell that unfolded slowly so that when he finally poisoned the wellspring itself at the winter solstice, which I believe was his plan, he would've been far, far away with an unbreakable alibi.

Tristan had already noticed some of his experimentation and reported it to the Protectorate. If he'd suspected Jasper, he never told me. But that night as Tristan was walking across the bridge to meet Malcolm Bellrose at Cypress Hardware, which was spelled with magic that teleported desired objects into it, he saw for himself what Jasper was doing.

I don't know what Tristan said when he confronted him, but I can imagine it was charming and persuasive, just like Tristan was. He was a popular man, and he wouldn't have expected Jasper, or anyone, to lash out with violence. Jasper had put on a convincing show of being a nerdy, unassuming guy who kept to himself and didn't have many ambitions. Tristan wouldn't have had his defenses up for magic intended to kill.

Probably via one of Jasper's potions, Tristan's heart stopped. But then Jasper was stuck on the bridge with the Protector's dead body. Had he known about Malcolm and the torc, he might have fled immediately, leaving Tristan there as he fell, not attempting to divert attention from himself. He didn't know Malcolm was coming to Silverpool to see Tristan, and he didn't know I could hear the wail of the grieving fairy beneath his feet. He couldn't hear it himself. So he decided to take the time to set up a scapegoat.

One fairy he could see was Launt, who had lost his human body at birth to the changeling Seth Dumont. Launt was twisted from his own life experiences and was willing or eager to serve Jasper as he killed the fae. When Jasper killed the Protector himself, Launt must've felt liberated. There was nothing to stop him now.

Jasper told the eager Launt to steal Birdie's car and drive over Tristan's body. One of his students had been an estate lawyer in Santa Rosa, and with everything else Jasper was doing, using truth potions on his students had to be one of them. He undoubtedly collected the secrets of every witch who came to see him. I shuddered to think what he knew about me that I hadn't intended him to know. Tristan's will, which left everything to a nonmag clerk at the hardware store, would've been the kind of prime secret he could've plucked out of a student's brain.

With his fairy gifts and human abilities, Launt stole Birdie's car, drove it over the body, and returned it to the garage without her noticing. And then, while Birdie was playing Yahtzee and I was stirring in my bed, hearing the cries of the fae, Jasper and Launt left Tristan on the bridge. Compelled by the cries for help, I ran to the bridge and found Tristan. Then I talked to the river sprite and went home.

Because I was delayed by the emergency crew, my father had time to get into my house before I did. He had a knack for teleportation and obviously burglary. Spooked by Tristan's body and the police, he would've wanted to unload the stolen torc as soon as possible—and what better hiding place than his own daughter's home?

He tucked it away—I still don't know where—and helped himself to my leftover pizza. When I arrived, he bonded Ethan to me, commanding the poor dog to follow me—not yet, in the morning, in his natural form as a mixed-breed black dog—until he could retrieve the torc for his master.

Unfortunately for Malcolm, Seth Dumont, who had been chasing Launt, came to see me at my house. The magical scent of the torc must've drawn him, and he stole it for himself. He said it was for me, but I didn't believe that for a minute.

In the morning, Ethan—Random—appeared as a dog, and with my father at a distance, was happy to enjoy life as nature had intended. Until he met Seth, he was just being the good dog he truly was. Once he'd smelled the torc on Seth, he was reminded of his commands, and when Seth actually pulled it out of his pocket, and then Malcolm told him to seize it, he did as he was told.

I didn't know if Random survived that battle with Seth, if he was in pain, if he was disabled, but I knew my father deserved what would be coming for him. Namely, me.

The day of the memorial service, Jasper must've thought he was in the clear when the police arrested Birdie. But then I rushed after her, obviously not believing she could be guilty, and he had Launt run me off the road before I could hire a lawyer, bail her out, or confirm her innocence with magic. He later pretended to have had his wallet emptied by fairies, just as mine had been, so that he couldn't help me.

He'd also seen me at the memorial service talking to Nick. Nick, who wore the silver chain of his ex-girlfriend because without it, he could've told everyone about the Free-witch movement she'd always talked about, the one that her tutor Jasper belonged to as well. But the chain ensured his silence only so far. Jasper obviously thought it hadn't been insurance enough and had Launt push his truck off a cliff.

And all for what? To trigger a war that would've died out within a week. The Freewitch meetings in Berkeley were famous for their bake sales, not their hard-core dedication to overturning the Protectorate. All Jasper had done was hurt a few dozen fae in the North Bay, and they were more like rabbits and kindergarten teachers than demons. Launt was the only fairy I'd ever met who would kill a human being— and no surprise, he was one himself.

WHEN I WAS DONE SPEAKING, Raynor locked his gaze with mine. "You're going to come to work for me," he said. "You belong here at the Protectorate."

"No way. No way on this fine planet, my demon-hunting friend."

"You have gifts."

"I have an Incurable Inability," I said.

Raynor shook his head slowly. "Thanks to you, Jasper Holland is dead."

"By his own hand," I said. "His own magic. If I've ever wanted to kill anyone, it was him at that moment—and I couldn't. I'm not like him, Raynor. I'm not like you." I slapped my hands on the armrest and stood up to go.

"You forget, ex-Agent Bellrose," he said, holding up a hand. "You need to repeat everything you just said, minus the parts about hearing and seeing fae who don't request to be seen, for the recording app."

I groaned. My dry throat burned from speaking steadily for the past hour.

"Unless," he said, "you answer one small question. Then I might be able to have your words recorded magically as I would like them to appear in the formal statement. The app won't remember either way."

I glanced at the app. Her head was slumped forward, and the drool had puddled on the notebook like a miniature, bubbling wellspring.

Because I knew what he was going to ask, I sighed. "Yes?"

"Where is the torc now?"

I stared at him, trying to keep my face as blank as the dazed app next to me. In my account, I'd try to suggest my father had reclaimed it when he took Random. But it was too risky to give a wrong answer to a direct question—the oak leaves might work on a little lie but not that.

The app let out a loud snore that made me feel sorry for

the other agents upstairs who shared living quarters with her. It was hard enough to sleep under a desk without such a horrible sound interrupting the few hours available for sleep.

"You can wake her," I said. "I don't mind repeating myself."

He pursed his lips but didn't seem surprised. "As you wish." He made a reverse spiral in the air with two fingers and then clapped his hands. "Act lively, Flint! What's the matter with you?"

The poor woman jerked upright, grabbed her pen, and surreptitiously wiped her lips with the back of her hand.

When I thought she'd recovered enough to write, I took a sip of water and got comfortable in my seat.

"Jasper had studied fairies for a long time," I began.

Chapter Forty-Nine

❦

W hen I got home around midnight, Willy greeted me at my back door with a basket of blackberries, apologizing for the two gnomes, his friends, who had attacked me the night before.

"They didn't know you were going to kill the evil one," he said, bowing his head over the berries.

I squatted down and took the basket. "I'm sorry too. For everything."

"Your animal is gone," Willy said.

I was still too sad to talk about that, so I thanked him again, and he returned to his tree.

My house was quiet, empty. No dog greeted me, and even Birdie had gone home. After spending last night on my couch, restored by a mug of ginger tea spiked with a drop from the wellspring, she'd felt good enough to leave the protection of my enchanted property.

She'd asked me to teach her magic. I didn't know if she had any power worth nurturing, but I'd felt so bad about letting Jasper and Phoebe hurt her that I said yes. She even offered to pay my rent for a few months, courtesy of the riches she'd inherited from her father. I didn't know yet if I could accept that. Probably not.

As I brushed my teeth and prepared for bed, I tried not to think about my own father. After a heist, he could stay underground for months, even years, and I didn't expect to see him for a long time, if ever. Tristan's murder, Jasper's fairy revolt, his own daughter's evidence against him—if Malcolm cared about his own skin, which was the only skin he did care about, he'd never set foot in Silverpool again.

Which was why I was surprised when Random appeared in my bedroom after I'd fallen asleep. There was no moon, and the clouds covered the sky, blocking the stars. Random's dark fur blended in perfectly with the shadows, and if he hadn't jumped up on my bed to lick my face, I might not have realized he was there.

I smiled, letting the tongue get me wet, but didn't make a sound. I didn't even sit up for fear it would alert his master. He was shaking with the effort of disobeying a direct command by making contact with me. My heart jumped to see him—well, smell him. I could feel the pain, the distress, in his furry body.

A flash of power outside suddenly moved him to action. He turned away from me, a slight whimper in his throat, and jumped off the bed. I heard the scratching of his toenails on the hardwood floor as he went to the filing cabinet in the other room.

I got out of bed, put on a robe, and touched the two beaded necklaces and four bracelets I wore now at all times before I followed Random.

Nobody was fooling anybody now, so I flicked on the lights. If my father had been able to get into the house, he wouldn't have sent the dog.

Random sat bolt upright in front of the cabinet, staring at it, then at me. He was pleading with me to open it.

I removed the staff—I was going to need it—and, after a pause, I opened the bottom drawer. Random began to shake harder, with joy this time. When I drew out the torc, encased in a black velvet bag, he jumped to his feet and wagged his tail so wildly it knocked a candle off the coffee table.

"This is what he wants, isn't it?" I asked Random, holding it up.

Random suddenly sat down, rock steady, as if waiting for his favorite treat.

That's why he'd appeared in my house that morning; Malcolm had sent him in to retrieve what he'd hidden there the night before after learning Tristan was dead. Never got caught with the goods when heat was around, that was my dad. Dear old Dad.

But this time Malcolm had gone too far. With Random so close to the object of his command, I could feel the spell that bound him to it and my father. It was no innocent spell, nothing cute like being a dragon for parties. This binding spell carried the penalty of death, and if I broke it, I might break my dog.

And he was *my* dog, dammit. Time to make that clear to my father.

I put the torc in the pocket of my robe, went into the kitchen, and opened the door, careful to block Random from following me. The bond would compel him to chase the torc wherever it led—which is why from the beginning he'd demonstrated such affection for Seth.

"Come inside," I said in the doorway. Because it was my house, and my house was powerfully spelled, my invitation carried weight.

Against his will, Malcolm appeared from the shadows, walked up my steps, and crossed the threshold into my kitchen. "So nice to see you," he said. "I didn't want to bother you so late."

I set the tip of the staff on the floor between us. "You'll speak the truth in my home."

He opened his mouth, as if to speak, and his smile faded. Pressing his lips together, he nodded.

Glad to see that spell at least was working, I moved on to the next. "You won't leave this house until you agree to my terms."

This one was more tricky. If he didn't agree, and I knew he wouldn't want to, then he might be there for a long time. But at least that way, I figured, Random would be there with me. I was willing to put up with my father's slippery presence for the remainder of a good dog's life, if that's what it took.

"Break the bond you have with this dog," I said. Then I tapped the staff for good luck. Good luck was no small thing.

"I don't want to." He moved his lips in a funny way, stretching and wiggling them as if he wasn't used to the taste of honesty in his mouth.

"You want to live here with me instead of leaving without him?" I asked.

"You'll get sick of me before I get sick of you, daughter. And you know I'm not lying when I say that." He smiled triumphantly as if he wanted extra credit for his paternal feelings.

"Break the bond," I said.

Still smiling, he went over to my refrigerator and took out an apple. "If we're going to be living together, you should know I've gone vegan." He held up the apple. "Buy in bulk. Costco might be worth the trip." Then he took a bite, still smiling at me as he chewed.

Unfortunately, he was right. I already wanted to kick him out. Instead, I took the black velvet bag out of my pocket, took the torc out of the bag, and casually regarded it in my hand. Random came running over and sat at my feet, on point again.

"Break the bond," I said, "and you can have this."

He stopped chewing. His eyes shone, watching the gold torc in my hand. "Your magic ensures *my* honesty, not yours," he said.

I gave him a hard stare. "I'm not a liar. You are."

"So what does that mean—your word is good?"

I gripped the torc harder. I hadn't realized how difficult it would be to give it to him. The deal I'd made with Helen would need to be settled a different way— I didn't like to think how creative she was going to get with my debt—but I had to free Random.

"Yes," I said tightly. "That's what it means."

Eyebrows raised, he took another bite of the apple. After a long moment during which I had to watch him chew, he finally nodded. "All right. I'll let Ethan go." He scowled. "It'll break the dragon spell though. He'll just be a dog all the time."

"Exactly," I said.

"And he's not even a golden retriever. That was another spell. This is what he really looks like." He threw the apple core in the sink. "Good for night work, you know?"

I thought of all the black hooded sweatshirts, knit caps, scarves, leggings, and boots I'd worn as a child. "I know."

"You're crazy, you must know that. It's a ridiculous trade. No dog is worth that much."

"You're stalling," I said. "My boundary spells will hold. You can't get out of here without my permission."

His eyes went out of focus for a moment, and I knew he was testing me, testing my power. Eventually he looked at me seriously and said, "You're right."

I nodded.

"Did I teach you these? The"—he gestured in the air—"whatever magic you've got going on around here?"

I held up the torc. "No."

His hand shot out to take it.

"Random first," I said, pulling it away. "The dog. My dog."

"Won't you consider calling him Ethan? That's what I called him."

I noticed he was already using the past tense. "I'll call him whatever I like," I said, then added, "or what he likes. Now break the bond, Dad. Get it over with and you can go."

Malcolm sighed and squatted down in front of Random. He took his furry head in his hands and pulled him closer, looking him in the eyes for a moment. Finally he reached inside his shirt, pulled out a silver amulet on a chain, and tapped it on the dog's black burglar-friendly nose.

"It's done," he said, standing up with his palm out. "Hand it over."

"Hold on a second." I carried the torc across the room, watching to see if Random followed. I set it down on the floor, released it, pushed it toward him with a fingertip.

Completely uninterested, Random trotted out of the kitchen. Down the hall I heard the sound of the bed creaking and dog feet circling the bed covers, looking for the perfect spot.

"Take it," I told my father.

He rolled his eyes at the need to bend over and pick it off the floor himself, but he did, very quickly, with his usual grace, and then was at the door. He paused, not looking back until I released the spell that kept him in my kitchen. Next breath, he was gone.

I reengaged the boundary spells before I returned to bed, where my dog was already asleep in the center of the mattress. Curling up next to him, I stroked his silky head and smiled.

"Welcome home," I said.

Books by Gretchen Galway

SONOMA WITCHES (Paranormal Mystery)

Dead Witch on a Bridge (Sonoma Witches #1)

Hex at a House Party (Sonoma Witches #2)

A Spell to Die For (Sonoma Witches #3)

Charmed to Death (Sonoma Witches #4)

Murder by Magic (Sonoma Witches #5)

The Sonoma Witches Series Box Set: First Three Novels (Sonoma Witches Books 1-3)

❦

OAKLAND HILLS SERIES (Romance)

Love Handles (Oakland Hills #1)

This Time Next Door (Oakland Hills #2)

Not Quite Perfect (Oakland Hills #3)

This Changes Everything (Oakland Hills #4)

Quick Takes (Oakland Hills Stories Boxed Set)

Going For Broke (Oakland Hills #5)

Going Wild (Oakland Hills #6)

Oakland Hills Romantic Comedy Boxed Set (Books 1-3)

RESORT TO LOVE SERIES (Romance)

The Supermodel's Best Friend (Resort to Love #1)

Diving In (Resort to Love #2)

About the Author

GRETCHEN GALWAY is a *USA Today* bestselling author who writes mystery, fantasy, and romance. Raised in the American Midwest, she now lives in in Sonoma County, California.

For more information:
www.gretchengalway.com
gretchen@gretchengalway.com

Made in the USA
Las Vegas, NV
22 December 2023

83401673R00198